Praise for

REAL MEN KNIT

"If you're looking for an easy charmer, this is the novel for you."

—Shondaland

"Readers who adore snappy family banter and feel-good romance won't want to miss this one." —NPR

"A bighearted, warm, funny story of community, family, and unexpected romance, *Real Men Knit* is an absolute winner."

—*New York Times* bestselling author Kristan Higgins

"Such a fantastic read, complete with an emotion-filled romance and a cast of characters I'm so looking forward to seeing again."

New York Times bestselling author Nalini Singh

"Gorgeous, funny, sexy, smart."

—*New York Times* bestselling author Penny Reid

"I loved every word of *Real Men Knit*. It's a sweet and satisfying slow burn of a romance about what knits us together as family, friends, and lovers. I can't wait for the next installment of the Old Knitting Gang!" —Lyssa Kay Adams

"Kwana Jackson combines everything I look for in a story—family, heart, romance—and knits it into the perfect reading experience."

—*USA Today* bestselling author Farrah Rochon

"Kwana's characters and vivid world-building leap off the page in this hilarious and heartwarming frenemies-to-lovers story."

—*USA Today* bestselling author Andie J. Christopher

"This emotional, funny, and sexy friends-to-lovers romance introduces us to the enticing Strong brothers and has me clamoring for more!" —*USA Today* bestselling author Priscilla Oliveras

"Like a hand-knit sweater, you'll want to wrap yourself up in this delightful love story." —*USA Today* bestselling author Tracy Brogan

"Reminiscent of *Four Brothers* but completely original, *Real Men Knit* is heartfelt and romantic, hitting just the right notes of emotion."

—*Wall Street Journal* bestselling author Kennedy Ryan

"With love and laughter, Kwana Jackson's contemporary romance *Real Men Knit* captured my imagination and held it from the very first page. . . . I loved this book!"

—*New York Times* bestselling author Jenn McKinlay

"Jackson crafts a cute friends-to-lovers romance with a diverse cast of characters that emphasizes the importance of community and found family." —*Booklist*

ALSO BY KWANA JACKSON

Real Men Knit

KNOT AGAIN

Kwana Jackson

JOVE
NEW YORK

A JOVE BOOK
Published by Berkley
An imprint of Penguin Random House LLC
penguinrandomhouse.com

Copyright © 2022 by Kwana Jackson
Readers Guide copyright © 2022 by Kwana Jackson
Excerpt from *Real Men Knit* copyright © 2020 by Kwana Jackson
Penguin Random House supports copyright. Copyright fuels creativity, encourages diverse
voices, promotes free speech, and creates a vibrant culture. Thank you for buying an authorized
edition of this book and for complying with copyright laws by not reproducing, scanning, or
distributing any part of it in any form without permission. You are supporting writers and
allowing Penguin Random House to continue to publish books for every reader.

A JOVE BOOK, BERKLEY, and the BERKLEY & B colophon are registered trademarks of
Penguin Random House LLC.

Library of Congress Cataloging-in-Publication Data

Names: Jackson, K. M., author.
Title: Knot again / Kwana Jackson.
Description: First edition. | New York: Jove, 2022. | Series: Real men knit; 2
Identifiers: LCCN 2021051634 (print) | LCCN 2021051635 (ebook) |
ISBN 9781984806529 (trade paperback) | ISBN 9781984806536 (ebook)
Classification: LCC PS3610.A3526 K66 2022 (print) |
LCC PS3610.A3526 (ebook) | DDC 813/.6—dc23
LC record available at https://lccn.loc.gov/2021051634
LC ebook record available at https://lccn.loc.gov/2021051635

First Edition: July 2022

Printed in the United States of America
1st Printing

Book design by Alison Cnockaert
Interior art: Knitting set by Lytrynenko Anna / Shutterstock

For Will
I'm lucky to still be spinning with you.

And for those who give their all and get so little in return . . .
Thank you for fighting strong.

KNOT
AGAIN

1

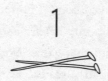

"YOU KNOW, YOU really are a little shit, Lucas Strong."

"Little"? How would you know?

The rebuttal was on the tip of his tongue, but instead of saying anything, Lucas scoffed to himself and ignored the insult that was hurled his way. He knew she was angry. She expected him to respond. To perhaps be thankful for her come-ons. But still it got tiring. The week had been crap, and now here was Michelle going on. Practically ready to tie him up with the new twisted wool blend the shop just got delivered. Lucas inwardly shivered. He needed to stay cool.

Not take the bait. And that's all this woman was doing with her "little" comment. Baiting him.

Hell, there was nothing little about him. Never had been. Not even when he was a kid and actually was little and faking it on falsified guts thanks to the fact that at times it was all he and Noah had keeping them together in the group home after their mom died and before Mama Joy came and rescued them. And definitely not since he'd become a man. No, nothing little about him since then, that was for sure.

So, when Michelle gave a loud "humph" and added a petulant foot stomp, Lucas thought only briefly about looking her way. But no. He wasn't playing into that game. Not tonight. He'd had more than enough. The day had already been plenty full of women throwing unnecessary fits at his expense. Right now, all he wanted to do and give any attention to was diving full force into his much-needed plan of rest and all-about-himself self-care. Sure, it might sound a little selfish, but after the hellish week he'd had, if he didn't deserve it, he sure as hell needed it.

But for now, here he was, stuck. Doing a shop closing and being insulted on top of it by this woman, with her long linger in the worsted section and suggestive pawing of the Peruvian highland wool.

Lucas squelched down a sigh. Tonight he'd only planned on barely passing through Strong Knits, the shop that he and his three brothers, Jesse, Noah and Damian, now owned since the sudden passing of Mama Joy, coming up on a year ago. They were now running the shop, though that term was used in only the most tenuous of ways, thanks to the help of Kerry—their longtime shop helper and now Jesse's full-time girlfriend.

Lucas threw up a silent but earnest prayer, one that he knew his other brothers probably said too, that Jesse stayed on the straight and narrow and never fucked things up with Kerry. She was way too perfect for him, the shop—hell, all of them. She had been running the shop since their mother passed away last year.

But today Jesse had pounced on Lucas before he'd gotten fully inside. Nowhere near letting him make it to the back of the shop and the steps that led to their living quarters and the glorious rest Lucas had been longing for. No, his younger brother was quick. Always had been when there was a potential payoff involved, and tonight, he guessed the potential payoff was high. Probably for all of them, so he shouldn't complain. Much.

Jesse wanted to take Kerry to the Bronx for a date at a new drive-in that had recently opened. Lucas was all set to tell Jesse where he could go with his teen dream Friday date night, but when he took one look at Kerry, with her sweet face and her big brown eyes shining, giving him that "You know you want to do it for me" look, Lucas knew he was sunk. Though Kerry had become Jesse's girlfriend—fiancée, if Jesse finally had his way—the truth was, she'd actually somehow made her way into all the Strong brothers' hearts and wedged herself in so tightly that she was now the sister from another mister who had them all wrapped around her little finger.

And what thanks did Lucas get for this finger-wrapping? Not a quiet few hours of watching the world go by outside the window of their Harlem yarn shop while he knit away the time until closing, like Jesse and Kerry had hyped up his night to be. No, he was stuck with Michelle, Ms. "I can't decide between the sock or the bulky weight yarn or the red or the green, but I know for sure I want to get tangled up with you, Lucas Strong."

As Michelle continued to babble on, Lucas continued to pretend to not hear her, instead keeping his focus on what he was doing. Knitting and people watching and trying his best to stay cool. It was what he needed to do. What he had to do. Keep his cool and keep his attention on something calm. Something more meditative than passes and insults and what had gotten him into the position where his life had become a constant loop of dodging both. With that thought, though, Lucas afforded himself a single silent groan of frustration, then wrapped the delicate yarn he was fingering around the wooden needles in his hands, gave a twist and—

"Did you hear me, Lucas Strong?!" Michelle's voice went up an octave to shrill, and his yarn broke, along with what may have been his eardrums.

Dammit!

He looked down at the broken threads. *Shit*. That's what he got for pulling from the shop's most expensive stash. Still, he shouldn't be surprised over breaking the yarn, given how tightly his nerves had been wound lately. He gazed at the ripped fawn-colored cashmere threads and forcibly pushed to the back corner of his mind all ridiculous comparisons to his psyche and the way his life had been going. He felt his shoulders tense as his stomach tightened. Even the thought of going that deep made him cringe. Not to mention how his brothers would react to such melodrama. He shook his head. Just nope. His family had been through enough with the death of Mama Joy and then having to get the shop finally off cash-flow life support. And that was just barely. His brothers couldn't deal with their supposed "got it all together" brother falling apart.

Lucas stood and placed his needles on the wooden stool he'd been leaning against. He suspected the old stool was probably even older than he was. A heavyweight piece in a gorgeous pecan color, it was glossy from many years of wear and loving care, being in the same spot where Mama Joy used to perch herself behind the counter, where she could look out at the shop and through the plate glass window, with its ever-changing seasonal yarn displays, onto the busy avenue beyond.

It was still so hard to believe he was sitting in this spot and that she never would again.

Almost a year now and Lucas still expected to hear her booming laugh, see her ever-welcoming smile when he walked in the door. That unshakable disbelief was probably the real reason he'd gotten caught out there tonight and had been wrangled into closing the shop. Out of habit, he and his brothers rarely used the outside entrance to their residence above Strong Knits—not during the hours that the shop was open anyway.

From the moment they'd each been taken out of foster care and into Mama Joy's care, she'd trained them to always check in when they made it home, telling them that's what family did. They checked in before they checked out, reminding them that they were no longer alone and had people waiting on them. People watching for them.

Lucas continued to look out the window while losing himself in memories. Though things were winding down in the shop and the hour was growing late, you wouldn't know it by looking out on the busy Harlem street. So many people were rushing here and there, most with that happy, just-got-paid, Friday-night look of anticipation. Summer was still on, but the end-of-season wind-down was in effect, and the air was thick with the energy of folks wanting to get in last licks before they had to bundle up again and go back under cover of layers of clothes to ward off the winter chill.

Once again, Lucas took notice of Michelle out of his peripheral vision. Shit, when was she going to either make up her mind or leave? He knew he needed to be better. That it wasn't her fault, being a new knitter—and if it was as he suspected, she didn't really care about knitting at all. But that was neither here nor there. She was a customer and he needed to get himself in check no matter how hellish his week and no matter that he was dog-tired and wanted more than anything to be deep into REM sleep. Lucas ran a hand across his neck and gave it a rub, twisting against the tight knots of exhaustion that had now fused into lumps.

Sleep had been hard to come by on his thin mattress at the ladder house, and he hoped that being back home and in his own bed for the first time in five days would do the trick. Now he just had to get to his bed.

Lucas did a mental countdown to the official closing time while trying to figure out how to get rid of Michelle and still keep up a good enough customer service facade. They needed all the customers they could get, whether slightly irritating, stalky or whatever.

He knew he shouldn't complain; it was his own fault again for not asserting himself, for playing fast and loose with his Mr. Nice Guy act. Well, that and Kerry having him wrapped around her finger—both of which got him thrown into this coming year's "FDNY's Bravest: Turning Up the Heat" calendar. He'd been tapped for it when a news piece came out about him and his brothers taking over the shop, and Kerry latched on hard, going on about how it would be great publicity for the shop and could bring in more customers.

Though it was against his usual "last Boy Scout," all-around-good-guy type of image, once Kerry got behind the pitch it didn't take but a minute for the rest of the crew to go in with the hard sell. Jesse was all for anything that Kerry was for, and Noah couldn't get enough of the idea of Lucas squirming shirtless in front of the camera. And as for Damian, anything that brought in more revenue was a win to him.

Since the calendar had gone on sale, customers like Michelle, who maybe wouldn't have given him a glance a month ago, were now suddenly indecisive lingerers who couldn't seem to make up their minds when it came to yarn and had endless pins on Pinterest.

No matter if they had never thought of picking up a needle, let alone knitting a scarf, before in their lives.

As he was thinking over his current predicament, Lucas continued to scan the block. The familiar night streetlights lulled him deeper into exhaustion, and as a response, his anxiety kicked up right along with it. Though he desperately wanted to sleep, he worried whether he actually could. His gaze started at the bodega on one corner and moved over the beauty and nail salon and past the brownstones and tenement entrances to the bright fluorescent wash of light that was the pink and turquoise neon sign that always pulled his attention.

Scrubs. The family-run laundromat was another neighborhood establishment, much like their knitting shop, and from what he'd heard from Mama Joy, it had been around even before her place. Not that that mattered to him all that much. What did matter was that it—no, she—had been drawing both his mind and his heart to that half-broke-down laundry for almost as long as he could remember. That was, until she'd left the neighborhood for the first and last time, leaving him with nothing but longing while she picked up a degree, then quickly went on to a fancy new house, a new man and even a new name.

Lucas closed his eyes against the pink lights and his admittedly useless thoughts.

"See, a real jerk. Call him cute, he doesn't respond. Call him a little shit, and he doesn't even respond to that." *Snap. Snap.* There were her fingers. Right up close to his face. Lucas felt his jaw tighten. He was trying. Trying really hard to be patient with Michelle. When she'd first come in, he'd pulled out hank after hank and bundle after bundle of yarn until he had the worktable practically covered, only to realize she wasn't paying any of his yarn suggestions a bit of attention, but just stalling while waiting for the other customers in the shop to leave.

He was a fool. What he needed to do was once and for all learn from the past instead of making stupid mistakes when it came to dumb things like patience and the benefit of the doubt. If the distracting lights of Scrubs and even his screwup at work this week had taught him anything, it should have been that. How often would he have to get hit over the head to know that patient nice guys don't end up anywhere but where he was—tired and alone?

2

WASH. RINSE. SPIN. *Repeat.*

If only her life could be so simple. A little detergent. An hour of time. And voilà—squeaky clean. Add a nice dry and fluff, and the stink of the night before is all gone. Nothing left but the faint odor of a faded memory.

Sydney snorted to herself as she took a moment to imagine what it would be like to be able to perform that sort of magic on her life. Or the past third of her life at least? Quarter maybe? Her snort morphed into a sigh. Why the hell was she negotiating with the Universe over something completely unobtainable?

Earth to Syd, how's about you join us down here back on Earth with the rest of the thirty-year-old, tail-between-their-legs, suddenly-back-at-home-with-a-kid-but-no-husband-in-sight masses?

She blinked, letting the voice of reason bring her back from her momentary musings to the present and the hypnotic swirling of the extra-large washer. It currently held the dirty linens from Sweet Ginger, the new Southern-meets-Asian-fusion place that had opened in their little part of Harlem. It was an odd culinary choice, since

Gerrard, Sweet Ginger's owner, seemed neither Asian nor Southern—judging by his Midwestern accent, anyway.

She would give his new restaurant six months, maybe a year tops, since he'd chosen to open it only two doors down from Great Wall Express, the long-established Chinese takeout place. Though it held only two well-worn Formica booths that were bolted to the floor, it had been standing strong for as long as Sydney could remember and had seen more than its fair share of restaurants come and go.

Fancy fusion and clean linens alone just wouldn't cut it.

In this neighborhood, it was all about the flavor and the people. Like over on the downtown corner at the Big Star deli, Ed had bacon, egg and cheese sandwiches and coffee on lock for at least ten blocks. And on the uptown side, at 5 Star, you couldn't beat Santi's chopped cheeses or any of his other famous concoctions. It was the stuff of legends. Hell, folks came in from the Bronx for his heroes.

Suddenly Syd felt an overwhelming sense of comfort at being back home, but still she forced herself not to look in the direction of Strong Knits.

It had been over a week and not a peep from him. Not a comment or even a like on her post about being back in town. Not that she wanted or even expected one after the way she'd so coldly ghosted him not once but twice. Still, he didn't have to be so stubbornly, infuriatingly goddammed Lucas Strong about it. Shit!

Syd felt her brows draw together and then did some quick facial flexing exercises to smooth them out. She hadn't packed herself and her daughter up to escape the wrinkles caused by one man only to come back here and get them from another. Screw that and screw him!

She sighed. Oh, but wouldn't it be nice to see him? Just once. Syd was heating up from head to toe when the sudden sound of a phlegmy cough from across the laundromat brought her heated face bolting up. *Shit*. What was she doing? She was in her family's very public laundromat fantasizing about a man she'd never have and who was, she'd bet money, surely not fantasizing about her.

She was sure he would have heard she was back home though. And the fact that she was in town and newly single—well, that was bound to get some sort of reaction. It wasn't that she had advertised, but it wasn't like she had to either. That's how it was in their neighborhood. Someone came in—especially if that someone was coming back home and down on their luck, and add in a good fall from grace on top of it—and that type of shit called for a parade. The neighborhood elderly gossip lines ran faster than Black Twitter. And the fact that Ms. Diaz and Sister Purnell had been in to do their wash and check on her grandfather not a minute after she was back in town ensured that the word was out.

But from Lucas she'd heard nothing. Crickets.

The last time she'd seen the elusive Mr. Strong and that beautiful face of his had been virtually, through her phone's screen when she was half-drunk and pissed at Red after once again uncovering the dark depths of her dear ex-husband's true colors—God, did she really FaceTime Lucas from the floor in the corner of her walk-in closet? Talk about embarrassing. And after him listening to her one-sided whining, she had had the nerve to use giving condolences over the loss of his mom as an excuse for the call.

But still, that call with Lucas was impactful. Enough so, at least to her, that here she was almost a year later unable to stop running the encounter over and over again in her mind. Thinking of how he looked at her with those dark eyes that reminded her of everything that felt right and every wrong turn she'd ever made. And enough so that right after it happened, she did a complete reverse, at least on social media, and for a while she doubled down on her efforts to look like the perfectly polished socialite wife. Happy with her life. Happy and in love with her husband. She never reached out to Lucas again. And when he checked in on her she practically pretended it was all a figment of his imagination.

If he didn't think her a first-class bitch before, he surely did now. She shouldn't be surprised he hadn't been around. Why would he be? He was probably cuddled up right now with some sweet-as-pie, not-a-bitchy-bone-in-her-body Little Miss Sunshine. Syd sighed. She bet Miss Sunshine baked for the guys at the firehouse and knit blankets for charity kids too.

Syd twisted her lips. She'd known when she'd walked away from the block the first time, right after high school, that blankets and charity weren't her future. That Lucas wasn't her future. And he'd known it too. At that thought she felt her lips smooth out into a sort of surrender as she realized that the future was now and she was once again back on the block, feeling the same old hurt over the fact that though she'd set the boundaries, Lucas Strong still didn't dare to cross them. Not with a call, a text, a fly-across-the-damn-street carrier pigeon. Nothing. Not even once.

Sydney scrunched up her brow again, then winced. Damned new braids. They were tight as hell. She'd only gotten a couple of cornrows around the perimeter of her crown and had the braid tech leave the rest of her naturally curly hair out so that she could either wear it loose and wild or put it up. At the time she was thinking perhaps she'd put it in a bun, or that maybe she'd even do a few Bantu knots for some variation, depending on her mood. But even with so much of her hair free, the rest still felt tight as all get-out.

Syd gave her scalp three quick pats to try and alleviate the pain without disturbing the braid pattern, but it didn't help. God, she must have been nuts. Of course, that had to be the reason she was here, back in Harlem and not at her house in Great Falls, with new braids and thinking about a new man who was never hers when she'd barely even broken from the old man who was hardly hers.

No matter—even with the pain, the tiny style change felt like an act of freedom; hell, it was almost a complete rebellion for her. A big, glorious style step into her new life. But just that fast, Syd found herself fighting against an internal shiver. What if this was all for nothing and she was about to fail once again? This time she wouldn't be failing just herself but her daughter, Remi, too. The shiver threatened to turn into a full-blown anxiety attack, and Sydney fought to put a quick lid on it. *Get it together, woman. You've got this,* she silently told herself. *The world is yours.* She'd first heard the expression from her grandfather and had been saying it to Remi since before she was born. For a while with Redmon, he'd made her stop believing it, and in her heart of hearts she had to admit she still kind of doubted it. For herself at least. But right now she had to hold on to the belief for her daughter.

Just then Syd's phone pinged, and out of habit she immediately pulled it from her pocket to check the alert on her IG. It had been days since she'd gotten a like or a DM, and she hated to admit it, but she was starting to feel invisible. But one look at the reply from Zara under her last post and she wished that she were. Shit.

> Syddie when you getting back to DC? It's not the same here without you. The Gate is dead.

Sydney read the message once more and cursed to herself again. Fucking Zara. She could have at least DM'd her that question instead of putting her on blast in the comments for the whole world to see. It wasn't like Zara wasn't privy, if not to all of her reasons for being in New York, then at least to the fact that she wasn't returning to Great Falls or The Gate, their exclusive subdivision and gated living community, anytime soon, and probably not ever. That life was behind her. But still, it wasn't like she was waving a banner and advertising the fact that her ex was a philandering son of a bitch either. That she wasn't enough to keep him content at home, as she'd portrayed herself to be during all their years together.

Syd knew this was just Zara's way of getting her to spill things publicly that she wasn't ready to spill. Not until things were fully settled and she had Remi established and comfortable with their new life, however that may look.

Oh well, screw it. Another day. Another lesson learned. That's what she got for mistaking acquaintances for friends. As if she'd ever had any real friends in DC. She'd been fooling herself to believe she had, almost as much as she'd been fooling herself that she'd had a faithful and loving husband. And this public, seemingly innocent little comment sealed exactly what had been niggling at her all along. Behind the smiles and the kikis, just like everyone else in The Gate's crew, Zara had been waiting for Syd to take a majestic tumble so they all could watch and document it on social media.

She sighed, taking in the stark differences in her current life: the silver dryers that could have used an upgrade years ago; the once off-white but now faded-to-beige walls that hadn't been touched up since before she'd gone away to college; the old black and silver washers that sometimes needed a hip check to get in gear. Yeah, she'd tumbled, all right. Tumbled her ass all the way back home, making room for the next new housewife hoping to make it onto the executive board and up to VIP Gate status. Well, they could have it, Syd thought, forcing a small smile, if it meant she didn't have to deal with any more of the type of fake crap that Zara was pulling.

But then Syd looked back down at the photo Zara had commented under. Fake ass. She was tempted to write that comment herself—about herself! She knew she had gall thinking the way she was when she had practically been the ringleader and head VIP of The Gate's Fake Is the New Real Club for so long. But after being back home with her grandfather and doing laundry for others, she hardly recognized the image of herself as "Syddie," smiling back at her from her top-of-the-line megapixel phone screen. It was as if the Sydney of her youth had only been napping and just needed a breath of Harlem air and a dash of Scrubs, her family's laundromat, to wake her up again.

She stared harder at her old self on the screen, fighting to connect with the face that she knew was her own. "Syddie" was seemingly carefree, her hair freshly blown out and expertly tousled in that way that looked as effortless as it came. *Problems? Stress? Sorry, never met or heard of those things. Can you spell it? Are they for poor people?* In the photo she had one arm draped around Remi's shoulder. They'd just gotten back to New York, and she was still in high-level damage control. One World Trade Center was their backdrop. The sky framed them in crisp cornflower blue, and both she and Remi had huge smiles of delight. Sydney had captioned the photo "There's no place like home."

Poor Remi. Syd had taken so many shots that day to get this one close-to-perfect pic that was good enough to post. But she had to do her best to put a positive spin on this move back to New York. She'd left DC damn near mysteriously, giving no real answers to her crew there as to when she'd be back. She just let them know she had "family business" to take care of in New York, assured that if the word "family" didn't resonate with that set, the word "business" would, since it implied money, and that would buy her some time and keep her in good social standing.

Sure, it was odd that she was leaving so close to the beginning of the school year and that she was taking Remi with her when she could just as easily have left her with her in-laws or, shock of all shockers, home with her father. But she held on to the fact that most of the Gatekeepers, as they were called, sent their kids to either boarding school or private school and had them in so many activities that they didn't really bond with them at all. The fact that she and Remi spent any amount of time together already made her an oddity. So fine, let them think it. As long as for the moment they weren't babbling on about her failed marriage. There would be plenty of that soon enough if Zara kept up her commenting. But she'd rather it come later, when Remi was more settled here in New York and in school—and when she herself had had more of a chance to get on her feet and out of the suds, so to speak, and had a handle on her next steps toward rebuilding her own life.

Tongues would wag with speculations, but they would have to keep wagging for a little while longer, until she could figure out a way to spin this and make sure Remi's future stayed as she'd always intended it to be and financials were finalized with Redmon.

She didn't want to consider the ramifications once the Gatekeepers got wind of her situation. Syddie Hughes, the grand dame, head Gatekeeper, Mrs. Perfection herself, was currently a by-the-bag, $3.75-a-pound paid laundress. Nah, couldn't happen. The social media blowback would be too much, and the pie-in-the-sky dream she had of launching something for herself would be shattered. What she had to do was keep up appearances. At least until everything was sorted out and she secured a better settlement. One that kept her, for appearance's sake, in good standing as the style tastemaker that she'd made herself out to be.

Sydney swiped at her phone and glanced over the facade that was her past life: the McMansion and the three-car garage with two luxury cars along with the mountain bikes that had been taken out approximately twice ever.

Purposefully, her eyes only skimmed over the photos of herself and Redmon, most of them so perfect, so sickeningly sweet, they could almost make a person's teeth ache. Sydney studied her image. "If only there was a best fake smile by a wife award," she murmured. She knew she'd win it hands down. She also knew it was probably the reason that Red, though he was all "Fine, pack your shit and go" when she first brought up leaving him, was steadily blowing up her phone now. Sydney knew how to put it on. Though the pictures lied, they didn't lie about that. Looking at any of their photos, it would take an extreme expert in body language to spot any flaws. To the untrained eye, they were the perfect picture of enduring love and admiration. The only possible giveaway to a glimpse of her true feelings was the hint of a shadow in her eyes, almost imperceptible and only visible when the light hit her a certain way and bounced off the furl of her top lip.

Sydney frowned as her focus shifted and she looked at her daughter. Her heart went soft as her anger at Red amped up. Remi did that to her. Took her emotions on a whole ride. She was her reason for everything and had been since before she was born. Syd stared at the photos of her nine-year-old daughter and saw herself in Remi's smile, which, when spread wide, extended her full cheeks even fuller. Syd smiled at how her daughter had even picked up the habit of putting her hand on her hip and placing one foot forward.

Sydney peered deeper, and there it was. That look. The one that told her that leaving had been the right choice. The one that had let her know she had to make a change. How long would it take that look of hesitation to disappear from Remi's eyes? And when had it appeared? She hated that she had been asleep at the wheel and missed the moment when her daughter had first started to fade. But when she did see it—saw the parts of herself she didn't like, the fake smiles, the calculations and the shrinking away to make yourself smaller to accommodate a man—that was when Syd knew she had to take action.

Sydney could accept it in herself. She was prepared to do so indefinitely if it meant a better life for Remi. But the moment she saw Remi changing around her father in the exact same ways that she herself was, well, Sydney knew. She knew right then and there that it was time to go.

It was horrible to think, but using her grandfather and his health scare had been her perfect opportunity for a way out. At least it gave her a cover to give to the women at The Gate. Which only added more weak sauce to the way she was running. Running when she should have been walking and doing proper planning. She and Red were through and had been through for a long time. He didn't love her and was in fact spreading his love rather freely, but this way at least she could leave with some semblance of her reputation intact. And so far, no one knew of his cheating, or even that she was no longer Mrs. Sydney Harris-Hughes.

She was surprised that Red had agreed to give her a divorce so easily. She suspected that the current woman he was screwing around with had some sort of magical pull, but that wasn't her problem. Now that the divorce was final, here he was calling her again. It was strange. But Syd knew now was the time to smarten up. Look at things through the lens of distance and clarity. She'd left too quickly, without fully thinking things through, only thinking of out. Not for herself, but for Remi. To save that light in her daughter's eyes. But now that she was out, she needed to think about getting paid. All other thoughts didn't matter. At least she knew her mother would understand that through her disappointment.

Just then the washer in front of her revved up and started its final spin. It sped up so fast and shook so violently that for a moment Syd thought it would knock over the rest of the machines to its left and right. The little numbered yellow sticky note she had stuck on the front, indicating the customer ID info, came unstuck and flew up in the air just as the machine finished and came to an abrupt stop with a loud buzz. Syd sucked her teeth as she watched the little yellow sticky as it floated and landed just out of reach between the machines, where all the old dust bunnies went to die.

She scrunched up her face and immediately winced, reminded again of her tight braids, and sighed. *What to do first,* she thought. *Put this load in, start folding the next client's clothes out of the dryer, or send Remi up for a fine-toothed comb to start taking these tight-ass braids out?* She didn't think she'd make it through the night shift with her scalp being pulled as it was.

3

AT THE SOUND of Michelle's fingers snapping, Lucas opened his eyes from his thoughts and saw Mrs. Campbell and her granddaughter, Maia, on the other side of the window. Maia was pointing at the new display of fall yarns that Jesse and Kerry had just put out, with cute little handknit bears hidden in the yarns. Lucas loosened his tight jaw and smiled at them both before turning to the maker of the "little shit" comment.

"Do you mind, Michelle? There are kids around."

Michelle gave her head a slight shake and rolled her eyes. He could tell he was testing her patience a bit too. Good. Maybe she would get the hint and go. But no, instead she flipped her features and smiled, not acknowledging his kid comment but instead batting her lashes his way.

Lucas frowned, noticing the lashes she was batting. If his tired eyes weren't playing tricks on him, those were different lashes from when she had been in the shop the week before. Way longer and much thicker. Michelle flipped her long, silky hair over to one bare shoulder, and Lucas caught a whiff of the slightly lingering smell of blow-dry afterburn. He sighed, hoping all this extra effort wasn't for him. He didn't need the type of entanglements that came along with the pretty package she was offering.

"You know I was just teasing," Michelle said as she took a pair of expertly crafted wooden knitting needles, with an expertly crafted price tag to go along with them, from the bin by the register and waved them suggestively his way. "Well, only kind of teasing," she added with a shrug. "Besides, your last customer just left, and it's not like anyone can hear me out there," she said, lowering her voice now.

Michelle leaned in closer. "I was only making polite conversation. Complimenting you, is all. Your moles really are sooo cute!" Michelle's voice went up high on the C in "cute," making it sound like a sharp Q.

She then leaned forward, finger pointed, and Lucas added a manicure to the lashes and blowout tally. Her fingers came perilously close to his eyebrows. He took a quick step back. She giggled. "Why are you so jumpy?" Her eyes narrowed. "You really are surprisingly sexy."

He almost grinned at that. "'Surprisingly,' huh?"

Michelle did grin then and licked her lips.

Fuck, he thought. Wrong choice of words there. But then again, were there any right words with this one?

"And this here," she said, her fingers now coming way too near the scar above his brow. It was long-faded and usually missed unless a person was really close, and in this case, she was really close. Too close. Lucas inched back some more.

"How did you get that?" She smiled. Her invasiveness stoked his anger back up to a blaze as memories he'd long tried to forget threatened to escape from their tightly locked box in the back corner of his mind. "I bet there's a good story to go with it. Probably something about getting into it with your brothers. You four seem like a real wild bunch."

It had nothing to do with that, but let her live in her fantasy world. There was no way he was sharing his worst nightmare with the likes of her.

Lucas shook his head, then cleared his throat. "Looks can be deceiving."

She nodded. "I bet. Look at you. You're a tough one to crack. Walking around half the time with that sweet, innocent, shy smile and wouldn't-hurt-a-fly look." She leaned in closer and stared. "Those eyes though." She smiled. "The way you're looking now. All that sweet, boy-next-door innocence dropped. You look like you could fuck a woman till she forgets her first *and* last name."

Lucas wasn't going to argue that last point, but he wasn't going to comment on it either.

Michelle giggled before resting her hip on the wooden farmhouse table in the center of the shop.

It wasn't lost on Lucas how she angled herself, showing off her legs, which were long despite her average height. She twisted so her breasts jutted out, then gave a little shake in an obvious—well, close to obvious—invitation. Letting Michelle linger till past closing and falling for her story about waiting on an Uber that had yet to show was pretty damned dumb. He should have been doing his best to get her out of the shop instead of getting lost in his own head. Hell, she hadn't looked at her phone or out the window for a car in the past fifteen minutes.

"Listen, have you made a decision on that sock yarn yet? It's getting late and I should close up," Lucas said. "And maybe you should check on your car?"

As if he hadn't spoken, Michelle sat fully back on the table. "Oh, I've got something in mind. But it's not for that type of sock."

Oh, just fuck this day. It took all Lucas had not to physically yank the woman in front of him off Mama Joy's table. He let out a slow breath, reminding himself that she was the customer and he was polite, civilized and in no way the raging brute he wanted to be at the moment or the grieving child he was stuck as and afraid he'd never stop being. Instead, he schooled his face into an expression of unreadable blandness. "Could you not, please? The table is old, and we need for it to hold up for classes."

Michelle let out a puff of air and pursed her lips into a little pout. "Like you're gonna tell me your brother and his girlfriend haven't christened this table plenty of times."

Lucas felt his lips tighten. He didn't need the image of Jesse and Kerry and their table antics running through his mind. Not when he associated this table with Mama Joy and the long days and nights she'd spent patiently sitting with him and his brothers and countless others from the neighborhood, teaching knitting classes, helping with homework, sharing meals. It was a perfect family and neighborhood gathering spot, and he didn't want that fantasy ruined. He needed something to stay pure.

He glanced at the shop's window again, remembering the newly installed privacy blinds that were a so-called essential security expense. Damned Kerry and her finger-wrapping. Lucas shook his head. No, that had to be Jesse's doing, because there was no way Lucas would put that kind of deception on Kerry Girl. Just then the pink and blue lights from Scrubs caught his eye again, right before the M2 bus sped by, jarring him back into the moment.

Lucas took three quick strides over to the side wall, along the way picking up another pair of needles. "How about you take this sock yarn, and I'll throw in these?" Lucas leaned forward toward Michelle and gently took the size nine straight needles from her hands and walked back toward the checkout counter to place them back in their bin. He flashed Michelle a smile, one he'd perfected over the years that said he was sincere, could be trusted and was someone you should listen to. Lucas Strong, dependable, firefighter, the last goddammed Boy Scout. "This set of double points should get you started. Check out the videos on YouTube I mentioned before and follow the directions. You'll be fine." He looked at her again and said a prayer that she'd get the hint, check out and leave.

Michelle stared at him a long time while he held up the self-striping Fair Isle yarn. "I had it right when I said it before. You really are a shit, Lucas Strong."

He couldn't help but smile, and it was genuine this time. "Hey, it's not the first and I'm sure it won't be the last time I've been called that. Now, do you want this yarn or not, and can I check on that Uber for you? I really need to lock up."

Michelle sighed. "Fine, I'll take the damn yarn."

Well, shit. With the way she was putting down the shop's carefully curated product, Lucas had half a mind not to sell it to her at all. But a sale was a sale, and they needed each and every one to keep the lights on.

Michelle continued, talking half of knitting and the rest of his inability to knit or get off the pot, so to speak. She let out a frustrated snort. "But it's your loss, dude. I was sending out all the signals"—she gave him an up-and-down, lingering more on the down than the up—"and you couldn't pull the trigger and just make your move."

Lucas didn't know what to say by way of a comeback to that one. Not even to himself. *Couldn't pull the trigger and just make your move*. Michelle surprised him by how perfectly she'd hit the nail that had been squarely on the head of his most recent thoughts. Instinctively his gaze went toward the twenty-four-hour laundromat across the street, full of rickety machines, but mostly full of memories of his past regrets and missed opportunities.

KNIT 1, PURL 2, *knit 1, purl 2*.

The mantra went on repeat over and over in his head but frustratingly was still no help in lulling him to sleep.

Groaning, Lucas rubbed at his eyes, then pushed his half-naked body to a sitting position. Shit. He'd be screwed if he didn't start to get some real rest. The final alarm call and his last screwup proved that. But even after getting stuck with closing the shop, and dodging Michelle and her advances and making a sale regardless, plus adding a quick workout on top of it all, here he was still resorting to old tricks of counting stitches. It had always worked in the past, but now even it was failing him. If it was night, his body was determined to believe it was time to be up, mind racing with thoughts he didn't feel like thinking or dealing with.

Lucas stretched out his legs, then vaulted forward, touching his toes, giving his back a stretch. He quickly twisted, then "Ouch!" He couldn't hold back the word as it came out on a rush of air. *Okay, not doing that again.* Whoever said thirty was the new twenty clearly wasn't doing thirty with the proper effort. He reached for his lower back as annoyance and remembrance hit him with a hard one-two combo. Not that his age wasn't a factor, but his pain could be thanks to that whack job who worked with Kerry at the center and had made his final call of the night a near disaster. How the woman was allowed

to work around children was beyond him. With her over-the-top the-
atrics, she'd nearly succeeded in making him a local trending topic.
*Come get an up-close look at and mouth-to-mouth from this year's hot
firefighter.*

Lucas groaned as the debacle ran through his head once more. He
had half a mind to sue the woman. A faulty coffeepot? But Lucas
knew he didn't have a case. Yeah, the coffeepot probably was at fault.
And who knew with the way these buildings were quickly remodeled to get new tenants in at triple and quadruple the rents, maybe
the wiring too. But as for the rest of the mess, the fault was all on her.

Once again, Lucas groaned. Fine, maybe it wasn't all on her. He
knew he could have stopped a lot of the ridiculousness in its tracks
if he'd been more alert and on his "A" game. That had been all his
fault. He had been tired and not sharp enough to avoid getting
caught up in some bullshit. At this point all he could do was be
thankful that his reputation wasn't jacked up any more than it had
been, and most of all that no one had gotten hurt. He knew good
and well the dangers of not being fully responsible and aware of
everything going on in your surroundings and not keeping your
head completely and fully in the game.

The cost was at times immeasurable.

He thought of what Mama Joy would say about this latest screwup.
With her sense of humor, a small part—okay, maybe a big part—of
her would laugh it off. And he knew she'd also be bragging her behind off about the calendar. Probably bring out some yarn and do a
theme window around it to show off her "famous" son, no matter
how cringy it was. But still, these little mistakes he'd been making on
the job, with those she wouldn't be happy. Not at all. It wasn't him.
Not the him she knew.

She never expected these kinds of screwups from him. Noah, maybe. He was more impulsive. Led with his heart and always leapt before thinking. Damian maybe too, though he was a hard one to catch out there. Not one to easily bend, being held together by a giant steel rod up the ass and all. And when it came to Jesse, well before the tragedy and his big turnaround, "Screwup" was practically his middle name, though Mama Joy would lay the smackdown on anyone who said it in her presence. But not Lucas. He was supposed to be the brother who had his shit together. The one who never gave her or anyone a moment's worry.

His only saving grace with the blonde and her coffeepot was that, though he'd gone minorly viral and trended in New York for a moment, he'd gotten a certain amount of sympathy from the Harlem neighborhood folk by being a part of the local firehouse and being one of Mama Joy's boys on top of it. The *New York Post* ran a tweet with an attached photo linking his calendar pic and their old article about the shop. In the end he guessed Kerry's calendar idea had saved him as much as it had screwed him over.

It was a mess. All because some woman decided to fake passing out when she noticed he was the firefighter who came knocking on her door. Gotta love a slow news day.

It was things like this that put his facade in dire need of superglue.

Truth be told, Lucas honestly didn't know how much longer he could keep it together. How many more nights could he go on like this before he eventually crashed? And not crashed in that good sleep-like-the-dead way, or even crashed like someone who'd said screw it and lost themselves in a liter of brown liquor. But literally crashed. As in hit the wall or worse. Lucas knew from experience that when a person was overly tired, or preoccupied and off their game, that's when they could very much end up in the "worse" category.

He closed his eyes, letting out a long sigh as he recalled his clear display of incompetence on the job. He'd been running on empty for way too long, as his response time and ineptitude would attest. His reactions, zoning in and out . . . it all had proven he wasn't himself. A person didn't get promoted in the FDNY by getting photographed while lip-locked with someone he was saving. No matter how many calendars it may sell. That shit was still frowned upon by the higher-ups.

But that was neither here nor there. This thing today was his fuckup and his entirely. Lucas knew he needed to get a grip for the most basic of reasons—and soon, or it would be more than just him or his reputation that would suffer from his lack of sleep and poor concentration. Lives were at stake when it came to his job, and he genuinely couldn't afford to be out in these streets and on calls while wandering aimlessly in his head.

Since Mama Joy died, Lucas had been trying to put on a brave front for his brothers, and an even braver one in front of his colleagues at the firehouse. But all that effort was wearing on him. He thought of the call he'd gone out on earlier that evening. So close to the end of his shift, he'd been looking forward to his downtime, dropping his facade, chilling out with some music, some video games, knitting or a run. Most of all sleep. But no, the call had to come in at the worst possible time, just before the shift change and right in time for him to fuck up before he was out of there.

His station, Engine 69/Ladder 28, was just a few blocks from home—which was in some ways convenient, but lately was starting to feel more like a curse. In the past he liked being so close to home, near his brothers and most of all Mama Joy. It gave him a sense of family he felt he needed and was even more grateful to have for Noah. Sure, there was the fact that everyone knew your name and thought they knew your business too and didn't hesitate to chime in with their opinion on it. That, he could admit, was a bit of a pain in the ass. Case in point with his most recent screwup.

He groaned. With this thinking, sleep for sure wasn't coming, and it looked like another washing night was ahead. Getting up, Lucas pulled a tank on over his naked chest and raked his hands a few times through his hair, knowing it was probably still defying gravity and sticking up in all sorts of directions, thanks to him flipping and flopping for the past hour.

Pulling on gray sweats, Lucas debated whether to wash them with the rest of his laundry or make them last until he did another load. Pausing in thought for an extra moment, he finally decided they'd be fine for now, plus they were his only option, since he'd gone too long between washings.

He really needed to talk with Jesse about getting the house machine fixed, though it would probably make more sense to just throw it out. But approaching that subject was still touchy for all of them. Changing anything since Mama Joy's passing was touchy for them, so it was better to travel across the street. Even if that had the tendency to rub him raw too. In this case, better he be the only one in pain instead of all four of them. He and his brothers had gotten that old machine for Mama Joy back during the first summer they all had jobs. Even Jesse had worked to put in some cash. Just a couple of months after her passing and their world turning upside down, the machine had decided it had had enough too.

He'd look on the bright side: even though it was hard for him being over at Scrubs, over the past year it had come to be a place of slow closure for him, and he'd grown to like checking up on old Mr. Harris and keeping him company. Especially on late nights like this when he couldn't sleep. Mr. Harris wasn't one for a lot of chatter. One or two words on how he was and then he pretty much left Lucas alone. Sure, Lucas was polite, and it was a given that he'd ask Mr. Harris about Syd. They had gone to school together. Graduated in the same class. Spent many years across the street from each other. It was only logical that he ask.

And though Mr. Harris didn't go on about his granddaughter, he did let Lucas know that she was fine. And he had no problem beaming over his great-granddaughter, Remi, and thankfully didn't have much to say about his grandson-in-law. Then, for the most part, he left Lucas alone to sit in silence for however long his wash-and-dry lasted and didn't bother him with added unnecessary questions about how he was feeling, Mama Joy, the shop, his future, a family or anything else he didn't want to face.

He noticed then how the foot traffic had died down and worried a bit for Mr. Harris. The old man really should get more help. These OGs thought they were indestructible, but they weren't. The elderly man had had a very real recent heart scare, and without his family checking on him regularly, Lucas couldn't help it if his mind wandered to the worst-case scenario. He felt his lips tighten.

Putting his Jordans on, Lucas grabbed his laundry bag, and his current knitting project, before heading down the back stairs and into the night. He could now hear slight whispering from Jesse and Kerry coming out of Jesse's room and made his steps lighter before barreling down at his usual pace once he'd passed. Despite the earlier inconvenience, he hoped they'd had a good time tonight and that his little brother's newfound efforts at being that attentive, planner-type boyfriend hadn't been all in vain. His gut said they hadn't. That Kerry seemed like she was now having the time of her life, as she very well should. Hell, even if Jesse was his brother, make the brother earn that forever. Kerry was worth it. When they all needed her the most, she didn't let any of the Strong brothers down, and he sincerely hoped for the best for her and Jesse's relationship.

Before he knew it, Lucas was standing on the street's median watching the flashing red hand as a Lexus SUV went by, filling the air with the sound of Cardi B, followed by a Durango right after blasting Nicki Minaj. He scrunched up his face at the ironic chase scene just as the breeze kicked up while he waited for the light to change. It was getting cool, with hints of the fall that was soon to come, and the hairs on the back of his neck suddenly stood at attention. He didn't welcome the idea of what an early winter would bring when it came to his job. The thought of small apartments being heated by gas stoves or faulty space heaters sent a chill down his spine. Lucas shook his head at the thought of the impending danger.

Not to mention yet another winter without Mama Joy. And who knew how long his younger brother Noah would be out on tour dancing? Not that he wasn't happy for Noah. He was happy for all his brothers. They were doing Mama Joy's memory proud. Noah was living his dream, and Jesse had gotten the shop back to running and was now coupled up with Kerry, and Damian was, well, being Damian. But still, he was working and successful and never let anyone forget it. It seemed that everyone was either moving forward or moving on. All except him. When would he, if not move forward, then at least move in some way?

FDNY pinup calendars notwithstanding.

SYDNEY QUIT HER reminiscing and hit the camera button to take a quick selfie. She paused and frowned. Had she gone too far with the braids and rocking her natural hair? Maybe this style looked too young. Like she was trying too hard?

Because I am trying and it is. Hard as hell.

Redmon always hated braids or any sort of natural style on her—even though he never failed to praise the look on other Black women, especially when it was for his benefit. Like when flirting with a cute barista and attempting to get a little extra foam on his latte or some such shit. Well, then the cornrows were A-OK, but when it came to his wife and wearing a beautiful natural twisted updo to one of his firm's conservative dinners, then the style got a quick shutdown and Red was swift to let her know, even going so far as to make emergency appointments to change her style before they went out.

It was as if anything that might have pointed out their status as a Black couple was a definite no-no. As if they could hide their obvious brown skin behind cash, cars and trips to the salon. It was beyond ridiculous. Still, on Sydney, Red said he preferred a sleeker, more conservative look. But she knew the whole preference excuse was just that. An excuse, and it had nothing to do with what he liked. It was more about getting her to conform to what he wanted and what he thought would frame his professional image best.

But hell, if she determined her look by what Red went for, then she could do whatever the hell she wanted. There were women with braids, bobs, weaves and buzz cuts. Thanks to a sexting video sent while he was in the shower, she knew that the last woman he'd cheated with was blonde with expensive highlights and breasts that were filled with enough silicone to make Sydney wonder if her skin hurt from being stretched so much.

Sydney sighed to herself, letting go of past thoughts and coming to the present. No, with Red it was about control. More specifically, control over her. That was always the way it was with her ex.

That was how it always was with her. She gave Red way too much power. This control thing was on her too. Somehow, she'd always let the people in her life lead her around by some invisible leash. First, she was controlled by her mother, and her mother had been controlled by a need to be looked at a certain way in society, and damned if she still wasn't controlled by that one. And now what? All Syd's efforts to do right—live right—be right—had gotten her where?

She looked around the now semicrowded laundromat where she'd spent so many of her growing years and snorted to herself. She was right back where she had started. It kind of felt like a cruel joke. Older, but hardly any wiser.

Syd thought of the Harlem she'd known when she went away and the one she was faced with now. So much had changed, and yet it seemed nothing had. The bodega and then the other one on the opposite corner were still there. Tresses Beauty Salon was gone, replaced by a barbershop called Blades. Nail City was now Pinkys4, and the family-owned pharmacy had been replaced by a Duane Reade run by, to let her pops tell it, "snippy-assed gals with eye problems."

And then there was Strong Knits. She couldn't believe the shop not only had survived Mama Joy's passing but was once again thriving. That part she was happy about, but losing Mama Joy was hard on everyone. She thought of Lucas again, then turned away from the window just as the M2 sped by. Better to stop her mind before it went down that path again.

She'd sent condolences. Well, general ones from her family. A nice potted lily from Mr. and Mrs. Hughes and family. She twisted her lip as a slight pang of guilt washed over her when she remembered how she had felt when the generic prayer card came back in the mail. It wasn't even personally addressed—though why should it have been? An impersonal response for an impersonal gift. And keeping it real, it wasn't like there was anything all that personal between her and Lucas Strong these days besides crossed wires and mixed signals. Keeping things at a distance was way better than her showing her ass and crying again in his video DMs. Anything was better than that.

She shook her head. For the life of her she didn't know what had made her reach out into his DMs that night under the guise of sending condolences, or what had made him hit her up right back. That part was even more unexpected. Their conversation had ended up being long and intense. Mostly on her part. Looking back on it, honestly it was pretty tame. *How are you? I'm sorry for your loss. I hope you're okay. Thinking of you.* But it was what was said in between the sentences that felt so intense. The long silence when he asked about her family, but not about Red. The bit she volunteered but shouldn't have, saying he was fine. He was always fine. His eyes that went hard, then way too soft, that had her overcompensating and pretending the whole encounter with Lucas didn't even happen and putting on the biggest social media happy wife show ever for the weeks following.

All it had been was a freaking conversation. But in that talk, in his eyes, it felt like he'd seen more of the real her than Red, her DC friends and even her family had in years, and it scared the shit out of her. It scared her and made her so mad that part of her wanted to get in her car and make the four-hour drive to New York to tell him off and ask him why he hadn't looked at her like that before she'd left. Why he couldn't put those looks into words. If he had, maybe she never would have left.

But pretending was better. She was good at it. So to fight temptation she ended up pretending it never happened and never responding to his DMs on top of it. She went so far as to make her IG posts for the next few weeks always with Red and always alluring. Even staging shots of morning breakfast in bed with the hubby, out to dinner with the hubby, shopping with the hubby, captioned, "What did I do to get so lucky to have such a fine fucking hubby? Talk about smug married." Then a family pic with her, Red and Remi. "Me and my 2 loves," she'd captioned it. Lucas gave a like to that one.

And then she'd sent the flowers. A boring peace lily, as if she didn't know Strong Knits was probably overrun that week with chicken, collards and peace lilies.

So yeah, she probably deserved the generic response card, but she was Sydney Harris-Hughes, and there was no way she was letting go of a sure thing like Red when a forever-maybe who never did shit or get off the pot was just standing around doing nothing when he was free and clear to hit her back up based off a random FaceTime call.

Still, now here she was, tail between her legs, no longer a Hughes, and once again pining over Lucas Strong like a lovesick puppy. "You're a real joke, Syd," she mumbled to herself. "Get back to reality and get to work."

She did a quick scan of where all her sticky notes were for by-the-pound wash. She was doing pretty well. Maybe not as well as her grandfather, but she was keeping up. She suddenly remembered the phone in her hand and let out a frustrated sigh as she clicked her favorite filter and snapped off three fast selfies.

"That will have to do," she mumbled to herself again. It wasn't like she was uploading them anywhere. Though it would serve Red right if she did. Let him explain his culturally cool ex-wife to the partners at his ultra conservative financial firm. Her gated aesthetic was just Black enough to be a safe fit at whatever client dinner he dragged her to. The strange thing was that a part of Syd understood it when she got wind of his mostly opposite taste for his mistresses. And a part of her felt sorry for the next Mrs. Hughes. She really hoped he could reconcile his public and private personas by then and not screw up the head of another woman. But that was for her to get over. The actual caring about him or the next woman.

Suddenly antsy, she tapped her feet as she watched the machine's countdown clock. Lord, how had her grandfather been doing this for so many years? It seemed so much more exciting when she was a kid. Just a minute more, then into the dryer. Just enough time to transfer Mr. Johnson's load.

Sydney dashed over to two machines and pulled out the clothes inside, tossing them in a basket. She gave a smile to Remi sitting in the employee area as she passed. She hated that Remi was down in the shop with her at this hour, but they hadn't gotten a routine set up for her just yet. Besides, it was still summer, and thankfully, this whole "DC girl in a Harlem laundry" thing was still feeling like a bit of an adventure for the nine-year-old, though Syd knew it was starting to wear thin.

Syd glanced at her daughter and got a moment of relief, despite feeling like a failure, when Remi gave her a sleepy smile. At least they were together. She looked a little more closely at her daughter for any signs that she was stressed, and she didn't see any. Hopefully she was seeing right.

All she wanted was for Remi to be happy.

Remi stuck out her tongue and then scrunched up her nose, giving her a goofy expression, making her chuckle before she looked back down. She seemed content as she colored, though if Syd stared too long she could see the slight boredom in the way the little girl frustratedly let out a puff of air as she looked for the perfect color before seeming to settle with the meager twenty-four-hue set she was working with. She caught Remi stifling a yawn and thought for a moment about telling her to lie down on the cot that was behind the front counter. It was pretty late, and Syd's grandfather was probably long in bed. He'd said he'd stay up for Remi, but Syd didn't want him to do that. She was there to help him out, not to put sitting and bedtime duties on him. But it was now close to eleven o'clock, and she didn't know how her grandfather had handled doing doubles when Mr. Bill called out sick. He needed more help or needed to change the laundromat's hours. Going the full twenty-four-hour route just wasn't making it anymore. That had to be modified somehow.

As it was, Syd was already beat and doing her best to stay on her feet until Mr. Bill came in for the midnight till eight a.m. shift. *Oh well,* she thought to herself. Maybe now that she was there she could talk to her grandfather more about the hours and getting an extra person. She needed to be there for him, Remi and the shop, and he needed to cut either his or the laundry's hours drastically if he didn't want to end up in the hospital again.

With that thought, Syd looked at her daughter once again, and fear rushed up at her from Scrubs' linoleum-covered floorboards and grabbed her by the throat. What would she do with the start of school? Staying up until eleven p.m. or midnight was not an option Remi could live with and be a functioning student. And putting it all on Syd's grandfather would do him no good either. She looked at her daughter again, and Remi blew her a kiss, then put her head down smoothly on the desk, closing her eyes, reminding Syd so much of herself at that age. Remi let out a contented sigh, and Syd let out a breath. They'd figure it out. Not tonight, but they'd figure it out eventually. She'd been fine growing up here. Well, for the most part. Maybe it was that, as with all children and childhoods, she just hadn't recognized the hidden charm of her old home. But she hoped Remi would, and she prayed it wouldn't take a quarter of a lifetime for her to do so. Syd let out another breath. As long as her daughter could rest and not be haunted or have to walk on eggshells, well, she was already ahead of the game.

Syd pulled off the yellow sticky note numbered 42 from the front of a machine and rolled the load over to a dryer. Sticking the note on the door, she loaded the dryer up. Syd carefully pulled out Mr. Reed's two pairs of khakis—the old man was a stickler when it came to these and insisted on them being hung dry and pressed, though she knew the dryer would do them better. Sydney paused. Shit. She'd only been back home and doing this a week and already she was firmly in the groove, as if she'd never left. If only her friends could see her now.

She looked around her family's laundromat and her current, depending on the way one looked at it, either refuge or prison. Whichever it was, there was surprisingly brisk business going on for one of the last beautiful New York summer nights of the season, before the chill of fall kicked in. These nights were precious, and she could think of quite a few places she'd rather be than here. Sydney paused. Could she though? Her mind drew a blank. Surely not back in DC, where she'd just practically run from. A flight to someplace where nobody knew her name and she had no connections to anyone and no one who cared for her? Hell, she could have stayed in DC for that, with her fake friends and even faker husband. Syd let out a sigh. This little laundromat maybe wasn't so bad after all.

Still, she'd thought that the place would be empty with everyone out and about, taking in the hot Harlem nightlife, but there was a young couple who seemed to be making a date night of their wash-and-fold. They were a little too in heat for her taste, but whatever. She wouldn't let her current personal disdain for romance interfere with business.

There was also a tall guy. Maybe late twenties. He looked to be finishing up a load of casual jeans and tees. He was just stuffing his laundry bag and slinging it over his shoulder. Sydney thought he was alone; he'd kept his head down and to himself and his phone the whole time as he leaned against the folding table and waited for his clothes to finish. But just as he was wrapping up, a cute caramel-skinned young woman came in wearing a cropped top, booty shorts and thigh-high boots, and he perked up. She leaned up as he leaned down and kissed her, then they headed out. Sydney guessed their date night was just beginning. Damn! What had happened while she was in DC? Had Scrubs become the hot pickup spot when she wasn't watching? Look out, Tinder.

Sydney looked at the rest of the customers. The older woman, who was about seventy, doing her laundry alone on a Friday night made Syd sad for some reason. She couldn't help the sudden fear that this could be her future—or perhaps she'd be living in Remi's basement and would be doing late-night laundry there. She groaned to herself. Great, now she was being pathetic and bringing perfectly fine strangers along for her ride. As if hearing her thoughts, the patron looked up and gave her a "Don't include me in your mess" look before she turned away to finish her business. It made

Syd think of her grandfather, and she was once again glad she'd come back home to help him out.

Sydney pulled her attention back to her work. She only had a certain amount of time to get it all in. Mr. James's load was on the next phase of the washing cycle, so it was back to the linens for her. Time to focus and get her attention away from the nighttime activities. Speaking of focusing . . . she turned and leaned to look back at the employees' counter where Remi was—or should be. *Where did she run off to?* Remi knew she had to let Syd know if she was heading to the bathroom or upstairs. Syd looked around, her heart instantly beating a little faster, though she told herself to just stay calm.

"It's so cool, mister. Your hands are moving so fast, I can barely keep up."

What the hell? And "mister"? Who the hell is "mister"?

Sydney swiveled her head toward the sound of her daughter's voice coming from the far-right corner of the laundromat. Who was she talking to over in the waiting area at this time of night? Just a moment ago she was in the employee area.

Sydney dropped the linens in the basket in front of her and stormed toward her daughter's voice.

"Remi," she started, her voice short even to her own ears, "who are you talking to over there?"

"Come look. It's so cool, Mommy. He's going so fast and said I could learn it easy."

Oh yeah. No freaking way!

Sydney could only see the two of them from behind. The man wore a bucket cap, but his head was bent down toward his lap and her daughter sat, though not quite next to him, close enough to be considered next to him. *Way too close.* Not a full connected chair away, the space that separated them was, by Sydney's measurement, not even a full arm's length. Remi knew better. And the man—she didn't care what he knew, just what he was gonna know.

It took all her restraint, and the fact that she knew she couldn't make the jump, not to hurtle herself over the chairs, yank Remi back and drop-kick the guy in the bucket cap.

"What the hell's going on here?" Syd spat out, rounding the chairs at the same time she reached out and pulled Remi harshly toward her.

Remi looked up with shock and fear in her big round eyes. Sydney didn't blame her, but she didn't have time to coddle her either.

Sydney looked down at the guy on the bench as he raised his head, bringing his dark eyes into view as they met hers with a bold challenge. It was Sydney's turn to be shocked. Emotion flipped and doubled back onto her as it seemed to physically hit her in the chest.

Remi continued to point. "We were talking about his knitting, Mommy. Isn't it cool? I want to learn too."

He cocked his head to the side then, the movement so familiar Sydney found herself mirroring it. "Yeah, Syd, we were talking about my knitting," he said. His voice was the same, but deeper now. More manly, with a raspy edge that hadn't been there when they were younger and that she strangely hadn't fully grasped over their video call. But then he shook his head at her as if he were somehow disappointed in her. Then he tsked. *Motherfucking tsked!*

"Same old Sydney," Lucas Strong said as he looked up at her again now with a raised brow. Then he looked down and smiled. Changed his tone. "Yep, same Syd. Jumping to conclusions and looking down on people," he mumbled.

Sydney grabbed her daughter's hand and turned on her heel,

stomping back toward the employees-only section. But mid-stomp his last words overtook her. She looked back at him looking at her. How was it the perfect boy from her past had the nerve to be sitting there looking every bit the perfect man and still give her the same off-kilter feelings he had stirred up all those years ago? Making her speechless. Able to do nothing but retreat.

She pointed at him. "And you're still the same old Lucas Strong. Minding other people's business like a know-it-all when you really don't know a damned thing."

He raised a sharp brow, and his lips quirked again. It seemed for a moment like he was about to say something, but he glanced at Remi and stopped short. Instead, he smiled at her daughter. "I guess you're right. A straight-A student like you"—his eyes went wide and he raised his voice into a mimicking tone—"now a whole 'smug married' woman!"

Sydney felt her ears go hot, and she silently prayed he'd just stop talking, but he didn't. No, the words still came as he continued to challenge her with his deep voice and that dark, glinting stare. "Why wouldn't you know the situation? Exactly what was up? You always knew everything," he said.

A "fuck you" was so near tumbling out of her mouth, but the fact that she knew Remi was glued to this whole convo had her biting it back hard. She seethed. Damned Lucas Strong, getting the last word.

Syd blinked, momentarily stunned, before finding her inner "screw that shit" and not giving up. "Just finish tangling with your yarn and your dirty laundry, why don't you? Some of us have real work to do," Sydney said before finally pulling her daughter away to an area of the shop where the drama was less dramatic and she could hopefully breathe again.

LUCAS DIDN'T KNOW why he was surprised to see Sydney again. But he was. Of course she should be here, with her grandfather's ailing health. But it had been so long that part of him thought, sick grandfather or not, she must have given up on Harlem entirely. He paused in that thinking as guilt crept in. Shit, her grandfather's health issues must really be serious if she was back. It had been so damned long. Not that he'd been counting the days, weeks, years . . . much.

He sucked in a breath as he thought of the little girl with the shining eyes and the smile so reminiscent of what Sydney's had looked like long ago. His insides practically turned to jelly with the thought of what his life could have been had he not let her slip away.

He slid a glance toward the end of the laundromat where Sydney was shoveling clothes into a dryer with determined force. He felt his lips quirk. He wasn't just surprised—he was actually happy to see her once again, though it wasn't like those feelings mattered. Lucas sighed. *Shit*. Like all his past run-ins with Sydney over the years, he'd screwed it up straight out of the gate.

Her storming off, already angry at him after their first time seeing each other in almost ten years, showed she still had her shit about her. The last time, he remembered clearly, she'd been back as a newlywed and a new mother, showing off her shiny new husband and even newer baby. Lucas's small bit of joy over seeing her now faded thinking of the husband, who'd probably come with her this time too, attached to the sweet girl Lucas should have recognized as Syd's.

Lucas did his best to keep his staring covert. He'd known Mr. H had been sick, but he hadn't figured that upon Syd coming for a visit, this would be how she would help out. Not with the way her

life, or what he knew of it from online, had become. Surely she'd
be the type now to hire her grandfather more help at Scrubs and
not take on the work herself. Washing and folding didn't really fit
the socialite she'd turned into. Hell, it had hardly fit her when they
were young and he'd watched from across the street as she regally
folded pile upon pile of clothes while still in her school uniform.
Her hair in its neat, high ponytail, not a baby hair out of place even
after a full day of school. Knee socks, still to the knee. She was
dubbed the Ice Princess of Harlem, but to him she was just Princess. What a fucking dweeb.

Lucas didn't know why he was suddenly so angry, but he was.
Seeing Syd back to work in the shop made him wonder just how
much he'd missed this week and just how sick Mr. Harris really
was. It had to be serious to bring her back home. Instinctively he
started to get up and move her way. He should ask. Act like an
adult and put the past behind them. She sure had. Besides, he
didn't want there to be something really wrong. When maybe he
could help out. But the stiffness of her movements, the sharp snap
as she separated the clothes before putting them into the machine,
let him know he didn't dare approach her and ask. Not now, at
least.

Lucas shook his head and looked back down at the project in his
hands. Crap, he'd lost count of the simple two-by-four ribbed hat he
was working on and was now off track, purling when he should have
knit. Having apparently done it for the past ten rounds, he'd now
turned the hat into a whole new design. It was either call it that or rip
the rows back. He sighed and ran his hands through his hair, scratch-
ing along his scalp in irritation. See, just fucking perfect. Two minutes in her presence and he was even more off his game. Not to
mention that there went his sometimes-secret place of refuge. There

was no way he was getting any peace here at Scrubs now. Not while Sydney Harris was anywhere within twenty feet of him. Better to keep quiet, let his load finish and get the hell out of here before he screwed things up any more than he already had.

He looked over at his machine and checked the cycle. Fourteen more minutes. Dammit. Might as well be four hours. How much of an ass would he look like if he waited out his fourteen minutes and then lugged his clothes home wet, screw the drying? Sitting through a thirty-minute dry cycle while Sydney Harris steamed in the same space as him might be more than he could take.

But he couldn't run. That level of ass bordered on super ass, and cowardly ass, and though all the monikers fit, it didn't fit the image he'd crafted for himself in the years since she'd been gone. He was a fucking literal lifesaver now, for Chrissake!

Lucas let out a breath, then glanced at the machine again. *Twelve minutes.* Fine, he'd sit and wait. Lucas looked down at his hands again and stilled. And he'd knit. Sit and knit like the same emo loser she left in the same spot when she went off to her fancy school and ended up meeting and marrying her big-time corporate dude, only to hardly ever look back his way again.

Lucas stared at the project in his hands. But all he could see over the swirling haze of the fall yarn colors was the heat of the flames that shot from Sydney's eyes when she realized it was him talking with her daughter. Granted, she was plenty pissed before she knew it was him, and rightly so—he'd give her that. Stranger danger. He should have at least had the good sense to not go talking to somebody else's kid like some weirdo.

But that's what giving lessons to kids in the shop and lack of sleep did to him. Clouded his judgment. Still, there was no denying that Sydney's pissed-off-ness had gone up about three levels when their eyes met and she realized who her kid was talking to. He wondered if her husband was ever on the receiving end of that look. Probably not, but he didn't want to think of that. He hated thinking of that. Of him. Of him and her.

Of how she, at one time—hell, maybe two times—had given him hope. Shit, if anyone should be pissed, it should be him.

Suddenly Lucas's mind went back. All the way back to when he used to do anything to see that fire in her eyes. Maybe not that particular type of blaze or all that much heat, but still he remembered when getting any type of reaction from her, the always staid and stoic Sydney Harris, was all he needed to make his day complete.

She'd had an innocence back then, when they were kids together in school, an innocence that had teased at the edges of his adolescent hormones, sending them off into all sorts of acrobatics and making him do things that bordered on the ridiculous. Which, of course, usually kept him high on her shit list, something it was plain to see had not changed in all these years.

Lucas looked over to where Sydney was still taking her frustration out on the clothes and caught her pause as she quickly turned away from him and back toward the dryers. He couldn't help his smirk. She never changed. Same old Syd as when he was feeling teasy back when they were in middle school together. She'd played it so straight back then, her nose always buried in a book or high in the air; of course she didn't have time for a cutup like him. She never missed a class, never was without her homework and was always ready for every pop quiz. And for some reason her cool demeanor and over-the-top cuteness made Lucas want to flap at the beautiful, unflappable, untouchable Sydney Harris with everything he had.

His raging hormones had told him she was worth risking it all. He'd cultivated a persona of being cool and collected, of being the perfect middle brother, the one who didn't fit in anywhere but somehow made himself fit everywhere. But not with her. With her he was just a straight-up goof, dropping the wall he'd built and for once letting his real self show, the Lucas he'd buried and never shown to anyone else except, at times, Mama Joy. Before Mama Joy, he'd worked hard to fit in where he could and not be separated from his younger brother.

His younger brother Noah, with his skin tone a few shades darker than Lucas's and his easygoing smile, acclimated faster into any situation with the kids at school and most settings in the group homes they were put into, but he had it tougher. Being full Korean, Lucas was instantly labeled an outsider and somehow harder to place. Black families didn't know what to do with him, and Korean families felt the same when it came to Noah, and then there were the white families that didn't want to take on the package deal of the two of them. Mama Joy was truly their end.

And though he didn't know how to be anything but Lucas, he'd had to quickly change into being everything that everyone wanted to see in order to just blend in when in reality what he really wanted to do at times was disappear. He knew he couldn't totally fuck up because he had to pull his weight and earn his keep for what Mama Joy was doing for him and Noah. She had taken them both in when they were suddenly thrust into the foster system and easily could have been separated. So he made sure he passed his classes. Not genius-level passed, but passed well enough to satisfy the teachers and not raise any academic red flags or get labeled the smart kid.

But getting Sydney to flap her wings wasn't easy. Back when they were in school, just the barest glance from her would cause Lucas to break character and pounce on his chance to cut up, make a face, give a wink, throw a heart, do whatever he could to try and illicit even a hint of a smile from her. More often than not she ignored him, but sometimes he'd get a headshake, a side-eye and, if he was really lucky, a sneer along with it. He ended up getting more attention from his teachers, which was all sorts of oh-hell-no as far as Mama Joy was concerned, or attention from Sydney's friends and the other girls in class, which wasn't the worst thing but was not his intended goal.

Lucas's machine beeped, taking him out of his musings. He got up to get a basket and pull his clothes out. Carting his load over toward the dryers, he drew closer to the woman who'd consumed his thoughts for way too much of his adolescent years. He stared at her back as he pushed the cart, and strangely, it felt like he was back in school being pulled toward her, as if by some invisible string. She hadn't changed much. Her back was still straight, her legs were still long for her petite stature and her waist was small enough that he could probably circle his two hands around it. He looked at the bare brown skin peeking from beneath her shirt, the curve of her spine as it dipped into the waistband of her sweats. His hands itched as his feet moved.

"Mom. I finished. What should I do now?"

He watched as Sydney's expression, at first pure old stoic Syd— flat, beautiful, unreadable cool marble—went soft as she looked at her daughter. Michelle was right. He was a shit. Here he was practically melting over someone else's whole-ass wife. A wife and the mother of someone's child. He was looking at a family. A family he had no right to think about. She'd made that abundantly clear in her posts. She had a family. A perfect one. The type he never wanted and knew he never deserved to have. Not with his track record of not being clutch for women he truly cared for. No, he knew the life Sydney had was hers, and he'd do what he always did: cheer her on from afar and do his best to be content with that.

4

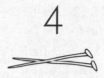

OULD THIS GET any more embarrassing? Here she was, looking like crap. Okay, not crap. She did just get her hair done — albeit in a style that she might not quite be pulling off. The jury was not back in on that one. But it didn't matter. Here she was, in sweats, no less, and sweating, while folding other people's laundry. The once-again laundress that she'd left Harlem telling herself she'd never be, and Lucas Strong had to show up looking just as strong and fine as ever. And had the nerve to still be giving her the judgy stink eye while his clothes dried.

Sydney tried to calm her mind and focus on what she was doing. To pay no attention as he loaded his clothes into dryer number 17. She should probably tell him that dryer was slow to heat and he should move down to 25, which was free, but that would bring him closer to where she was, so she kept her mouth shut. Let him deal with his own clothes while she dealt with her customer's.

She looked down. *Dammit!* She was messing up. There was a particular way the tablecloths had to be folded, first halved and then a trifold. What she was doing was nothing of the sort. Sure, she'd been rusty when she'd first returned, but it was amazing how quickly the old methods came back to her. Syd had been taught the ins and outs of the business at a young age by her grandfather, her mom even then not hiding her disdain for the fact that seven-year-old Sydney found more enjoyment at her grandfather's side in Scrubs than with the piano lessons she'd sworn would better her. But the truth was, Syd loved helping her pops in the laundromat, straightening the supplies and folding clothes brought in by the various businesses, busy working women and bachelors who would do drop-offs. She found comfort in the orderly, repetitive way things had to be done to avoid the chaos of the outside world, not to mention the sense of warmth and home she felt by her grandfather's side. Her time in Scrubs was way more fulfilling than going downtown to take the fancy lessons her mom had insisted on. Syd would spend the entire forty-five minutes on the M2 bus wishing she was back in her old familiar space and dreading the scrutiny that was to come. But it was hopeless. She'd begged her mother—if she had to take the classes, couldn't she at least take them in Harlem where some of her peers did at Harlem School of the Arts? She wanted to do modern dance and not ballet. But no, her mom was quick to shoot that down. Like the man she'd approved of her daughter marrying, Evangeline had definite ideas about what was and wasn't acceptable for her daughter.

Sydney let out a breath, then looked back at the misfolded tablecloth as she fought to ignore the prickly feeling of restlessness and unease that came whenever Lucas Strong was close by. It didn't matter. It couldn't matter. She'd known she'd see him sooner or later anyway, but she had naively hoped that when she did, it would only be in passing. But she should have known she'd have no such luck.

"Hey, um, Syd."

Her eyes closed for a moment. *Please don't let that be his voice.*

Please don't let that be his voice. Shoot, of course it was his voice. Who else could say a stupid name like Syd and make it sound like melted chocolate mixed with warm caramel, sending her into internal babblings?

"I seem to be out of money on my card and don't have change to refill it at the machine." Sydney looked up, begging her eyes not to betray anything but indifference as their gazes connected over his outstretched hand. It took all her strength not to shake as she reached out and took his card.

"How much do you want on it?"

He smiled. Dammit, he fucking smiled. Her legs had better not go and get weak. Not when she had to turn and walk over behind the counter, and not with her kid just over there, no doubt watching this whole exchange. She was a goddammed superwoman. She didn't do the whole weak-in-the-knees thing.

He reached into the pocket of his sweats as Sydney forced herself to feign boredom. Eyes forward. Do not look where his hands were rummaging and shifting things and pulling her attention. Shit! Gray sweatpants. They were the betrayer of women every time.

Suddenly her gaze was snapped back to where it should be by Lucas waving a bill in her face. She frowned and squelched her embarrassment as she caught the quirk of his brow that let her know she'd been caught peeking. "All I have is a twenty. So can you just put ten on my card?"

She shrugged. "No problem," she said as she turned to the register.

Play it cool, help the man and he'll be on his damn way. Lord, why are there so few laundromats in the neighborhood?

Sydney let out a breath and completed the transaction. "Here you go," she said, giving Lucas his change and his card back to use the dryer. She knew as well as he did that the "Finish and be on your way," though silent, was implied.

She didn't want to watch him walk away, so she only glanced. The broad shoulders had gotten broader. Firm ass, firmer. When he turned and bent to put his card in the machine slot, she could see just how defined the muscles in his arms were and how flat his abs still were. Damn. The years had treated him well, despite beating the shit out of so many other folks.

Sydney turned away and looked at her daughter. A moment ago, Remi had been complaining about being bored, and now she was reading one of the many books she'd brought with her in her backpack. She wasn't the biggest screen watcher (thankfully), but it was hard to keep her engaged. She was a smart and quick child. So it was no wonder she got excited seeing Lucas knitting. It probably looked like something fun that could keep her attention while she was sitting here waiting for Sydney's shift to end. It wasn't like Syd wanted her loading and unloading the machines or spending hours folding tablecloths. Sydney stilled, as the thoughts were so similar to what were probably her own mother's.

Her mind went to how Remi had seemed so immediately taken with Lucas. How her daughter, who knew better, still trusted him enough to get near his space to sit and watch him knit. It scared her. She'd have to have another talk with Remi about strangers and how they weren't in a gated subdivision anymore. And . . . oh, just screw it. It wasn't about that. It was about him. And why did Remi trust him, and why did Sydney not? Well, she needed to get over it.

It was safer to feel nothing than what she felt around Lucas Strong. He was definitely not safe. At least not for her. Not that it was an option. She knew from experience, hers and her mother's, that she should good and well listen to the gut instinct that made her feel that sense of danger. Here she was, despite all her mother's good intentions, sacrifices and, sure, at times out-and-out misguided tactics. She was the woman who'd almost had it all—the education, the man, the house and the kid—but somehow, she'd ended up right back here, just like her mother. A single mom with a daughter, and with a bachelor who was nothing but trouble hanging around her laundromat, asking for change.

Her cell vibrated, bringing Remi's head up as Sydney pulled her phone out of her pocket. Crap—Redmon. What was he doing calling at this time of night? It was now well past eleven, and he still thought he could just ring her up at any time. Probably calling to once again complain about the fact that she'd left. Well, not so much the fact that she'd left. As if her leaving didn't come with the divorce. She let out a sigh, suddenly thinking of the scene there would be when she did go back to divide up the contents of the house and clear out her things properly.

More than likely though, these calls had to do with him feeling shell-shocked over the real-life ramifications of life without her hitting him in the ass. Sex aside, everyone should have a wife like her. Hell, she'd take a wife like her. Besides his business—and Red was just good enough with the bullshit to keep lucrative at that—she'd kept his life in order. House, car, clothes and kid. He didn't have to think for himself with much of anything. It was probably why he'd had enough free fucking time.

She wondered if he was keeping up with paying the housekeeper. Because someone had to take his lipstick-stained shirts to the dry cleaner's if not his most docile wife, or wash his boxers and get the smell of other women off them.

She let the call go to voice mail, but she felt her blood pressure starting to rise as the phone started to buzz and vibrate again. She swiped at it fast. "What is it, Red?" Her voice was shrill and annoyed, and instantly she regretted it. Her face heated as most of the patrons, Lucas included, turned her way.

And then she heard a scrape as Remi shifted in her chair. Hell, Remi had heard that. She needed to dial it back for Remi. Syd turned and saw that her daughter was now absorbed with her iPad and wouldn't meet her eye. But Sydney knew by the straightness of her head and the ever-so-slight tenseness in her little girl's shoulders that she was listening. Her eyes darted over to where Lucas had been by the dryers. He was gone. She turned and saw that he was back at the other end of the laundry in the waiting area, head down, looking relaxed, with his knitting back in his hands.

She put her phone to her ear, careful to keep her voice even and her tone normal. "What is it, Red?" She could have sworn that for a moment Lucas's fingers stilled in their rapid motion. She shook her head. Nosy-assed Lucas Strong, still minding her business. She turned away from him and this time encountered the gaze of her daughter. "Syddie, are you there, are you listening?" Red's voice was its usual: demanding, ready to bark orders.

"I'm listening, Red." Remi continued to stare, her eyes wide and questioning. Sydney felt like it was an assault from all sides as tiredness suddenly hit her. Her voice lowered. "It's late. Why are you calling?"

"That's more like my woman," came the smooth purr that was now nothing but grating.

Once again, she felt her blood pressure start to rise, the heat licking up her body from her toes. But she had to keep cool. There were too many people around—not that a woman going off on a man on the phone would cause that much of a spectacle, but she wasn't going to do that in front of Remi. She wouldn't be that mother. Still, she had to make it clear. "I'm not your woman, Red. Not anymore." She could feel Lucas's presence and lowered her voice. "Now please, what are you calling for?"

"Whatever you say, Syddie, but you and I both know that a little paper don't make all that much of a difference."

Sydney couldn't help but laugh at that. "If you say so, Red. Now, it's late, and I have work to do."

"And if you didn't insist on that paper, there would be no need for that."

Shit. She was now clenching so hard on her teeth she was giving herself a migraine. "Time is money, Red," she said, keeping her voice even as she bounced one of his favorite sayings back at him.

She couldn't yell at him like she wanted, and she had a feeling that he knew it. He probably knew she was working at Scrubs and wouldn't make a scene by having a public argument. It was a tactic he'd used to keep her tethered and in check for years.

She didn't even have time for the niceties with Red. She had these tablecloths to finish and more loads to come after them.

"Seriously, Red, what is it?"

"So I guess you're too busy to talk to me now? I see how it is. Maybe it's not work. Maybe you're busy with other things?" She could hear the petty accusation in his voice. As if with his philandering he should be one to throw around accusations.

She frowned. "What do you care, and why is it your business?"

"A man should care about what his wife does after ten."

She let out a sigh. "Ex. And like I said—work."

Red laughed. The sound grated on her eardrum, practically vibrating annoyance throughout her body. It was sad, but she could still remember when that laugh used to give her a very different kind of vibration. "Good night, Red."

"Wait, wait. I didn't call just to mess with you. I want to talk to my daughter."

Sydney felt her body tense. She looked across the counter to where Remi was. She was back to studying her iPad, and Syd couldn't tell if her daughter was paying attention to the video or secretly listening to their conversation. The fact that she didn't know filled her with so much pain. This was why she'd left. Because she'd no longer been able to give her daughter a life where she could just freaking be and know that she was okay.

"It's late. She's sleeping," Sydney whispered the lie.

"She's fucking not sleeping, Sydney," Red hissed.

The impulse to recoil ran through Sydney's body, but he wasn't there, and she stood her ground. Besides, Red had never gone that far. Close, but never that far. Either way, something in her still wanted to edge back and shrink down, make herself small. Instead, she frowned and fought against it.

"What did I say, Red? You'll have to try her tomorrow. Or she'll call you."

She heard him let out a frustrated sigh. "You see that she does. It's bad enough you used that shit excuse of your grandfather to take my daughter from me, but if you think I'm just going to pay more on top of what I'm already giving in support, with you holding my daughter hostage in another state, you're dead wrong. No fucking way."

Sydney looked down at the tablecloths she'd been folding. They were clean and white and nothing like the filthy mess her life was in now. She suddenly wanted to throw up. Retch it all out and leave the stain of her years with Red right there on the tablecloths and burn them, never to be seen again. But no. Not here in this shop that was her grandfather's legacy and, right now, her lifeline, and not in front of these people. "You really must be a different kind of shithead, you know?" Sydney said calmly. She was barely able to keep the weariness out of her voice.

"I'm just looking out."

"If you say so, Red. Like I said, you can try her tomorrow. Or not." And with that, she hung up the phone.

She looked over at Remi and watched as her daughter's shoulders dropped an almost imperceptible inch. She *had* been listening. Sydney walked over and stood at Remi's side. She rubbed the top of her head and Remi leaned into her.

"That was Dad?" Remi said.

"Yeah, I told him you'd talk to him tomorrow. That it was too late tonight."

She felt Remi nod into her side. Finally, she spoke, her voice soft and low. "Yeah, tomorrow is good."

5

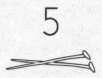

"SO YOU RAN into Sydney Harris?" Jesse said.

His youngest brother was in the kitchen when Lucas returned to the shop. He'd folded his clothes as quickly as he could after they were done in the dryer, which meant they were hardly folded at all. He'd have to refold them all once he'd settled upstairs. There was no way he'd let them stay in his duffel bag wrinkled like that.

He looked at Jesse and couldn't help but marvel over his transformation since Mama Joy's death and the shop's remodel. He seemed so much better. The way his relationship with Kerry had changed him was an astonishment. Talk about the woman making the man and all that. Not that his brother was a slouch, but he had definitely been a playa, and now he was totally a one-woman man. One woman and one career. A little over a year ago, Lucas would never have taken that bet.

Though they weren't rolling in the dough with the shop, it wasn't due to any slacking on Jesse's part. He, his brothers and the shop were still standing on nothing but grace and the fact that they were lucky to have so many people who loved Mama Joy and got behind them.

"Talk about a blast from the past. It's been a long time since she was in the neighborhood. I mean, I thought she would've been back earlier or made a few more visits. Her grandfather probably could have used the help. Although who knows, with how these older folks are. Set in their ways and unwilling to reach out for a hand. We know how proud they can be," Jesse said, and Lucas could do nothing but agree with him there. Even the four of them had had a hard time reining Mama Joy in and getting her to slow down—which she never really did. Not up until the very end.

Lucas fought against the rising tide of guilt that threatened to rear up and overtake him in that moment.

Jesse kept talking though. "But she is here now, so I guess that's good, especially since Mr. H hasn't seemed to be doing too well. I'm sure he can use the extra help over in the shop, and he'll be happy to have some family with him."

"Wait. Did something happen in the past week when I was working? We didn't get any emergency calls at the ladder house."

Jesse shook his head. "No, nothing like that. The one scare with his heart was enough. Yet it got Sydney here. Not that that's a reason to celebrate, but you, my brother, should take your wins when you can get them."

Lucas groaned. "You act like I'm some sort of sad case."

"And you act like you're not."

When he looked up, Jesse was staring at him with his head cocked to the side. He waved a butter knife Lucas's way, no doubt doing the midnight snack thing that had become a habit for him and Kerry.

"You want me to make you one?" Jesse asked. The casualness of his offer made Lucas smile. Yeah, Jesse had changed. The old him had been more apt to have a girl up and making his sandwich after sex. *Way to go, Kerry Girl.*

Lucas shook his head and lifted the brown paper bag he'd been holding in his duffel-free hand. "Nah, I'm good. I picked up something on the way back in. You and Kerry enjoy your"—he paused, remembering what Michelle had said about the table downstairs— "post-whatever feast and don't let me intrude."

He walked around his brother to grab a paper towel and a plate to head up to his room, suddenly feeling like he was more a third wheel on a prom date than a grown man who paid a portion of the mortgage. Maybe it was time to move out. But Jesse's voice pulled him back. "Wait a minute, you didn't finish your story. You saw Sydney Harris and . . . ? You can't leave me hanging. Did you two talk? Was she glad to see you? I know you were glad to see her." He waggled his brows.

Lucas let out a sigh. "Why should I be glad to see her? It's not like we have a history. And besides, she's a married woman. With a kid."

Jesse's brows drew together, and he looked confused for a moment. "First of all, stop with the lies. You two may not have been an official couple, but you clearly have a history, and everybody knows it. That woman has been your forever crush since forever." Jesse took a dramatic step back then and gave his brother a long up-and-down before clearing his throat. "And yeah, she's back in town with a kid, but from what I hear—the husband, well, he's no longer in the picture."

Lucas knew his jaw dropped, and the way he knew it dropped was because Jesse made a big show of cackling as he reached forward to close it.

KICKING THE DOOR closed softly behind him with his foot, Lucas put his food on his desk, then went immediately to work unloading his wrinkled clothes. He needed a distraction. Anything but thinking about the knowledge that Syd was now not a married woman—which, according to Jesse, had been double confirmed by no fewer than two members of the Old Knitting Gang.

Shit, this was huge. This could be his chance. This could change everything. This made him want to suddenly pack up his shit and head for the hills. It was way too dangerous.

With the clothes quickly put away, Lucas sat in his gaming chair to eat, hoping the greasiness of the food would lull him into some sort of state of non-Sydney-filled sleep bliss.

Better to think sensibly. Think of his job and the awful call and the damage control he still had to deal with once he was back to work, where he was most likely going to get chewed out by the captain again.

Lucas looked around his bedroom at the moving shadows from the passing cars on the street below. Dammit. Why was he thinking of this now, when he needed to be sleeping? He couldn't have more nights like the one he'd had last night. This time it was only his reputation that was bruised; the next time it could be so much worse.

There he'd been, so close to coasting for the rest of his shift, and then, as all other shoes do, it dropped.

Lucas was tired but pretending like he wasn't while standing around with some of the crew, just coming off a thankfully easy call where one of the elevators was once again stuck between floors in one of the local housing projects. Normally, they would have just let housing maintenance deal with it, but there was a person trapped inside and it could have turned into a distress situation. After going out on so many of these calls, they knew how to get high-rise elevator doors open, so luckily that call went by without a hitch. Well, without much of one.

When the other call came in, they were all back at the ladder house, standing around and listening to the comic recap being put on by Flex Edwards, another firefighter and their resident comedian.

Flex was going on about Mr. Henley's shimmy out of the space between the elevator and the floor above. The poor man, who could barely move a moment before, moved like a gazelle when the alarm suddenly blared on his phone, giving him a fright. The funny part was that it was only his wife scaring him with a new ringtone she'd installed. Just after Flex got to the mimicking portion of the Mr. Henley story, the firehouse's alarm blared out, and just like that, in the space of a nanosecond, Flex was transformed. The normally easygoing paramedic's expression turned deadly serious, and all laughter in the small group of firefighters that had been lingering by the truck stopped.

Lucas exchanged a quick glance with his colleague and friend since their training days, Danica Lewis. The second lieutenant's eyes went skyward as she shrugged her shoulders. "Sorry, my guy. You were this close to being out," she said, with a slight grimace.

Lucas gave a shrug back. "No biggie. It's part of the job," he said. "We'd better get going." His words were wasted on air and Lewis's back, since she was already gone, as were his other colleagues. They had already started moving to their stations with the first ping of the alarm. Damn, he really was slow. Finally falling in line with the rest of his crew, he grabbed his gear, suiting up as he got onto the truck, which was in motion as he took his seat.

The call was to a remodeled tenement on 138th Street. He knew the neighborhood—and the building, for that matter. Despite the recent remodel to high-priced condos, the general layout had not changed, and maybe that gave him a false sense of security too. Made him even more lax. He didn't know, and he hated that he was still looking for excuses. All he knew was that he was distracted from jump. He felt Lewis's penetrating gaze from beside him as she glanced his way. "You okay?" she asked.

He gave her a quick nod, then turned his attention toward the window, watching as Harlem went by in a blur. "I'm fine," he said, fighting to focus on the streets before him and not the fact that they were for some reason blurring with images that if he had his way would be long forgotten, never to resurface. Scattered and blown to the wind, just like the ashes of their long-dead bio mother.

Lucas smiled, and Lewis frowned, her dark slashes of brows furrowing under her helmet while her nearly black pupils went a deeper onyx.

Don't show fear, Lucas reminded himself. *Keep up the facade.*

He tilted his head. "You okay?" Then he raised a brow and jutted his chin her way, lowering his voice a bit, but not enough that Flex wouldn't hear. "Wait a minute," Lucas said. "Don't tell me you got a hot date going on when your shift is over tonight?"

That comment did the trick, and her eyes narrowed as her nostrils flared. He knew he'd pay for that later, but the distraction was worth it. She let out a rush of air. "Did you forget I now outrank you, Strong?" she said.

"Oh, sorry, Lieutenant," Lucas said with a tinge of mocking reverence that he knew he could get away with—but only to a point.

Then Lewis looked at him. "I wish," she said as she twisted her lips. "I've got a date with nobody but my dad and a pint of Ben and Jerry's," she said. Then she smiled. "Not that I'm complaining about either one. My last three dates were a bust before anybody could bust, so to speak. You're welcome to come over. We've got plenty. There was a sale."

Lucas and Flex looked at each other and cringed. Lucas looked back at Lewis. "Seriously? Did you have to?"

She shrugged. "You started it, jerko."

He shrugged. She was right, so he guessed he did deserve at least what he got. But the image of Dee busting it—ugh. Just no. It wasn't one he wanted to have.

Lucas nodded, ready to end this convo and be at the call, then done and off his shift. He leaned back in his seat. "I can't argue with you there."

They were silent for a moment, and in that space, he knew they were both remembering past disastrous dates.

"I don't know what's with you two."

Lewis turned toward the voice that came with the comment. Lucas could see in her sharp turn that she was less Dee and more Lieutenant Lewis in that moment. It was a fine difference, but it was there. "What are you talking about, Carroll?" she said to the firefighter, who obviously didn't know when a done conversation was done.

"I'm talking about you two. Why don't you just hook up already? Don't worry—I won't tell," he said jokingly. "At this point you're like an old married couple anyway."

Lucas watched as Lewis's nostrils flared ever so slightly, and then her full lips quirked at the corner as if she was going to smile, but then they dropped. Shit, Carroll was fucked. Goodbye to his dream shift or next planned vacation. With her promotion, Lewis was now in charge of scheduling, and she had a wicked petty streak. Lucas looked at Carroll, suddenly feeling sorry for the idiot—but then again, not. He should good and well know better.

"As if," Lucas blurted out and gave Lewis a look that said maybe cut Carroll a little slack and only put him on bathroom rotation. Besides, Lucas had started this and put her in a mood in the first place.

Lewis sighed. "Yeah, as if," she finally said by way of agreement.

Lucas breathed a sigh of relief. He didn't know why either of them was getting bent out of shape anyway. It wasn't the first and probably wouldn't be the last time they were in the situation. The fact they were friends who seemed to genuinely like each other and hung out together was bound to fuel the rumor mill. New York was the smallest big city there was, and the world of the FDNY was minuscule. Still, Lucas had thought they could at least relax in their home station.

He and Dee were nothing more than friends. And never would be. Yeah, there was that very awkward and very bland kiss that had happened after their academy graduation, but that had sealed the deal for both of them forever. It happened in the hazy space where—blame it on the alcohol and maybe being fueled by the peer pressure of the stupid rumors—she for a moment stopped being Lewis or even Dee and started being Danica. But with just one touch, they both stared at each other and knew. It was friend zone forever. And though Lewis was a top wingwoman, and he was good enough as a wingman, he didn't need to hear her using words like "bust." The visual went too far.

Thoughts of busting, old friends and all that went out the window when they pulled up to the scene a moment later. The crew was instantly back in game mode as they launched out of the truck and went about assessing the situation. A couple of newbies made a perimeter check, carefully urging away the quickly gathering crowd of onlookers on the tight Harlem street.

He looked up at the building and saw that there were no visual flames, thankfully, but there was dark smoke coming from a side window on the third floor. *Shit.* He blinked as an icy finger of remembrance brought forth the image that had been plaguing him lately and keeping him up at night, and it rooted him for a moment to the concrete under his feet. Smoke billowing from the window of an old Harlem tenement. A crowd gathered below and him, small, holding the hand of his younger brother Noah outside while his unsuspecting mother rushed back in unnecessarily to save them. If only he'd listened to her. Paid careful attention then. She would still be here. None of it would have happened. His "umma"—mother—practically the only Korean word that still came to him naturally, the rest gone in a flash, just as she was. It was the same with Mama Joy. If only he'd been paying attention, she'd probably still be here too.

Lucas shook his head and focused on the very real smoke coming from the third-floor window. Fuck anxiety. He didn't have time for that shit. His job was saving people, and that took movement and action.

So why the hell aren't I moving? Lucas jumped when Carroll's hand clapped him on the shoulder. "Let's hit it, man." Joe Carroll's voice was loud, and Lucas looked, expecting to see the man beside him, but instead he saw his back, since he was already on his way into the building. Of course. Carroll got it. No time to waste. It was time to move. Lucas rushed forward, pulling his mask down and heading into the building.

The stairs were dimly lit despite the remodel—something he was sure the new management would hear about. He looked up and noticed the flickering of the overhead light. The elevators had already been disabled by his colleagues. The ones much faster and more ready on the job than he was. It was okay though. That part wasn't his responsibility. Still, he continued to take stock and see where he needed to be.

There was a strange feeling in the air. Lucas knew that he was off, but still, nothing felt quite in sync as he made his way to floor three, now passing Lewis and Carroll as they made their way back down the stairs, already escorting some of the residents out of the building. Rodriguez pointed up, giving him the signal that he should keep going, that three was now clear. Lucas nodded. He was in the process of banging on doors when he noticed smoke seeping from under the doorway of one apartment. He pounded on the dark gray door but didn't get an answer. Lucas banged again, then yelled for whoever might be inside to step back, since he was going to ram it, when the door suddenly opened.

Through his visor he saw it was a woman. She appeared to be in her twenties, blonde, in a loose tank that hung past her shorts. She was coughing softly into her arm. Lucas frowned and pushed up his visor. He leaned in to check her breathing. She looked up at him. Her coughing suddenly stopped as she leaned fully on his arm and tilted her head back.

"Miss, you have to go downstairs," he said. "Let me check to see if someone else is in the apartment."

Lucas moved to her right as she grabbed his jacket sleeve, shaking her head. "There is no one else. Just me."

His brows furrowed as he looked into the apartment. The smoke was subsiding, but it still needed to be checked out, and she seemed fine. "Okay," he said, "but I still need to check things out inside."

She coughed again, a little louder this time, and leaned into him further. Lucas could see others from his crew coming up. He started to steer her toward the stairs, guiltily hoping to pass her off once they were downstairs. By now an EMT battalion should have arrived and they could take over and assess her. But just then she coughed once again and fell fully into his arms. Lucas looked down. "Oh hell." He groaned just as Rodriguez and Flex hit the landing. "What's up?" Flex said shortly.

"Check that apartment. There's smoke," Lucas replied. "I'm taking her out."

Flex nodded, but Rodriguez paused. "You good?" he asked.

"Yeah," Lucas said as he was starting down, the tenant's body tight to his side. Something twisted uneasily in his gut as he navigated the stairs with her. She was limp, but not really, and was seemingly responding to his nonverbal cues.

Once on the sidewalk, out in the fresh air, Lucas quickly looked for an ambulatory unit to help the woman attached to his side. Seeing none on the scene yet, he quickly shuttled her to the gurney that had been set up by their truck in anticipation of any need. He lifted her slim body easily and noticed her eyes were fully shut. Tight. Maybe too tight. Lucas leaned in to check her vitals, his fingers at her neck, and noted her pulse was steady and strong. He moved closer to assess her breathing, and that's when it happened.

Holy fuck! She was fast. But he should have been faster. He should have been more alert. He sure as hell would have been if he'd actually been getting adequate sleep during his allotted hours and not up in his bunk staring at the ceiling for most of the night. But it didn't matter now, because she had her thin arms wrapped around his neck and pulled him in for some nonemergency mouth-to-mouth. Thankfully he was at least quick enough to turn to the side.

"Con-sent!" he ground out, surprising himself with the word, but *shit*, she was clearly pulling at him without his permission. "I don't consent! What the hell is wrong with you?" he said as he tried to wiggle away. What was she, a low-key weight lifter? Damn, she was strong.

Finally, Lucas got a good hold on the woman's bionic arms. She grinned. He frowned. What was this lady doing grinning while practically molesting him on the street? Dammit, she was supposed to be in distress. Lucas pulled away, and the clearly not-in-distress woman followed, her upper body dragging along with his neck. Fuck again! Half—no, more than half—the crowd had their phones raised and were filming their little drama. Great. Just what he didn't need. A video of a woman with her arms around his neck would be fun to explain to the captain when it came time for his performance review. Their captain could take awkward situations as well as the next, but what he didn't take was any tarnish on his unit. If Lucas was to embarrass the team in any way, he'd have to explain his way out of it or he'd find his next promotion and pay raise slow to come. Yes, their shop, Strong Knits, was doing all right, but they were far from in the clear. The woman reached for him again, and he jumped back.

"Damn, that's cold," a woman in the crowd yelled, and there was a smattering of laughter around her.

The woman on the gurney whined and reached for him. "She's right—it *is* cold."

"Listen, lady, I don't know what your deal is, but I've got a job to do," Lucas said, moving from her personal space to the seemingly safer space of the potential fire.

"Hey, just shooting my shot," she came back with a shrug. "Not many chances a blown coffeepot will get you Mr. November at your apartment door."

Lucas found it hard to keep control of his emotions in that moment. *Mr. November.* Just perfect. The fucking calendar. Once again it was coming back to bite him in the ass. He would be so glad when this year came and went and he was no longer anyone's monthly fantasy.

He turned and was about to head back into the building when he saw the rest of his crew coming out. "All clear here," the captain said.

"Is it really, now?" Lewis chimed in from the foot of the apartment steps. She gave Lucas a raised brow.

"Don't start," he grumbled, over being his usual nice self.

"Ben and Jerry's?" Dee replied, not as surprised at the drop in his facade as most would have been, but picking up on the fact that he was done. "The offer still stands."

Lucas shook his head and narrowed his eyes as he gazed over at the blonde. Dammit. Now he knew why she'd seemed familiar. She was the weird one who worked with Kerry over at the center. The one she and Val were always annoyed by. And here he had thought she was harmless all this time. He looked over at the crowd with their cells up once again and thought of the almost lip lock with her potentially trending. "Dammit," he muttered. "I should go over there and tell her the hell off. Better yet, press charges."

But his friend was ahead of him and, thankfully, was thinking faster than his irrational mind was. "No, you don't," Lewis said, reaching her hand out and pulling him back by the forearm. "Hold on there, cowboy. You're a superstar." She grinned. "Or stupid star."

Lucas tilted his head as his eyes narrowed.

She laughed. "I'm just screwing with you. Though I can see this isn't your fault. With this crowd and all the cell phones, you'd just be giving them more fodder. Besides, you're this year's golden boy, and you don't need to do anything more to bring unwanted attention right now." She looked over to where the blonde was smiling for the crowd but still somehow putting on like she was playing the part of the victim in a fire tonight. Fake coughing as if she were ready to be sent in for emergency testing when she'd just had Lucas in a deadlock a moment before.

Lewis pulled her shoulders back and steeled her expression. For a moment it seemed like his friend had suddenly put three inches on her five-foot-six-inch frame as she trained her gaze on her target. "You leave her to me," Lewis said as she eyed the still-performing blonde. "Go and finish clearing the scene so we can get out of here that much faster." Her eyes got just a touch softer. "And please cool down. These days you seem off. You gotta get some rest. When you get home, that's the first order of business."

Lucas took a deep breath and looked at his friend. Her gaze showed her understanding. She was right. No matter how much he wanted to tell the blonde off, he knew that was the wrong move. Besides, there would be another right after her—at least until this whole calendar thing cooled off. He nodded and watched as Lewis strode over to the woman. Within seconds of Dee speaking to the blonde, the self-satisfied look vanished from her face. Lucas afforded himself the barest hint of a smile but stopped short of going full-on. He still had a crick in his neck from where she'd yanked at him. *Fuck*. Turning from the scene to go and assist with clearing, he made a mental note to pick up extra quarts of ice cream for Lewis during his time off this week. It was the least he could do.

REST.

Remembering Lewis's words brought Lucas back to the present and put a neon sign on the fact that he wasn't following her order, not for lack of trying though. Speaking of signs . . . He stared at the lights outside his window. They were always on and now seemed to shine even brighter with the knowledge that once again Syd was back and so close—but in some ways farther than ever before.

Lucas stretched, then groaned. He wasn't sleeping, and thinking of his screwups at work wasn't doing anything but pissing him off more than he was already, which damned sure wasn't bringing sleep along.

One thing that he did know though, and that this hellish week and now night fully reminded him of, was that women with problems, women with issues, women in peril—they weren't for him. He was unreliable. Despite his civil service rank and title. If he cared, it was bound to end wrong. He hadn't made the right decision when his mother needed him, and he hadn't been there when Mama Joy needed him either. And when it came to Syd, who knew if, in the process of pursuing her, he'd have let her down? No, it was better to keep his screwups light and local and definitely not personal.

At this point he felt like he'd been up for at least twenty-four hours, if not more. And then, seeing Sydney Harris had been more than enough to send him over the edge of exhaustion.

With a frustrated sigh he wrapped up the rest of his sandwich and slipped downstairs quietly to put it in the fridge. Reluctantly he went back to his room. But what else was there to do? He could go to the gym, but if he ran into one of his coworkers there and it got back to Dee, he'd be a dead man. Better to do what he should and try to get some rest, or at least pretend to do so. Back in his room, he thought of doing a mini workout to burn off some steam. Maybe get in a few burpees. But he didn't want to disturb Jesse and Kerry, who were sleeping downstairs, so instead he sat in his gaming chair again and swiveled until his eyes caught on the lights at Scrubs.

He thought of Sydney and her little girl with the smile so like Syd's had been. The one he had only caught rare glimpses of when they were kids. Against his better judgment, he swiped at his phone and went to her IG page again. Looking at it with fresh eyes, he wondered where her marriage had gone wrong and if it had ever been right. As he scrolled through her photos now, all he felt was sadness—and it was a type of sadness so different from the hopeful emotions he used to feel when he'd come across her page. Then, when he'd look, sure he'd be sad for what he couldn't have, but he was also happy for the life she'd made for herself. The beautiful picture she'd created. You'd think that hearing her dream had shattered would give him hope, but it left him nothing but hollow, empty in the knowledge that he knew he couldn't help her rebuild it.

Lucas leaned his head back on the chair.

WHEN NEXT LUCAS opened his eyes, it was thanks to a hard shove from his brother Noah. Lucas squinted. He couldn't believe it. The harsh but still welcome, surprising rays of the morning sun were now hitting his face. The last thing he remembered from last night was thinking of Syd, her smile intermingling with that tough glare she liked to put on, all mixed with manicured lawns and the tumbling of dryers. And now here it was morning. He didn't know when he'd last slept so soundly.

It was then that confusion grabbed him once again. *Wait. Noah?* Lucas looked up at his younger brother, taking in the mirage that wasn't even supposed to be in the country, let alone in New York.

He frowned. "What the hell are you doing waking me up on my day off?"

As per usual, his brother was unfazed and, despite his words, grinned at him. "Well, isn't that a fine welcome home to a road-weary traveler. Barely gone a few months and you treat me like an intruder."

Lucas snorted. "Shaddup and be happy you still have a room and we haven't Airbnb'd it out."

"As if."

"Do you know your brother Damian?"

Noah's face finally dropped.

6

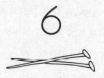

WAKING UP ANNOYED was bad enough. Waking up annoyed and more tired than when you went to bed was the freaking worst. But there was nothing new about either of those things, since "annoyed and tired" was her usual default these days. These past few years, if she was really telling it. It was like a *Groundhog Day* torture loop. But as was also her usual, she stretched, shook it off as much as she could and did her best to put on the mask of contentment that had become part of her daily uniform.

It was part of her daily reboot to transition from agitation and anxiety to go-get-'em, got-it-all-together wife and mother. She sighed and slipped through the partially closed door of her old room, where Remi was now sleeping, and peeked in. Scratch that. Go-get-'em, got-it-all-together *single* mother. There was a big difference.

While dressing, she thought over Red's call from last night. Maybe she should have let him speak to Remi. But then again, it had been late, and Remi still could use a bit of time to process what their life was now. Sydney knew she needed to tread lightly, since Red wasn't one to play fast and loose with. And she was quickly learning that she had to figure out a whole new landscape without his full financial support behind her. So far, all that was settled was the divorce and the barest alimony, but what was agreed on was agreed on hastily on her part, and not with New York rents and schooling in mind. All she had been thinking of was getting gone. But now that they were in New York, Syd was definitely regretting not slowing things down a bit, paying more for a better lawyer and getting more on the front end.

Here, with what she was getting in terms of spousal support, a private school would be out of the question, and she'd returned too late for the charter school lottery system—not to mention that there were the extras that were now necessary if you expected your child to get into a good college. The piano, dance, pre-pre-SAT prep courses. Whew. *Slow your roll, Syd*. That was way too much of Evangeline's voice coming through, she thought as the droning echo of mapping Remi's perfect life went through her head.

Still, the older she got, the more she knew her mom did have a few points, as misguided as some of them may be. And she knew that, just like with her mother and her relationship with Mr. Wiley, the same would be true when it came to requesting additional favors from Red. There were parts of Red she definitely needed, and those parts started with dollar signs and ended with zeros, and there would be no end to the quid pro quo he'd want in return.

Once again Lucas Strong popped up, unbidden, in her mind—a hybrid of the boy he was, all full of quirkiness and easy smiles, and the man he'd become. Broad shouldered; strong, slashed brows; slightly intimidating, deep-set, hooded eyes that saw too much. He still had that smile. The one that made his eyes shine like diamonds and melted her heart all at the same time. There wouldn't have been any quid pro quo if it were Lucas; something in her gut told her that. Sydney twisted her lips in frustration and shook her head. What did it matter? It was too late to worry about her faulty gut now. She needed to be thinking with her head. Anywhere lower than that was nothing but trouble.

Sydney gave herself a final shake before heading into the kitchen. It was just a little after six, and of course her grandfather was already up and dressed, and likely had been since his usual four thirty. She'd said she'd be down to help him early even though she'd gone to bed only a few hours before. He'd insisted it wasn't necessary, since Mr. Bill was working, but she was determined. If that's what meant she was putting in her fair share, then that's what she was going to do. She hadn't come home to laze about.

She took in her pops, dressed in his usual college pullover—how he had accumulated so many was still a mystery—long khaki cargo shorts, and sneakers with gym socks pulled up high above his ankles. His short gray curls were brushed back into tiny waves, and his deep caramel skin had few wrinkles to show his advanced age.

But Sydney knew that though he looked relatively healthy on the outside, there were underlying issues that told his true story. Arthritis and high blood pressure, plus back and hip pain from folding and toting everyone's clothes for the past forty-five years. Then there was the worst: his now-weakened heart and a diagnosis of cardiovascular disease.

There would be no end to the prayers of thanks she gave up to Mr. Bill for being alert enough to catch her grandfather's symptoms of overexertion that day. She knew her grandfather hated letting her know about his rapidly declining health and slower work rate, and her mother hated letting her in on it even more. Her mother still clung to the stubborn belief that nothing, not even family obligations, should come between her and Red and keeping up the sham of a picture-perfect marriage they'd built, as if her grandfather having an acute aortic attack that had him clutching his chest and gasping for breath when Mr. Bill found him didn't trump likes on social media.

The wild thing was, Syd knew her mother was the last person she could complain to about Red and his other women, her being a longtime mistress herself. Syd would get no sympathy but be told to stay in and bear it, not move an inch, just as Mr. Wiley's wife had and was still doing.

Maybe Syd was her mother's totally twisted revenge—who knew? If Evangeline couldn't have the life she'd dreamt of, she'd make damned well sure her daughter did.

Well, no more. Sydney was living her own life now, for however little it was worth. Let her mother stay out on Long Island, the side woman living on the fringes of Mr. Wiley's married life. One thing her mom's experiences had taught Syd was that if she couldn't be the main character in her own marriage, then she was better off the star of a one-woman show.

"Here it is a bright and sunny new day, and you're walking into my kitchen with that kind of face on, Syd?"

"Face? I don't have any kind of face on," Sydney said, knowing she definitely did have a face on. "And I wouldn't be making the face that I don't have on if I didn't smell bacon cooking in this kitchen, when you know good and well that you can't have bacon in your diet."

Pops gave her his you're-not-the-boss-of-me look. It was full of annoyance and frustration, with no small amount of "I've had it up to here." But then his eyes that had rolled skyward toward the kitchen ceiling came back to her and softened as he smiled. "Now, I've been cutting and cooking slab bacon since way before you were born. I don't need you thinking you're going to come in here, missy, and in any kind of way stop me."

Sydney opened her mouth to argue, but Pops raised a hand, silencing her. "Ah. Now, before you start, the bacon is not for me but for you and Remi. If you look over here, I've got some lovely, though not all that appetizing-looking, turkey bacon. Lean, hardly any fat, hardly any flavor, just waiting on me. All that blandness should make you happy indeed."

Sydney glanced to the side of the frying pan, where Pops had indicated. There was the one plate covered with a napkin soggy with grease from the heavenly-smelling slab bacon drippings, and next to it was a small saucer with a neatly folded napkin and three slices of rather sad-looking turkey bacon. Poor Pops. Sydney fought to keep her face straight and not relay her thoughts on the turkey bacon.

It wasn't fair. A man should at least be able to eat what he wanted after fighting to keep his business open and available for the people in the neighborhood over the decades. Having to give up his beloved bacon on top of so many other things he enjoyed . . . it seemed ridiculously unfair for a man who gave so much to so many.

Still, Sydney stood firm as she looked back at her grandfather and gave him a sure nod. "Excellent, that's what I like to see. Me and Remi need you healthy and in good fighting shape so we have you for the long haul, Pops."

"Long haul?" Pops turned around toward the frying pan and went to pulling out the last of the bacon and adding it to the rest of the bunch. "I might as well be out to pasture," he grumbled.

Sydney frowned. This was unlike him. Pops was usually the

most upbeat person she knew, even in the most trying of circumstances. He hardly ever scolded her, even when she deserved it, and was one of the most generous people, often taking on more than he needed to. So what was with the grumbling and the talk of pastures and all that? "What are you grumbling about, old man?" Sydney asked.

Pops coughed and turned back toward her, giving a shrug. "I'm not grumbling about anything. Maybe just a little mad I can't have my bacon and have to resort to this turkey crap. But hey, the way I figure it, it could definitely be worse." He smiled at her then. "At least I have my looks, all my good teeth. Hell, Grady went to the dentist the other week and his ass had to get six teeth removed all at once. Bet he wishes he could have some turkey bacon this morning. Best he can do now is oatmeal or a turkey smoothie." He picked up a piece of turkey bacon and took an exaggerated bite as if it were crunchy, but it only crumbled, and he had to quickly reach out his other hand to stop the droppings from falling to the floor.

Sydney shook her head. "Yeah, poor Grady, huh? How about poor all of us? Seems if we look hard enough, we can all find something to gripe about. Just let me make you a quick egg white omelet and then we can have something to eat together before Remi gets up."

Pops shook his head. "Now, you go on and get your coffee. I don't need you handling eggs and working around hot flames without some caffeine in you first."

Syd frowned. "Come on, Pops. I'm not that bad."

Her grandfather shrugged, then looked her up and down. "Well, I guess you've gotten a little better over the years," he said as he took in her appearance. "I mean, at least your socks match today, and your shoes too."

"One time, Pops, one time. And I only went two blocks before I noticed I was mismatched." Normally Little Miss Perfect growing up, she knew it hadn't been without the help of her grandfather keeping her straight and up to her mother's exacting standards of dress and good decorum in the morning as a kid. For all her years, Sydney had not been a morning person and was terribly hard to get up and out of bed, so it had usually taken no less than three tries by her grandfather, the laying out of her clothes the night before, and a little hint of sweet tea when she was younger, light and sweet coffee when she got older. All that and she was daughter of the day before she headed out to school. That may not have been the way with most kids, but it had been the way with her.

She remembered the time she told Pops she was going caffeine-free, as was a trend with so many of the other kids. Well, that lasted about a good three days, during which she'd misplaced notes, been irritable, and then forgotten to match her socks right. And now here it was almost twenty years later, and Pops was still bringing it up.

He laughed at her. "I know, I know, it was a long time ago and you were nothing but a kid. But such a perfect kid that it's about the only thing I have to tease you about. So what else is an old man supposed to do? Now get your coffee and let me finish making your breakfast."

Sydney made her coffee and let her grandfather fry her an egg. She watched his movements carefully and tried hard not to let what could've happened had Mr. Bill not caught his dizzy spell in time take over and send her into a fit of fear, anxiety and guilt. She felt horrible for not being there for the past year—well, the past few years—though he had never given her any reason to feel guilty. Still, she felt it all the same. Being a full-time trophy wife was no excuse for being a shit granddaughter.

But her mother, who'd spent so many years in the laundry, felt she'd broken out and past their little hood thanks to the not-so-free benefaction of her lecherous boss, yet another by-the-pound bachelor. (Turned out later that he wasn't the bachelor he'd claimed to be, but had a whole other side family. But by then that was neither here nor there.) Mr. Wiley had come into the shop and, in his own words, "saved" the young single mother. He'd had a business and needed a secretary, and he knew Sydney's mom would do anything to give her daughter a life that was better, or at least what she perceived to be better, than her own.

And when Sydney thought of it, what had she really been running from when she went running toward Redmon? Was it from her mother, or was it to gain her mother's true pride and acceptance once and for all? Would something like that ever be achievable when her mother couldn't even achieve it herself?

All her life her mother lived on the outskirts of a life she never quite fit into, and here Syd was running away from one she'd molded near perfectly to make fit.

Syd thought of Lucas and how seeing him the night before had brought up such an instinctive, almost visceral reaction. She sighed. It was nuts, but even on his worst days, Red hardly made her that mad or excited or anything. Not unless it came to Remi. He hardly made her anything. Barely moved her needle. Now, who could she be mad at for that? Lucas? Red? Or her own foolish self?

Pops put a plate in front of her with a perfectly fried egg, two slices of bacon, and one slice of lightly toasted bread with butter and jelly, all just like she used to like it. Sydney twisted her lips and took a deep breath as she picked up the toast and took a bite.

"You and your melancholy ways, Sydney Harris."

She looked at him as he sat down across from her with his

sadder-looking plate of scrambled egg whites and two slices of turkey bacon. He had a cup of black coffee in his hand, and she knew how much he hated it bitter that way without his heavy cream.

Still, she protested, because with him she knew she could. "What are you talking about, melancholy?" she asked. "How am I being melancholy? I'm just sitting here enjoying this fine breakfast you made for me. If anything, it's you who might've woken up on the wrong side of the bed this morning. You feeling all right?"

His eyes narrowed a little and he gave her one of those looks— the ones where his rich chocolate eyes latched onto her and saw more than she wanted them to see. Sydney looked down, taking her fork and using it to slice at her egg, knowing she had lost this particular round of chicken.

Her grandfather let out a humph sound. "Yeah, melancholy and overthinking, way too much. It's always been that way, so nothing new there. Still, I would've thought things would have lightened up, with you coming back home and being out from under that ass chap of a husband you went and married."

Syd's eyes snapped up as she looked at her grandfather. It wasn't all that shocking that Pops used the word "asschap." He was always making up ridiculous-sounding words. What *was* shocking was the way he put so much venom behind it. And the really surprising part was the fact he was using that venom in reference to Redmon. Sydney thought she'd done such a good job hiding the troubles in her and Redmon's marriage. Whenever she called back home, she did her best to put on a convincing "everything's fine" act for her grandfather. If she'd known that Pops knew all along, she wouldn't have wasted her time. Shit. In that moment, guilt engulfed her. Who knew, maybe if she would have put a little more effort into her marriage or had been better with her cover-ups and acting skills, Pops wouldn't have had the extra stress of worrying about her and wouldn't be sick now.

Her grandfather was staring at her with serious eyes, and Sydney felt the urge to hide. To protect the lie she'd built her life on.

"What you talking about?" Sydney asked. "You've always liked Red."

He shook his head side to side in a nonchalant kind of way, then shrugged. "I didn't like or dislike him. What mattered was how he treated you and if you liked him. So I guess I liked him for as long as you did, and when you stopped, I stopped." He stared at her hard once again and added the word "Quickly."

Syd swallowed, knowing Red was getting off light, being that her pops wasn't up to his old speed or strength.

He continued. "I guess it's been four or five years, then, since I stopped liking that asschap of a husband of yours."

Sydney couldn't help but laugh. "Really, Pops. Asschap? You couldn't come up with something better?"

"If the ass and the chap fit, then I say go for it." He reached out his hand and gently took her own. "I should apologize to you," he started. Syd immediately wanted to protest, but he was talking too fast. "With me knowing that he wasn't treating you right for so long, I should have gotten you out of there sooner."

Sydney shook her head. "What you talking about, Pops? I don't know what you think you know, but it wasn't like I went into this blindly. Staying with Redmon was my own decision, and I appreciate you giving me the space to let me choose."

Pops let out a breath, and though he looked a little relieved, she could still see the worry tightening his brows. "I appreciate you saying that, but I can't help but feel some amount of guilt. I was trying to give you space to make your own decisions, but as your grandfather I should have stepped in. You deserve more happiness than what you've gotten."

Suddenly he brightened. "And speaking of happiness, there is walking sunshine and light, right when I need it."

Remi came bouncing in, her eyes filled with sleep. She greeted Pops with a big hug around the waist, then came and snuggled on Sydney's lap like the five-year-old she used to be instead of the nine-year-old she was now.

Syd leaned in and got a good whiff of Remi's hair. It was almost ready for a wash but still had the lingering scent of hair oil and soft innocence that were undeniably her. She closed her eyes for a moment, wanting so much for her daughter to be able to hang on to that sweet innocence, but there was nothing she could do, because once it was gone, it was just gone.

"What will it be for you today, little princess?" Pops asked Remi.

"It'll be whatever we're having," Sydney said, giving Remi a nudge off her lap. "As a matter of fact, she will help me make her breakfast."

Syd started to get up, but Pops was ahead of her, already moving toward the stove. He turned around. "All right then, that's enough out of you, Ms. Sydney. You may be helping me run Scrubs, but this is still my kitchen, and that is still my laundromat. And while this is still all mine, if I want to cook breakfast for you both, then I will." He smiled at Remi in such a sweet way that once again Sydney had to push down guilt for staying away as long as she had and letting the rift with her mother and the pain of seeing Lucas keep her away so long. She was an awful granddaughter, and keeping Pops working like this and Remi away from precious memories had just been cruel.

She gave a nod and said "Knock yourself out," then went back to finishing off her breakfast while Remi sat beside her.

"That's more like it," Pops said. "Everybody happy, everybody getting along. Now let's talk about better things. I hear Lucas Strong came in to do his wash last night. I'm sorry I missed him, but it must have been great for you catching up, Syd." He turned to Remi. "Did your mom tell you that she and Mr. Strong used to be old friends back in high school?"

"Mr. Strong?" Remi giggled. "That's a funny name."

"A ridiculous one is more like it."

Her grandfather shot her a look at the same time as Remi turned to her with a face full of confusion. Then she turned back to Pops. "Who is Mr. Strong, Grampops? The only man who Mom talked to in the laundry was one who didn't seem like an old friend at all. But I thought he was cool, with his knitting." She paused then, and Syd saw her wheels turning, her daughter's quick mind clicking things into place. "Wait. Mom, you did say his name. You called him Lucas Strong." Her face went all quizzical, looking too much like Pops. "If he was an old friend, why did you pull me away from him so fast?"

"It was just that it's been so many years that I hardly recognized him at first, so I thought he was a stranger. And you know you're not supposed to talk to strangers."

Remi nodded.

Sydney could feel her grandfather's hard gaze even though she'd decided to put all her concentration on her last piece of bacon.

How was it she was sitting back in this kitchen at the same old yellow table, the subject once again Lucas Strong, and once again feeling all of fifteen years old and sweating over her crush while Pops saw through every barrier she attempted to put up? But she wasn't fifteen now, and Lucas was nothing more than an old acquaintance, one of the many who made up the blurry history that had turned her into the woman she was today. She let out a breath. And that's where he would stay—in her past and part of her history.

But of course, Pops being Pops, fifteen years in the past to him was no further than a week ago. He looked skeptical but then got serious. "Your ma is right. You can't talk to strangers, Remi. A friend is one thing, but you've got to have your wits about you. New York is not DC. Hell, DC is not DC anymore." He let out a sigh. "No matter. Pops will teach you right. Not that you have any worries when it comes to Lucas Strong. He and his brothers are pretty all right." He looked pointedly at Syd. "If you ask me, that is."

Syd shot him a look, and Pops went on. "I mean, they all have been an invaluable resource to me these past few years. And I always thought of Lucas as just one of the kids you went to school with and nothing more. I was right about that, wasn't I, Syd?"

Sydney looked at her grandfather, wishing to all hell they could just be done with this conversation. "He was, and he still is. Nothing more," she said, adding a tight smile.

Pops nodded. "I'm glad to hear it. Because I'd hate to think there was any real animosity there. Not after the way we've become friendly and all the good work he does at the firehouse and in the neighborhood. It would rub me raw to add him to the list of jerks who chap my ass."

Sydney chomped down hard on her last piece of bacon, took a final swig of her coffee and nodded. "Don't worry about that, Pops. You can consider that list officially closed."

7

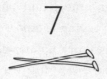

LUCAS BLINKED HARD three times, barely registering the situation. Seriously, how did it get to be morning when just a moment ago it was still night? The last thing he remembered was sitting here like a lovesick fool spending way too much time on thoughts of Sydney and the past. Maybe he really was just finally hitting that wall he'd been so worried about. Or maybe it was something more.

"Who has got you so whipped that you've got that stupid-assed look on your face this morning?"

Lucas felt his brows draw tight. And maybe he needed to get his head out of his own ass and figure out what Noah was doing back home months ahead of schedule instead of on tour.

"What are you doing back home?" His stomach did an involuntary knotty twisty thing, and he looked hard at Noah, doing a quick assessment for anything visibly amiss. But his brother looked the same, just as tall and fit as ever, and the immediate relief that overcame him was welcome. Still, something must be wrong.

"What are you doing sleeping in a chair and not your bed?" Noah countered, ignoring Lucas's question entirely. "And since when do you leave crumpled laundry all over your bed and, to top it off, sleep past eight o'clock?" Noah continued.

Lucas shot his brother a quick and hard glare, then rubbed his hands over his face, still trying to knock the fogginess out of his head. He gave him another quick up-and-down. Now that he looked again, though not too the worse for wear, Noah did look a little thinner than normal. He was still tall and fit and muscular, his dancer's body kept in shape with nightly shows on tour. But Lucas could see a little bit of fatigue around Noah's eyes, which were almost exactly like his. Their mother's eyes. Noah had so much of her that sometimes it hurt Lucas just to look at him. Noah got his height from his African-American father, and he never let Lucas forget the fact that he stood taller than his older brother by a good three inches. He'd also inherited his father's hazelnut skin tone, soft curly hair and strong bridged nose, but the rest was all their Korean mother, and every time Lucas looked at his brother, the memories of her came flooding back with a mixture of happiness and heartache.

"You avoided my question. What you doing here? You never said you'd be coming back home. Aren't you supposed to be, what, in Amsterdam right now—or is it Italy?"

Noah let out a sigh. "Not like I didn't notice you avoided my question too, bro." He shook his head as his long legs brought him over to the bed in one and a half strides. He shoved Lucas's clothes over to the side and lay down on the bed with a groan, putting his arms back behind his head. "Well, as you can see it's neither of those, because here I am back in New York. Freaking Jett."

Lucas looked at his brother and almost laughed hearing him say "Freaking Jett" yet again. The initial enthusiasm Noah'd had when he got picked up as a replacement for an injured dancer with the mega-famous R&B and hip-hop singer Jett Hathaway's tour had worn off pretty quickly when the rumors of Jett's diva ways turned out to be true. "So what happened? After the cancellations last year, you guys seemed pretty booked up, so the tour shouldn't be over. What you doing back?" Lucas was fully awake now and leaning forward in his chair, staring at Noah.

Noah looked his way, his eyes going wide. "Don't look at me like that. It's not like I got fired. The tour really is over. Or at the least it's over for now. 'Postponed.'" He put his hands up and did air quotes at the end of his sentence. "That's what they are officially calling it for the press, but who knows," Noah said, his voice now laced with pent-up annoyance, which was so not like him. Out of all of Lucas's brothers, Noah was the least likely to show any thread of annoyance. He was nearly un-annoyable. Little Mr. Sunshine, as Mama Joy had dubbed him. Noah lit up a room. But here he was now. Back home and, dare Lucas say, a little pissed.

Noah sighed. "Postponed. Just like almost all of our principal rehearsals were postponed. Which in turn had us turning into low-key jokes on tour, the grand dame somehow always coming out un-scathed. It was always someone else's fault. The choreographer, a backup dancer, one of the stagehands, but never the fact that the diva couldn't get her shit together and put in the time it takes to perfect a show." He let out an exasperated groan and slapped his hands on his thighs. "There are nightmares and then there is Jett Hathaway. I have never worked with anyone so unprofessional in my life, and that includes the time I was the lead choreographer for the pre-K group at Dumble Downs Broadway Stage summer camp up in Scarsdale."

Oh damn. He didn't like to revisit his summer in Scarsdale. Now Lucas knew his brother was really pissed.

His normally rose-colored-lenses brother gave a groan. "So

many shows will now be canceled due to her lack of professional-
ism. I swear, that woman was a total nightmare to work with."

Lucas leaned back in his chair and shook his head. "So, what
are you doing for now?"

Noah let out a breath as he pushed himself up off the bed and
stretched, arching his back farther than any human man should be
allowed to do. When he came back up, he gave Lucas a bored look
and a yawn. "Well, the first thing to do is take a shower and then
sleep. I feel like the tour is stuck to my body, and right now I just
want it off and slept away. And then . . . well, I don't know what. I
guess I'll help out around here. I'm sure Jesse can use it. And though
the tour is postponed, it's not like I'm going to be destitute. The
Queen Diva is taking her sweet time to rest and recharge, but in the
meantime, to not lose what she calls her"—he rolled his eyes and
put up air quotes once again—"'family,' she's keeping all of us on a
minimum retainer. She sold it to me and the rest of the crew by saying she'd be coming up with new songs and a new set list and sending it soon, so she needed us to stay on call and at the ready. As if
she was ever ready. For anything." Noah grunted in uncharacteristic frustration and leaned his head back as he pushed at his temples
with his thumbs.

Lucas shrugged and got up to hug his brother. He gave him a
quick double pat on the back before pulling back. "Hey, as far as
gigs go, I'd say you're lucky to have it." Then he stared at Noah
harder, taking in the shadows beneath his eyes and the gauntness
in his jawline. "Before you go to bed, let me make you something
to eat? I can't speak too much about her being a diva, but I can say
she could have fed you better while you were on the road."

Noah yawned but nodded, despite his tiredness. "Fine, Mom.

Feed me if you must, but then it's lights out, because your boy here is wiped."

"Okay, little smartass, cut the mom comments and come and eat. Remember who the older brother is here. I can still beat your ass at the drop of a hat." Lucas winced internally as he heard his own very mom-like "I brought you into this world, I can take you out" comment and watched as Noah started off down the narrow hallway. Suddenly he remembered the night when they were both kids and had gotten into a wild fight after living with Mama Joy for just shy of a year. Strangely, now Lucas couldn't even remember what the fight was about, but what he did remember was telling Noah how he was tired of him being underfoot all the time and in his space, and how Noah said *Fine* and that very night stomped down to Mama Joy after half dragging his mattress to the middle of the narrow hallway and told her he was moving to the other side of the attic and he'd had it with his older brother.

Noah stood his determined little ground. Mama Joy and Lucas didn't expect him to last an hour on the other side of the house, but still Mama Joy helped him drag the mattress three-quarters of the way over there and Lucas the rest. Lucas remembered staying up till nearly dawn waiting for Noah to come back to their room fearful because he'd had a nightmare or crying for their mother and saying he couldn't sleep without Lucas nearby. But he never did. Finally, when Lucas went to check on Noah, he was fast asleep, his mattress pulled even farther to the other side of the attic room that he'd now made his, next to the dirty window with a view of the sun rising in the east. His little brother was growing up, he'd realized. Trying to break away. And there Lucas was, still awake and watching over him.

Lucas blinked out of the memory of the boy Noah used to be and looked now at the man he'd become. "I shouldn't be long. Let me just go wash up, then I'll make you some breakfast. I'm sure that Jesse and Kerry have already eaten, but if not, maybe they'll join us," Lucas said.

Noah turned around. "Cool. I can't wait to hear what's been going on since I've been gone. Catch me up on everything from when I left up until last night when you ran into your old crush, Sydney Harris." Noah grinned then, all cheeky and little-brother-like.

Lucas frowned. "What the hell? You're back home, what? Three and a half minutes, and already you've got the scoop on the latest gossip? I swear, Jesse has turned into a Little Mr. Chats-A-Lot since he started running the shop."

"What Jesse? I heard this from Sister Purnell as I was getting out of my Uber and coming into the shop first thing this morning. She happened to catch me up on a few things when she was heading over to Mount Neboh Baptist for the sunrise senior praise line dance class."

Lucas shook his head. *Perfect.* Sister Purnell was already talking about the two of them running into each other last night? How did she know? She hadn't even been in Scrubs last night. And Lucas hadn't seen any of the usual missionary church–slash–gossip gang when he was going over to or leaving Scrubs. He groaned. If Sister Purnell was talking, then that meant the rest of the OKG was privy to the news too. Just fuck his life. One thing was for sure: if those women knew and if Mama Joy were still alive, she'd definitely be up on the news. Not only had the Old Knitting Gang been Strong Knits' best customers, but they were Mama Joy's ride or dies and held her strong by helping with keeping an eye out on the boys after she'd fostered and then adopted them.

Oh well. At least this would take the neighborhood talk off his almost-lip-lock with the wild blonde from the smoking-coffeepot call.

Exciting old dish, even served cold, was always tastier than new news, which was an acquired taste. Folks around here liked the feeling of the familiar. And if they knew about him running into Sydney, then they probably had already known, even before he did, that she was here with just her daughter and that she was no longer with her ex.

He didn't know how long she was staying, but he had a feeling that for however long it was, even if he tried to lie low, he'd somehow get wrapped up in some mess. Knowing them, they probably knew how many pairs of underwear he washed last night too. Harlem really was the smallest little village ever in the biggest city in the US.

8

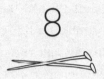

"HE STREETS ARE calling my name! The streets are calling my name!"
Syd looked up to see her oldest and dearest friend, Kat, making a
grand, gorgeous and quite noisy entrance into Scrubs. She pointed at
Syd, then put her hand dramatically to one ear. "What is that, Streets?
You're calling my friend here's name too?" She clapped her hands to-
gether. "It's your lucky day, my girl. The streets are calling our names.
Stop the presses! You and me are going out tonight!"

Sydney was glad to see her friend Katherine Bell stride into Scrubs
like her same old self, loud and full of fanfare. Even better was the
feeling she got over seeing Kat's daughter, Aisha, coming into Scrubs
behind her. As soon as Remi caught sight of Aisha, she perked up
from where she'd been sluggishly shifting an empty clothing cart
back and forth and quickly pushed it to the side, running toward
Aisha as if she were a long-lost friend.

The girls met in a tight embrace and spun around, instantly reminding Sydney of how she and Kat used to greet each other when
they were kids. Kat was the only friend from New York she'd kept in
contact with. Kat hadn't gone for her starting-a-new-life bull—she

was just that tenacious. When Syd didn't come back home, Kat made her way to DC for lunches and getaway spa overnights with her friend. And when they both had their daughters, she vowed that was it. They were co-aunties for life, going through the raising-girls game while trying to stay sane through thick and thin.

"I'm sorry it took me so long," Aisha said. "But I was visiting with my dad for two weeks, and we went to Disney with his new girlfriend and her kids."

Sydney watched as Remi gave Aisha a "Poor you" look. "That must've been something," she said, sounding way more mature than she should have at her age. But then she brightened. "Got to go to Disney though? That's really cool."

Aisha nodded eagerly. "It was really cool. The girlfriend and the kids weren't all that bad. They didn't get in my way too much, and she's a huge *Star Wars* fan, so it wasn't a problem that I wanted to spend most of my time at that park area."

"Wow, you're so lucky! I wonder if my dad will suddenly want to take trips to Disney now that we're divorced?"

It was on the tip of Syd's tongue to open her mouth and say that it wasn't Remi who was divorced from Red, but before she could, Kat had spoken up.

"Yeah, yeah, she's a real lucky girl. But what about me?" Kat said. "You've got no love for your old Auntie Kat?"

Remi looked up and laughed, wrapping her arms around Kat's waist. "You're not old, Auntie Kat. You're the youngest adult I know."

Kat's eyes went wide, and she stuck her tongue out, giving a smug look to Syd, who rolled her eyes and stuck her tongue out right back. When it came to Kat, they all but dissolved into twelve-year-olds, usually within ten seconds of seeing each other.

"Don't let it go to your head," Syd said. "I've taught the girl the finer points of flattery. She's all talk."

"If you say so. But I'm going with the kid knows a good thing when she sees it."

Syd nodded. It wasn't like Remi was exaggerating. Kat looked fantastic. Her short-cropped hair was shiny and looked freshly styled. She was wearing high-stacked sandals and tight camo ankle jeans, along with a flowy top that showed off one shoulder. Even though this was her Saturday chill outfit, the way Kat carried it, she could easily walk into a boardroom and command a meeting. Which was probably why she was a top media ad VP, despite her young age, and was always being scouted by other firms.

Syd was proud of her old friend. On the surface, they seemed so similar and had lived very much parallel lives— coming from this neighborhood, destined to break out and get into college on scholarships, they had even ended up getting surprise pregnant the same year. But that was where the similarities ended. Syd's world had seemed to stop and become all about Red and Remi. But Kat hadn't let her dreams get swallowed up.

She used the motivation of her daughter to fuel her to go farther just that much faster, and when she saw cracks in her failing relationship with Taye, she dropped him like a bad habit. Hell, as a matter of fact, she dropped him, processed food and sugar. Said she was giving up all the dead weight in her life. So many times Syd had thought that if only she'd followed her friend's track just a little more closely, maybe she wouldn't have wasted so many years. Maybe she wouldn't feel so behind that catching up didn't even seem worth the start.

Taking her head out of regrets and a past that couldn't be changed,

Syd turned her focus to Aisha. The little girl had grown a lot. Aisha was so much like Kat had been at that age: tall and thin, all arms and legs, with bright brown eyes that seemed to take in everything all at once. She was so pretty, with her wide mouth and her lips that appeared constantly poised to smile. What was it, two years since their day trip to the Smithsonian in DC? So much had changed since then. Remi was now a child of divorce, like her friend, and both girls had not only grown taller but matured in many ways—some to be admired, and others that just saddened her. Not that they wouldn't both thrive. Syd had to believe that. But still she couldn't help feeling that in some ways she'd let her daughter down, that she hadn't lived up to the promises of the sacrifices she'd said she would make for her even before she was born.

"What about me, little Aisha? You're just as bad as your friend here, with no love for your Aunt Syd."

Aisha came over and gave her a hug. It felt good, and she took it, eagerly and gratefully.

"It's good to see you, Aunt Syd," Aisha said. "I love your hair! Your curls look cute! I've never seen you wear your natural hair before. I like it!"

Syd gave a wink Kat's way. "Looks like this one knows how to flatter too."

Kat grinned. "I'd say we both aren't doing too shabby."

Syd's heart filled with warmth. Their girls were so special, and having her friend show her this support gave her a feeling of contentment she hadn't had in a long while. Her smile was wide as she watched Aisha run back to Remi, and the girls went and huddled over by the front window. Syd and Kat looked their way, and Syd knew they were both seeing their old selves coming back in the present.

"Talk about the past coming back to smack you, huh?" Kat said.

"You got that right." Syd sighed. "Now what's all this about going out tonight? How am I going out? What about Remi? I can't just leave her with Pops, and besides, I have work here."

"So I'm not supposed to be insulted by that?"

Shit. Of course Pops would walk up right when she said the exact thing she didn't want him to hear. He'd taken a moment to go up to the residence and grab some fruit for his after-lunch snack.

"Hey there, Kat. It's good to see you, hon," he said, no longer addressing Syd.

"Good to see you too, Mr. H. You're looking fine." Kat went in for a hug, hesitating at first and giving Pops a hard stare as if confirming he was okay.

But Pops took her bare hand in his and pulled her in close. "It's fine, dear. I'm fine. I'm keeping well, and I've got these two with me now. All that's plaguing me is a touch of age." His eyes shifted to Syd. "Though to let this one tell it, you'd think I was one foot in the grave already."

"I was not saying any such thing."

He shook his head and gave a slightly annoyed wave Syd's way before looking back at Kat. "Please take her. She's been home over a week and you'd think she was older than me, the way she mopes and pokes around."

"I don't mope or poke." Syd pouted.

"You poke and mope plenty!"

"But what about Remi and the shop?" she asked, knowing she'd never win this particular argument. "You can't take care of them both."

Pops shot her a look then that took her back about twenty years in the space of a nanosecond. "I can, and I can take care of double that." But then he quickly calmed. "But it's not like I have to do all that much these days. We have Bill, and if need be, I have Glen. He doesn't mind working to make some extra cash."

Sydney had to practically bite her tongue. Glen was fine but really the most unreliable part-timer. Call on him when you needed and hope his pockets were light, or you were shit out of luck. But Pops was stubborn and loyal and a little bit jaded, and besides Mr. Bill and Glen, he didn't trust anyone else to work there.

"Bill will be in soon to take over the evening shift. Did you forget he's helping out tonight?" her pops said.

Kat raised a mocking brow. "Yeah, did you forget he was helping out tonight, Sydneyyy?"

"He doesn't need any help," Pops said.

"No, he doesn't," Kat said. "But how about you let me give you a double night off?" She turned back to Syd. "Come on out with me and do me a favor and let Remi stay over with Aisha tonight. My sister said she'd watch them for us. Aisha would love it."

At the words "stay over," the dynamic duo over by the window showed their hand and the fact that they were totally eavesdropping on the conversation. "Please, Auntie Syd," Aisha said. "Can Remi come over?"

"Yes, Mommy, please. I'm bored. I want to go over to Aisha's. Her dad got her the latest *Animal Crossing* and I want to play it."

"Oh, the latest game, and Disney World too." She raised a brow at Kat. "Really? You letting Taye slide with that type of easy bribery?"

"I know you're not talking to me about bribery right now."

Syd opened her mouth for a comeback but quickly shut it when she realized she didn't have one.

"I thought not."

She looked at Remi, who was going all in, making faces, even attempting to bat her long eyelashes. "Fine. You can go."

Immediately she and Aisha started jumping up and down and shrieking, sending heads in Scrubs whipping their way. "Girls, girls—keep it down."

"Oh, leave them be, Syd. It's fine," Pops said. "It's been silent in here long enough. I never thought I'd say it, but I miss the ruckus of children running around this place."

"Okay," she said, giving in to her grandfather, and to Kat and the girls too. "I'll need to get her bag together, and my things. What time are we going out? You could have just called, by the way. You didn't have to come all the way here."

"What all the way? I moved from the projects and slummed it three blocks south to my overpriced condo."

Syd laughed. "Yeah, slummed it. Sure." She knew for a fact that little three-block move was nothing to laugh at and a huge leap for Kat. For anyone coming from where she came from. The woman was badass.

"But really, we didn't just come here to see you," Kat stated. "Aisha is eager to get back over to Strong Knits for some yarn and to pick up where she left off taking classes before her trip with her dad."

"Well, isn't that interesting. Talk about perfect timing."

"Don't go giving me that look, Miss Harris. It's not like I have anything nefarious going on. But it's good to see you haven't changed in your everything's-about-you thinking."

Sydney just shrugged. Kat was trying to guilt her into feeling like she was overreacting, and she was sure that Aisha probably did have some interest in knitting, but she also knew her friend, and her friend definitely knew about her past feelings for Lucas and her regrets over not having pursued him like she really wanted to. "Oh, no, it doesn't matter anyway. Aisha got you over here. And that'll get Remi out tonight. She's going to be so happy."

Once again Remi came bouncing over with Aisha. "Mom, can I run over to the knitting shop with Aisha? She says if I bring some yarn to her house tonight, I can do some knitting too. It looks like fun, and I really want to learn. Please?"

Syd turned to Kat again. *I'm going to kill you,* she mouthed silently.

Kat's eyes went wide as her shoulders went up in mock innocence.

"Sure, Remi, she'll let your Auntie Kat take you over there with Aisha." Kat looked down at her watch. "You better hurry up, because it looks like the next kids' lessons are starting right about now. I'm sure you'll be able to sit in and get some basics down with Miss Kerry."

"Wait a minute," Syd started, "I didn't say yes to lessons."

"Please, Mommy?"

"Remi, you know we can't go jumping into just anything without researching the time, the cost." Not to mention the fact that it was run by Lucas Strong's family. Of course, Sydney didn't say that part out loud. The time, the money and figuring out the logistics of it and how to keep it up in the future were enough to worry her. She ran a hand over the back of her neck, squeezing the tight knot that was starting to form there.

"It's fine, Aisha, you go ahead without me. Maybe I'll come with you to class the next time." Syd felt Remi take her hand in her own as she smiled at her friend in a way that tried to say she was fine and wasn't all that interested in the knitting anyway. Syd's heart got a definite crimp in it with that one, a dull pain that could only be described as disappointment worse than her own.

She slipped her hand out of her daughter's and gently pushed her forward toward Aisha. "You go over there and pick out something nice to make, okay?"

Remi looked up with her eyes wide and full of tentative hope.

"Pick out some yarn with blue. You always like the color blue."

Remi's grin spread wide. "I don't know, Mom. I'll see what they have. Maybe they'll have green or orange. You always like orange, Mommy, that's your favorite color. I'd rather make something for you."

Kat moved between the two girls. "Okay, you two, we better get going, or there'll be no deciding for any of us." She turned back to Syd. "It's my treat, so don't worry about that part. You just go on and throw a bag together for this one here so that she can go back home with Aisha. Then give me a little time after that and let's say we meet up tonight about eight for hanging out like we used to, SK style?"

"SK style? What is that?" Remi asked.

Kat seemed a little too enthusiastic for Syd to take the "hanging out SK style" with anything but trepidation, but she'd go along with it.

She looked at her daughter. "'SK' stands for anything with the Syd and Kat flair. It was the name of our little club back when we were your ages. I guess you'd call it our squad."

Remi stared at her blankly and then looked sad, her eyes full of pity. "Oh, Mommy. You two only had a squad of two."

Kat gasped. "Excuse me, little girl —I'll have you know that's all we needed. There were girls dying to get into the SK crew back in the day, but we were tight." Kat twisted her first two fingers around each other in an exaggerated gesture. "We didn't need any others messing up the good thing we had. Let the rest watch and learn. Just like they will tonight." She beamed over at Syd.

"Okay, okay. It's your show tonight. I'll come."

Kat was already pushing the girls toward the door. "You just be ready for anything," she said before hitting the Harlem streets once again, leaving Syd even more nervous.

9

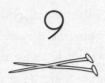

I CAN'T BELIEVE THIS is the same old Lenox Club." Syd looked around at the lounge that had been a Harlem staple for years, and could barely recognize it. It wasn't like she'd been a frequent patron back in the day, but still she remembered the lounge from when her mom would get done up and slip out for cocktails there with Mr. Wiley. Syd recalled a part of her admiring her mom, thinking she looked classy, with just a hint of sexiness about her that she worked hard to keep in reserve the rest of the week as she went about her day-to-day as his secretary. What that man told his wife about staying out every Thursday night in the city, Syd still didn't know. But she'd long since stopped caring.

Syd remembered sneaking off to the lounge with Kat when her cousins, Taylor and Tina, were in town the summer they were seventeen. They'd been up from North Carolina and wanted to see all of New York and make all the stops young girls should and maybe should not. And of course Kat was one hundred percent game to be the NYC tour guide and insisted Syd tag along. It didn't matter that the girls were underage   height, hips and ass got them through the doors. Still, with no head for alcohol and no straight face when it came to lying, Syd was the designated buzzkill and stuck to Diet Cokes with lemon during their illicit club outings. It was fine by her though, because the hour she'd been in the Lenox Club she'd spent not chatting with the girls about being in the big city, but instead taking in the lounge's art deco decor: the deep crimson leather banquettes, which somehow worked perfectly with the zebra-print wallpaper and dark black tufted leather in the strategically wide lounging areas. There were mirrors with ornate frames everywhere and the perfect soft lighting to set the mood for something decadent to break out at any moment. The whole while, she sipped on her Diet Coke, though Syd couldn't help imagining her mom doing her best to use the venue to capture another woman's man, another woman's life. And she came so close too. So very close. Perhaps if her mom had been born during another time—but sadly, Syd had come to learn that for some, no time was the right time when it came to being open about love.

At one point, Syd had romantically believed that her mother too maybe thought if she'd been born during another era, things could have been different between her and her boss. But Syd knew in her heart that wasn't true. Her mother was too pragmatic for that. Mr. Wiley was a comfortable means to an end, and her mother was his dark secret—perfectly accepted as his secretary and undercover sometimes-bedmate, but wife material? No way.

When Syd had gotten back to New York, her mother was just as relieved as she was full of admonishments for Syd's not giving her a date for going back to DC and home to Red. As for the divorce, her mother's reaction was pretty much just as she'd expected it to be.

"What do you mean you don't know when you're going home?" Evangeline had said. "I don't understand."

She was lying. She understood. Perfectly. She was just willing
to give Red every pass in order to keep up appearances of Syd living a perfect life.

"He's been messing around, Mother. It's over. We're done," Syd
told her.

Evangeline just rolled her eyes at the "messing around" comment, as if Syd had said he'd brought home powder instead of liq-
uid detergent, then had proceeded to move the lint traps that Pops
had been cleaning on the dining table, exaggeratedly picking them
up between her manicured nail tips. Syd loved her dearly, but why
did she make making a caricature of her so easy?

Syd snorted. It was low, but still, she gave herself credit for it.

Evangeline twisted her lips, letting her daughter know the snort
wasn't missed. Finally, she let out a breath and turned a steely gaze
on her daughter. "I don't know what you mean by 'done.' How can
you two ever be done? You're married. Thank goodness you at least
have a child and the legitimacy of documented paperwork to secure
that." She muttered that part, in reference, Syd was sure, to the
phantom father who had never appeared on Syd's own birth certificate. Finally, her mother let out a long sigh. "Whatever. You are going to do what you want right now anyway. You'll come back to
your senses soon enough. I just hope by then it won't be too late and
he won't have truly moved on." She looked Syd up and down. "You
keep yourself right and he'll be back. At least with you here I won't
have to take that long drive over every time your grandfather
coughs or teeters a bit. I've got to hold on to my job too. I wasn't
lucky enough to have as much support as you have. You think you'd
be more grateful with the way I set you up."

Syd bit the inside of her cheek to keep from screaming. She
couldn't handle Red, getting Remi settled and fighting with her

mother over her divorce and her unwillingness to back her up all at
once. It was just too much to take on. She knew her mother would
never see her side of things.

The fact that her mother lived in two worlds where she actually
pretended her job and her "job" were separate was both delusional
and commendable. Maybe it was why she was able to last as long as
she did without both her and Mrs. Wiley completely losing their shit
and plotting together to kill that turd of a man they both claimed to
care for. Who knew? But one thing Syd did know was that she
couldn't live the life her mother lived, and she wouldn't subject her
daughter to growing up that way.

A jarring clash of dishes from the bar area brought Syd back to
the here and now. She put on a quick, well-practiced smile and
tried to remember she was supposed to be having fun. If she didn't
at least show it, then Kat would call the night a wash and have her
do it all over again. The place really had changed. All the mysteri-
ous allure of the past was gone, and in its place was a Gen X calam-
ity that didn't know if it was going for S&M sex dungeon with the
deep eggplant hideaway alcoves or something out of *Tron* with the
tubular lighting that made a person feel like putting on a track outfit and zipping around the space. The lighting in question went up
and around the tables and the bar to the ceiling—just everywhere—
and framed the egg-shaped DJ stand that was in the back corner
where the lovely stage and upright piano used to be.

Sydney took in the decor, loud music and tight crowd and immediately wanted to leave. She turned to Kat. "You think the girls
are going to be okay?"

Kat grinned. "They are going to be more than okay. They have
Netflix, Hulu and Disney+. Not to mention enough snacks to start
their own candy drives on the side. Then there is the new yarn I

bought them, and I'm sure they'll be chatting about that cute little knitting phenom, Errol, who takes classes at the shop. I don't know what it is about Strong Knits, but even without Mama Joy, the most darling boys still flock there."

"Boys!" Syd stopped in her tracks. "What are you talking about, boys? They aren't even teens yet!"

Kat waved a hand. "It's fine. And as if we had to be teenagers for our heads to be turned. Besides, the boys that hang out at Strong Knits are the best. That little Errol is just a kid himself. Cute as a button, a total sweetheart and a wiz at knitting. A little older, so he's in the higher, more advanced division. But he helps out the younger kids. I think it makes them feel more comfortable. And it's been great seeing how with their new programs and outreach they are taking the gender stigmas out of crafts like knitting. Don't worry. The boys who hang out there are harmless."

Syd pursed her lips together and slid Kat a side-eyed glance. "So say you."

Kat burst out laughing. "Keep your dirty mind on your hot fireman, why don't you!" She poked Syd in the side. "Don't go getting wayward thoughts about messing this up for our girls. I'm just happy to see them happy and hanging out being normal together." She slung her arm around Syd's shoulder now and pulled her in, forehead to forehead. "Just like I'm happy to be hanging out with you again."

Syd's chest went warm, and she felt the usual knot in her belly start to loosen a bit. She nodded. "Fine. But don't expect me to be queen of the crafty train."

Kat pulled back and frowned. "That makes no sense, you know."

Syd shook her head. "Doesn't matter. You know what I mean."

Syd thought again of Lucas and how sexy he'd looked right before she'd laid into his ass. It *was* kind of hot the way he'd handled his sticks. Or whatever it was they were called. The knot in her belly began to tighten again. She shook her head. Maybe it was too soon for her to be going out. This was the first time she and Remi had been apart since they'd gotten to Harlem.

"Listen. I know we're having our super bonding hangout, and so are the girls, but can we not do this tonight?" she said to Kat, tugging at her arm before they were fully inside. Kat turned around, looking at her with confusion and a hint of disappointment. Of course, she looked great in a black catsuit with her short hair parted on the side and slicked back. Her dark oxblood lipstick was perfect on her deep brown skin.

"Why? The girls are getting their groove on, and it's high time you got yours on too."

Syd frowned. "Groove? Are we heading into some sort of nineties throwback or something?" she asked.

With that, Kat's eyes shifted ever so slightly, and she let out a nervous laugh. "Of course not. Who would want to do that? All that blue eyeshadow, and those high-top fades." She shuddered. "Now come on, Syd." She took Syd's hand. "Please? It will be fun." She bit her bottom lip, and immediately Syd's hackles went up.

"What. Is. It."

"Nothing much," Kat said, pulling her farther into the club. "Promise you won't hate me."

"Oh hell no. I already do, with that prep. What did you do?"

"Oh, just come on. You need to stop hiding in Scrubs and let the powerhouse Syd I know and love out! So . . . I maybe invited some of the girls."

"No." Syd shook her head. "You're supposed to be my friend.

The only friend I'm up to seeing. Wasn't that you telling our girls how we were the only crew we needed?"

She nodded. "Yeah, that was me, but you've been a lone wolf long enough. And there's power in numbers."

Syd let out a long sigh. "Fine. Who did you invite? Why did you invite anyone?"

"I am your friend, and that's why I did it. Just Chantelle, Joslin, Mia and Shaya."

Syd's eyes bulged. Shaya. Freaking Shaya. She was a high-level-ass high-school-nightmare type of pain.

"I know, I know, but she's Mia's third tit, so you know how those two travel. And either way it's better to let everyone know the bitch is back and better than ever." She looked sheepish. "I know you're mad, but I also know you better than anyone. You're a fighter. Not someone who hides in the dark. Even in your silence, you still know how to give as good as you get. My Syd is no shrinking violet."

Syd tried her best to untighten her lips, but they stayed stuck in a firm grimace. She closed her eyes a moment, then opened them. Kat did have a point. There would be no hiding that she was back. And she knew her friend had arranged this little ambush out of love. Besides, she'd been dreading seeing old friends, and this way it would be like pulling the Band-Aid off all at once. Finally, she looked at Kat and put on her best smile. Kat frowned and took a step back.

"And now I'm scared."

"As you should be," Syd said, taking a step forward and walking past Kat. "Now come on and lead me to our happy reunion."

"Oh, and one more thing," Kat said softly from over her shoulder. "The club is having a charity auction for the FDNY tonight, so . . . probably not, but you might just happen to see Lucas Strong here."

Syd stopped walking, and it seemed everything else stopped right along with her as she turned to look at Kat. Could she really have said what she thought she'd just said? "Woman, are you serious right now?"

"Well, hello to you too, sunshine."

She looked up into the dark pools that were Lucas Strong's eyes.

"Yeah, I kind of was serious," Kat whispered in her ear.

"You will pay for this," Syd said. She pointedly ignored Lucas and his dark eyes, but she knew from her stumbling trip and step back, and the fact that he had to quickly reach out and pull her into his wide chest so that she wouldn't knock the drink out of the hand of a woman standing behind her or step on the pretty pedicure of another woman, that he was not ignoring her.

She practically collided with his wide chest, where she was completely enveloped by the ridiculously-out-of-place-for-Manhattan, earthy smell of him. Shit. There was no way she could avoid him now. All she could do was look down and mumble her thanks as her face, ears—hell, her whole body—heated.

"Are you okay?"

It was Kat. Syd did her best not to growl at her friend. Instead, she gave her a smile, which still had Kat narrowing her eyes. Good. As long as she knew. "I'm fine," she said through clenched teeth. "Now, where is our table? I could use a drink."

10

WHAT IN THE *hell is she doing here?*

Lucas ignored the fact that she looked hot as hell tonight with her hair all sexy down around her face. That she smelled hella good too, her sweet scent of lavender mixed with something deep and musky. What he couldn't ignore was that once again there he was, left looking at her back—her sexy back, encased in tight black jeans and a loose racer-back tank top that showed off her shoulders. He bit his bottom lip; damn, her shoulders were gorgeous.

But he'd play it cool, Lucas told himself. He'd just take a cue from the Sydney Harris playbook—he tried to not grin so hard over the fact that he could freely call her Harris. Not that he'd ever really stopped in his mind, and not that he wasn't a shit for secretly celebrating her marriage's downfall, but it did make him feel like less of a jerk for still liking her as much as he did.

Instantly his stomach knotted. *Even if this isn't going anywhere?*

He stilled as the horrid inner demon of doubt tried to make its way from the back of his mind and out into the club. Fuck. Couldn't he just have one night of fun?

Fun—that's all he wanted. Not for forever. But one night doubt- and anxiety-free would be fine. And if bonuses were added, if he could get a smile from Syd, perhaps he could sleep happy tonight. But he knew that was probably asking way too much.

Back to the plan of playing it her way and hoping to make it out unscathed. It was probably safer for them both. She was newly di- vorced and had a kid to consider, and he was barely keeping his head on straight and a paycheck coming in. She didn't need an- other man screwing up her life.

He'd ignore her as if his life and his sanity depended on it, be- cause it kind of felt like they did. He was unraveling as it was, so having her back screwing with his head was the last thing he needed. Still, it was weird. Why was she so hell-bent on going out of her way to be so cold toward him? Yeah, sure, he should be used to it. It was always her way. But by now they should be past it. Well past it. What was she covering up?

Sure, he may have teased her when they were young. Gotten her to laugh a bit. It had been clear he liked her, and he'd thought—no, hoped—that she'd liked him too. But just like now, all he ever got was her back. And just like then, they were once again right back in each other's orbits. Once again fucking up each other's balances and throwing things off kilter. Lucas chuckled to himself and looked over toward the VIP table area, where she was heading with Kat. Maybe that was why this past week had been so hard for him. The dreams, the screwups at work. He should have known that hurri- cane Syd was on the way to kick up a fuss. She was more reliable than Mercury going into retrograde.

She for him and he for her. It was probably part of the reason she had stayed away so long.

Harlem was her home, but it wasn't her heart. Never was. He

remembered how happy she'd looked when he glimpsed her that day telling Kat about her college acceptance and getting to go away.

They were in the school stairwell, and he was about to head down. Kat hugged her tight and squeezed her friend's hand. "I'm so happy for you. I'll miss you like crazy, but I'm so happy for you. What are you gonna miss about here?"

Syd snorted, then squeezed Kat's hand back. "Only you. I can't get off this block fast enough."

It was as if another fire was extinguished in his heart that day. He had felt small and useless and hated himself for loving her and had been proud that he'd never let her know just how much.

Lucas let out a breath then, as the past faded and the sounds of the present came back full force. Oh well. It had all worked out as it should.

He shook his head. Whatever. He'd smile, play it up on the stage for this damned charity night like the last Boy Scout and then go back home to another sleepless night.

Lucas let out a chuckle he didn't feel and turned around, directing his next comment to Flex, who had talked him into coming out tonight and filling in for this charity auction. "Okay," he said, clapping his hands together and letting out a breath, trying hard to tamp down his frustration, both emotional and sexual. "So, what have we got going on? You said this wouldn't take long, and already I've been here ten minutes past too long."

"Somebody's got his hose in a twist."

"Keep trying me, Flex, you going to feel exactly what I got in a twist."

Flex just shook his head, not intimidated at all by his half-assed threat. Lucas knew that being part of the calendar also meant this sort of ambassadorship was part of his obligation, but it was getting to feel like a bit much. The club was nearly full, with tight pockets of people all ready to drink and dance and have a little fun with one of New York's Bravest. Though he had a hard time letting go of the image of Syd's retreating back, the proof was here that there were still plenty of women out for a good time. And he had been and would continue to be just fine with or without Syd. Shit, maybe it was high time she knew just how fine.

"REMIND ME WHAT the hell I'm here for," Sydney whispered on the side of her cocktail straw toward Kat. A good time she definitely was not having, though she was doing her best, smiling and nodding and putting on her best impression of Sydney Hughes, Gatekeeper. But it was tiring, and it felt like her facade was cracking under the weight of these women.

She knew of course about their work and personal lives from social media updates, but sitting and drinking with them while they went on about careers that were stressful and boring and so busy that it just made them want to get out and get wasted made her ridiculously jealous, and for that she felt stupid and petty. It wasn't as if they were purposefully trying to make her feel like crap. Well, maybe not much.

Yeah, sure, the night had a certain amount of potential. She had gone and hyped herself up to a moderate level, putting on her best skinny jeans and a top that she knew was sexy and showed off her curves in just the right way. It even felt good to put on a pair of shoes with a bit of a heel after so long with her feet and her mood flat on the ground. But that feeling of being out just to be out had gone out the window with the revelation that she'd have to be on again for a crew who were hella judgy back in high school. Add to the mix that she couldn't help thinking she saw Lucas Strong in every other broad-shouldered back, and suddenly all she wanted to do was go back to the relative safety of the laundromat.

"We're here to get you out of your little spin-dry comfort zone and back into the real world," Kat said.

Sydney looked up toward the raised stage, where Lucas was with a group of other guys she assumed were firefighters. They all had that annoying, too-good-looking-to-be-trusted look about them.

She watched as one of the guys tapped Lucas on his chest, then pointed to a beautiful brown-skinned woman with a tiny waist, full hips and at least thirty inches of curly platinum extensions who was waving from the crowd. Lucas looked and then broke into a smile as he bent down and shook hands with the woman and her equally follicly endowed friend. Suddenly Syd missed her blowout and thought a few clip-ins wouldn't be the worst idea. Shit, what was she thinking? One look at a woman in a good wig getting eyes from a man she was hot for and she was back to doubting herself.

The MC of the night, a local comedian who couldn't be more than thirty but had the delivery of a seasoned professional, walked between Lucas and the woman whose hand he was holding and separated them. The MC shook her finger in front of Lucas's face while she pulled him back toward the middle of the stage.

"No, no, honey, what we're doing here is a charity auction. So, despite what you might normally do on the regular, you're giving nothing away here for free tonight. If little mama wants it, she's gonna have to pay up like the rest. All proceeds are going to the very fine widows of firefighters, with a little cut for the bar, of course. Side note—don't forget to tip your lovely MC."

She did an exaggerated hand wave across Lucas's chest, going down, down, down until he stopped her right at the top of the button on his jeans. She made a shocked face as if she was offended. "Now I see you're a fast learner." She raised a hand, stilling his movements. "But save it. You don't have to use those techniques on me."

Lucas leaned forward and spoke into the mic. His voice came out deep and seemed to vibrate throughout the room, or maybe it was just her body that felt the vibration. "It's like you said. I am a fast learner." Then he looked out at the waiting crowd. Was that seduction in his eyes? "So you all remember that when you're making a bid, all right?"

There were catcalls and squeals throughout the audience while Sydney took a long draw of her drink and rolled her eyes over the cheesiness of the whole thing. She turned back toward Kat. "I can't believe they charged a twenty-buck cover for this. I mean, *Magic Mike* it's not."

"I don't know what you're complaining about. It's not like you paid the cover charge. Just sip your drink and cut it out, or you and me are going to fight."

"Oh, I'd like to teach him a thing or two. Get all tangled in his yarn." At the sound of Mia's declaration, Sydney forgot about Kat and the cover charge and flipped her attention to her left. Was Mia, a spa owner and massage therapist, talking about Lucas? Should Syd even care if she was talking about Lucas?

"Don't you know it," Joslin, Mia's good friend and business partner, said. "Hey, maybe now's your chance. All it takes is a bid. I mean, technically, you're only supposed to be getting a drink with your bid on a man, but where it goes from there is up to you. And from what I hear these days, Lucas Strong is a changed man."

"He sure is," Chantelle, a computer forensics specialist, chimed in. "And it seems everybody wants a touch. Some wild-assed woman the other night even tried a reverse CPR maneuver on him. It was a whole mess. Ever since the calendar came out, he's become a wanted man."

Sydney couldn't believe what she was hearing. The last Boy Scout, Mr. Do Right, never-make-a-move Lucas Strong had turned into some sort of fucking man whore? She looked toward Kat with wide, questioning eyes. Kat shrugged and shook her head slightly.

"I didn't hear anything about him getting around all that much."

Syd's eyes went even wider. *All that much*? Not that it was any of her business, but wow . . . that was a change she hadn't expected to come across when she came back home. Maybe it was a good thing she never got back to him when he asked how she was after her closet meltdown.

She turned and looked as a couple more guys gathered on the stage. They were all pretty good-looking, various heights, all of them fit since they all had to take those firefighter tests. Each had a certain swagger that seemed to come with the whole firefighter-hero thing. But still, there was something about Lucas as she looked at them all. He was the only one who made her nipples go rock-hard, and she instinctively had to cross her legs. Sydney turned away.

"Well, that's it. I'm going for it," Shaya said. "After months of being in a not-shopping mood, not to mention not getting any, I might as well take a shot and bet on him." Shaya bit her lip, then paused. "Aw, fuck," she said.

"What's the matter?" Mia asked.

"I forgot that I went and put a new bag on my credit card last month. I only have so much money. Dammit, just when a girl wants to get some. Now why did I have to go and buy that Louis?"

Mia nodded sagely like she totally understood and patted her on the arm. "Don't you worry, girl, I got you. If it gets you some good dick, I will definitely lend you the cash."

Shaya let out a little squeal and wrapped her arms around her friend. "This is why you my homegirl. I love you." She blinked hard past her new eyelashes, which were fluttering to the point of worrying everyone about their fate.

"Ladies," Kat started, "are we forgetting that we're here to celebrate Syd? This is her night. If anybody should be getting a bid on, it should be her."

Sydney coughed, choking on her own saliva, since she had finished her drink. She waved her hand. "Oh, I'm good, not to worry about me."

Shaya looked at Kat like she'd gone mad. "See, she's good. And what are you talking about? I've welcomed her back. Right, Syd? Don't you feel welcomed?"

Syd raised her empty glass to Shaya. "Abso-fucking-lutely."

Shaya suddenly burst out laughing. "Do you all see how mad she's getting? Look at her about to break that poor glass. Abso-fucking-lutely," she said in an annoying mimicking voice. Chantelle, Joslin and even Kat joined in the laughter.

Syd looked at them all and waved her empty glass their way. "Okay, the laugh would be nice if I was in on the joke."

Shaya leaned forward and patted Syd's thigh, then took the glass out of her hand and waved it in the air in order to get the attention of their waitress, who gave a nod, indicating that she'd be back with a refill. "Girl, I was only screwing with you. We were just testing out a long-held theory, and I guess it's true."

Syd turned to Kat and narrowed her eyes. Kat immediately threw her hands up. "Don't look at me. I had nothing to do with this."

Sydney stared at her friend for a couple of beats but felt inclined to believe her. Kat was the only one who knew that she'd had a . . . whatever in the past for Lucas. Key word being "past." She looked at Shaya. "I don't have any idea what you're talking about."

Shaya shrugged. "If you say so. I don't want to go and ruin the whole untouchable, Mrs. Perfect vibe you got going on."

Mrs. Perfect. If the lie weren't so absurd, she would burst out laughing, but as it was, all she could do was take the drink that the waitress brought over to her and gulp down a huge swallow.

"Slow it down, tiger, I said I was only playing. I'm not planning to mess with your hot little firefighter over there."

"He's not little," Syd started, then caught herself. "I mean, he's not my—"

Sydney gave up and stopped right there. One look at her crew for the night and she knew talking was just a waste of time. They weren't inclined to believe her anyway, at least not tonight. Who could blame them, with the way he used to follow her around in school, which had her ending up being dubbed his girl without ever being anything of the sort. Not even close. She'd always been more of a huge joke to him than anything else. A plaything. She was a cat, and he was always throwing bits of catnip and distracting yarn balls to take her off her path.

Abruptly the relatively tame music went up about ten notches to a hard-thumping hip-hop track from Megan Thee Stallion; the MC came back on to the roar of the crowd. Syd turned and looked at the stage. What the hell? Suddenly it really was a mini *Magic Mike* night with the stage full of hot men, all clearly fit enough to take on a fire or whatever else needed hosing at any given time. The scene had caused most of the women in the club to gather around the stage and jockey for the best posing position while looking up at the men adoringly.

The MC knew she had a live crowd and was funny while getting things going at a fast pace. Up for auction were essentially package dates with the men under the guise of more PC activities. There were tours of city landmarks, CPR lessons and what she knew was Lucas's: one-on-one knitting lessons.

When it was his turn, the MC walked slowly around him, making a big show of shifting her hips and bumping into him as if by accident. "And now we have our little troublemaker from earlier. This here is Mr. November, ladies. And you know what they say about Mr. November. He's so good you'll go back for seconds." With that line, Lucas blushed. He was putting on a hell of a show, and the crowd was loving it.

The MC played it up. "To those of you with the dirty minds, I'm not talking about that. This man's talents go beyond the bedroom, so get your minds out of the gutter. He's offering up a free knitting class to show you how well he uses his hands and his stick."

Once again, with a roar from the crowd, the bidding began. It all went so fast, and before Syd knew it, Shaya had her hands up, making a ridiculously high bid for a knitting lesson from Lucas. Syd was pissed, but she had no right to be, so she bit down on her anger. When Shaya was outbid by a woman down on the floor, Joslin raised her hand to counter. Then Joslin was outbid by someone else on the other side of the room. That's when Mia put her hand up, and Syd turned around and looked toward Lucas, who looked at her with the same type of confusion. There was another bid from the same woman down on the floor, who wasn't giving up. Kat raised her hand then, bidding two hundred dollars over the woman on the floor. Sydney turned Kat's way. "You out of your mind? There is no knitting lesson worth that much—unless it comes with more than knitting."

Kat grinned. "Well, maybe it does. Besides, I just might be in need of a tax write-off."

The MC announced that Lucas was sold, and Kat pumped her fist in the air over her victory and ran up to receive her voucher. Heads swiveled in Kat's direction, though most of the women clapped. Ms. Thirty Inches looked at Kat as if she could claw her eyes out, but Lucas smiled and nodded his appreciation at Kat. The jerko. Guess that smile was his go-to. Syd shot him a sneer and thought he may have caught it when, for the briefest of moments, he flipped daggers back her way too. But maybe not. She looked down at her glass. How did it get empty again so fast? She thought about putting her hand up for another refill. Maybe she should slow it down? Remi would be home tomorrow, and then there was work at Scrubs. Her grandfather was relying on her, and she didn't need a hangover.

But Syd's eyes shifted again and she caught sight of Kat across the room in what appeared to be easygoing and, dare she say, intimate banter with Lucas as he handed her what she assumed was the voucher for the knitting lesson. But why was he also pulling out his phone—and wait, why was she pulling out hers? Were they exchanging numbers? Tax write-off her ass. Sydney threw her hand in the air, raising her glass. "Where in the hell did the waitress disappear to?" she said to Mia and the rest of the crew.

Shit. She needed a refill like ten minutes ago, responsibilities be damned. If she was going to get stabbed in the heart, she should at least be fully anesthetized.

Suddenly Mia's eyes went wide and Chantelle got a cat-that-got-the-canary expression on her face as Sydney's glass was smoothly slipped from her hand. The sizzle that went from her index finger straight through her body for some reason let her know that it wasn't the waitress who had taken her glass. Syd let out a breath before looking and sincerely hoped in that moment that it actually was the waitress who had gotten her nipples in a tizzy.

Of course, she had no such luck.

"How about you let me get you that drink?" Lucas said, cooler than he had any right to be.

"No thanks, I was just leaving." Leaving. Leaving was the exact right thing to do. The safest for sure. Syd knew it. Well, her mind knew it; her body was another story. She stood and caught a whiff of his distinctly masculine scent and her legs got all quivery and her traitorous nipples damned near sent out homing signals. Mind over body. She could do this.

"I'm going to turn in, y'all. It's been real, but today's been a long one, and I guess I'm not used to the New York nightlife anymore," Sydney said to the group just as Kat was walking back up to them with their waitress and a round of drinks in tow.

"What you talking about? We're just getting started," she said.

Sydney shook her head. "Well, you will finish it up for me." She slipped a side-eye Lucas's way, then quickly thought better of it when their connection hit a little harder than she expected.

"You're not even gonna stay long enough to accept the auction item that your friend kindly won for you?" Lucas said.

Sydney pulled back, shocked. Her eyes slid over to Kat. "I don't think that's for me, since I didn't ask for it, nor do I need it. So"— she paused—"I'll just let my friend here enjoy what she paid for." Kat gave her a hard stare that said she was more than a little disappointed in Syd. She knew she'd get an earful later, but still, Sydney grabbed her purse and tucked it under her arm, turning to leave.

Then she saw Kat's expression turn from disappointment to sympathy, and that was worse. She hated people feeling sorry for her. Despised it. Even when it was coming from her best friend, who was only trying to show her a good time—and who had even taken Remi for the night. But all this with Lucas here just felt like way too much. She gave Kat a look, imploring her to understand. Kat nodded. "Okay, go on, more drinks for me. Enjoy your kid- and laundry-free night. Don't say I never gave you anything—and remember this when it's time for my birthday."

Syd nodded at everyone else, then turned to walk away. She was surprised when Lucas was no longer next to her, nor behind her. Silly, but somehow, she had half expected him to still be there waiting, at least trying to change her mind about the drink or hanging out to drink with Kat or one of the other ladies when she had refused. Syd shook her head. Oh well, it was what it was. He must have figured her table was a lost cause, so maybe he went to join the hair weaves to try his luck over that way. Didn't matter to her—she'd had enough excitement for the night and was just ready to head home and get some sleep.

11

FUCK IT. HE'D had enough bullshit for one night and didn't have it in him to play games—well, more games—with Syd tonight. She'd made it apparent from the beginning she wanted to steer clear of him. If she couldn't at least accept a drink from him, well, he wasn't going to beg.

Lucas walked through the crowd to head out of the club, side-stepping the women who'd come for the charity auction with polite nods and brushing off his coworkers by telling them he'd fulfilled his duty for the night. He couldn't shake the feeling that things were murky and unsettled between him and Sydney. He hated the tension between them and didn't know why it was there, or why he even cared after all these years. It wasn't like he had to be friends or even friendly with her. He'd survived just fine without them being in each other's orbits, and clearly, she had too.

When he was just about through the crowd, Lucas turned to take one last look Syd's way and found his view blocked by one of the women who had been deep in the heavy bidding earlier. "Leaving so soon?" She reached forward, her hands coming out fast and eagerly, going for his chest.

Lucas slid back, glad he was at least quicker on the uptake this time and not caught unawares again. "Yeah, duty calls, as they say."

"Well, I can be that duty. It looks to me like your winning bid is not all that interested, and I've still got a pocket full of money. How about we make an arrangement?" She tossed her hair over her shoulder and licked her full lips. Her eyes sparkled. "I mean, it's all for charity, of course."

Just then the woman's friend came up behind her, laughing. "What's up, cutie? You can't be leaving so soon? And not alone. You were a big draw, and my girl here don't mind coming in second. Hell, I don't mind taking third. You look like you can handle us."

The first woman looked at her friend and nudged her playfully. Lucas looked back over to where Sydney wasn't. The same Sydney who'd rejected his offer once again. An offer he shouldn't have even made.

Maybe he should just take what he could get. She wasn't for him and had made that clear when they were back in school with the way she constantly ignored him, and she was still doing it now, going hot then cold when all he'd ever wanted, all he'd ever lived and breathed for, was to see her smile. But why should he be mad that she turned out to be just like everyone else when he was only doing what he always had—turning himself into what other people needed to see?

He looked back at the duo in front of him. They seemed like nice girls, despite all their big talk. But neither was what or who he wanted. He shook his head when the first one stepped forward, again raising her hand to grab his upper arm. He raised his own in an attempt to block hers and step out of the way when his hand was grasped by another. "Sorry, ladies, but I believe I had the winning bid tonight."

Lucas was dumbfounded. Syd was beside him, looking straight into the eyes of the woman who'd been coming on to him. No, not just looking, but staring her down while holding his hand. Holy shit, Sydney Harris was holding his hand as if she owned it. And dammit if he didn't fucking like it. The woman looked to Lucas. He tightened his grip on Syd's hand, held it up and grinned. "Sorry, she did win the bid. That means I'm all hers."

Syd growled and dug her thumb into his palm. Okay, so he'd gone a little far, but shit, even the thumb dig felt hella good.

He turned to Syd. "Come on—how about we dance before that drink?"

Her eyes widened, and the way her mouth formed a pretty O shape was so damned cute that Lucas couldn't help but smile as he pulled her away from the little posse and onto the dance floor.

"Hey," she said, pulling her hand back while her feet came forward, following him.

"Just come," he said. "You covered for me this far. Might as well keep up the pretense."

She shook her head. "I don't know what I did that for. I should just go."

"Please don't." The words came out quick, and they probably sounded more desperate than he felt. Or maybe they were exactly as desperate as he felt. He didn't know. All he knew was that he wasn't ready to let her go. At least not yet.

He was surprised once again when she looked back at the other bidders, then looked up at him, shrugged and nodded. "Fine, I'm here. And I did start this. Besides, I came all this way to be out, so I might as well be out."

She let go of his hand, and suddenly he felt bereft. It was silly, but the feeling was there all the same. After she let go she adjusted her purse, a small crossbody with a chain strap, making sure it was secure before she started to smoothly ease into the music. It was an upbeat track from a couple of summers ago that hearkened back to better times.

Lucas was amazed, seeing the way she quickly got into the music, showing a side of herself that was so unlike her norm. But really, what did he know of her normal self? All he knew was the girl back in high school and the woman she'd presented to the world on social media. Oh, and the other Sydney. The one who seemed to be unable to tolerate the sight of him for some reason but sought him out at the strangest times to share her intimate secrets and then go ghost on him.

She was so beautiful, almost like an ethereal dream. The music was a throbbing hip-hop beat but she seemed to be going with a beat that was in her own head or somehow dancing slightly above what was playing. The way her head tilted side to side, her hips going with the beat as she did a smooth-as-hell two-step, she was suddenly so cool. Even cooler than he'd always thought. This was a dance-girl version of her that he'd never even thought the normally reserved Syd had hidden. It made him wonder what other sides she had buried within her. She closed her eyes, long lashes coming to just above her fine cheeks, sending his attention lower to her beautiful jawbone and long, gorgeous neck. He swallowed against the pull to lean forward and taste it.

Syd shimmied her shoulders and raised her arms. They were bare and long and brown and looked so soft. His eyes danced with them. Moving with a rhythmic sway, he was mesmerized by the gold bracelets she was wearing as they inched down toward her elbow. But then suddenly she wasn't moving anymore. And then her hand was waving in front of his face. "Well, you wanted me out here. I'm here. Are you just gonna stand there?"

No, he absolutely was not. An opportunity was an opportunity, and Lucas wasn't missing out on this one. He picked up on her movements and matched her rhythm. Moving and grinding, almost but not quite touching, in time with the hard-thumping beats. Every once in a while her curls would brush his arm or graze right under his chin, and it took all he had to not make a fool of himself or, worse, bury his head in the intoxicating scent of them. He wanted more than anything to smell her deeply, to feel her all over.

She looked up at him for a moment, and their eyes locked. She bit at her bottom lip, and Lucas felt his balls tighten as his dick took on a mind that only had one thought: Sydney.

She turned away from him as the tempo of the music changed again. He watched as her hips did this magical figure eight thing and she dipped low, bending her knees and then winding back up to the Caribbean beat. Then he just about had a total heart attack as she took one small dip and stepped back and then another to the beat of the music, popping her ass out at the same time as she thrust out her chest until finally she was leaning right onto him.

Holy mother! He must have passed the fuck out. Maybe he wasn't even here and this wasn't really happening. Maybe he'd finally fallen into the deep sleep he'd feared and this was all a dream.

Well then, he was just gonna go with it. Enjoy it until he woke up.

Lucas moved closer to her, his chest to her back, his groin pressed to the upper curve of her ass. He dipped and she dipped down with him to the beat. He came back up and she did too. Slightly slower, the friction between their bodies lingering just long enough for him to harden against her.

He groaned. And she laughed.

"That's not funny, Syd."

She tilted her head back, looked up at him and smiled. "It's a little funny. Well, that groan I heard was."

Lucas laughed. She was really screwing with him big-time. "Are you drunk?"

She shook her head, and he saw some of the playfulness drain from her eyes. "Sadly, no. I was about to go when you showed up."

The music changed again, the tempo coming up a bit. For a moment Lucas thought Syd would move away, and instinctively his hand came out and went around her waist. His heart sped up in a bit of a panic when he expected her to immediately pull back. He was so used to her pulling away. So used to her retreats. And he would have accepted it. What else could he do? Everything was her choice. But she didn't move. She continued to dance, and this time she let her shoulders press into him.

"So?" he asked.

"So what?"

"So why didn't you let me buy you that drink?" he asked against her ear.

She moved now. Turned and faced him and looked him right in the eye.

Shit. The dream was over. He guessed it was time to wake up.

But then Sydney started to dance again. Dipping her hips and biting at her lips. Closing her eyes and spinning for a moment. Finally, she opened them again and looked at him. "I didn't want to

drink with you here. Not with a crowd watching and all your ador-
ing fans."

Lucas stopped moving—stopped trying to keep up with her or
play cute—and then something clicked as passion and anger started
to war with each other. He thought of her smiles and her calls in the
past and how they'd all only been for him. Never with a crowd.

"You mean, not with anyone watching."

Her eyes narrowed. "What?"

"You're the one talking about not wanting to drink with me with
anyone watching. But isn't that so like you. So like us. We can get
along and communicate perfectly fine when there's no one watching." He sighed, then mumbled, "Still same old Syd and the same old
games."

He remembered where he was and met her gaze. In a way, he
was shocked that she was still in front of him. But she was. And
she wasn't smiling or dancing. Hell, she wasn't even moving. She
was back. Back to angry. Back to Syd.

"Playing games?" She laughed, though there wasn't anything
funny behind it. There was nothing but a bleak hollowness. "You're
one to talk, Lucas Strong. Your kind of games is leaving what should
have been said unsaid. If you wanted me back then, why couldn't
you just say so? Why did it always have to be me?"

He looked at her dumbfounded and then blinked. "I thought I
did. I thought that's what I was doing the whole time. Not that it
would have mattered. You were leaving anyway."

Sydney shook her head. "How do you know what I was or was
not doing?"

He blinked again. "How would I not? I knew more about you
than just about anyone."

She was quiet, then let out a long breath.

How were they back here? All these years later, arguing as if they had some sort of stake in the game? The thought gave Lucas a hope that filled him with terrorizing fear.

"I swear, with the way you coasted through school and put on such a good act for everyone, I thought you were smarter than this, Lucas Strong. How could you get something so big so very wrong?"

He stared at her, feeling his nostrils flare while he sucked his bottom lip hard. "I could say the exact same thing about you, Sydney Harris."

With that, he was once again looking at her back. The small space where she'd just been standing seemed vast and cold.

But she wasn't completely gone. Not yet. And there was no way Lucas would let her drop that bombshell and then just leave—leave them in limbo, where they always were.

OUTSIDE THE CLUB, she was staring at her phone, eyes laser focused, lips tight, jaw rigid—almost as rigid as her back and shoulders. Lucas was hesitant about approaching her, but if he didn't, she'd no doubt hop into an Uber and head back home, and then tomorrow their dance, their flirtation, would be forgotten, for who knew how long?

She tapped her phone, and Lucas wondered if she could be texting the on-the-outs husband. He was ridiculous. Why was he even thinking about her if there was a husband, even if that husband may or may not be an ex? He thought of Mama Joy and what she would think of him, his current thoughts, hell—half his actions this past year, no less this past week.

Lucas gave himself a mental headshake. It was better to just go, or at the least just let her go. She, her daughter and whatever she had

going on with her husband, ex or whatever he was, didn't need any
of his baggage weighing them down. She had been right to leave all
those years ago. The dance had been good, and it would have to be
good enough to hold him for eternity.

He was about to step away when he noticed two guys standing
off to the side only about ten feet away, closer to the curb. They
were acting like they were deep in conversation, but the taller of
the two—brown skin, a low cut, full beard and fuller lips—couldn't
stop licking those lips every time his hooded eyes slipped Syd's
way. Shit. Lucas knew that look and knew he wasn't going anywhere except over to where she was. His feet set off toward her a
millisecond before old boy's did.

Kat: Is he out there yet?

Sydney: He just came.

Kat: Did he now? You telling me you got him
that riled that he couldn't hold back?

Sydney: Shut it you know what I meant.
Out here. He just came out here.

Sydney texted back to Kat as she tried her best to ignore the
energy coming off of Lucas as he tried not to stare at her.

Kat: I knew it. You two looked hot as hell
dancing together out there.

Sydney: I don't know about that.

Kat: Of course you do. I knew there was a hot
temptress in you just waiting to get out. And
when you walked off that did it. He was gone.
You don't play fair.

Sydney: I wasn't playing. I should just go home.

Kat: If going home means going to that man's
bed then yes you should go home. Don't worry
about Remi. I've got her until the afternoon.

Sydney: Wait. You don't have to.

Kat: Later Hot Mama!

Dammit. What was she going to do now? Here she was, a grown-
ass woman and a mother, and she was outside a club, past her bedtime, playing pickup games like she was coming from a high school
dance. She swiped at her phone, clicking on the Uber app and tapping in the address. A blue Toyota in four minutes. The license and
all its vitals were there. Syd was about to look up when there were
suddenly two sets of feet around her. She raised her eyes and saw a
tall guy with a beard and linebacker shoulders. She frowned when
he gave her a half smirk and licked his lips.

"You looking for something, chief?" came Lucas's voice from
by her side.

The bearded guy continued to smile at her for another moment
before turning an annoyed and slightly predatory look Lucas's
way. "Yeah, but what I'm looking for doesn't concern you, only the
lady here."

Lucas stepped forward, partially blocking her. "Then that definitely concerns me."

The hell? Sydney thought. He was sexy as all get-out, in an over-posturing, stepping-out-of-his-lane way, but still . . . *THE HELL?*

"Lucas, it's all right." She took his hand for the second unexpected time that night. This time when her fingers laced into his, it felt strangely right. As if she belonged. And it was even scarier than when she'd grabbed his hand when the woman was trying to pick him up earlier.

Beardy looked at her, at the hand grasp and then over at Lucas, who looked him in the eye, stepped forward and was now entirely too close.

Beardy put up his hands and stepped back. "My bad." He shrugged. "Do you, playa. I didn't mean to infringe."

Infringe? This was too much. Syd pulled at Lucas's hand. "Come on, let's go."

He turned her way. "Where? I thought you were waiting for a car."

"I was," she said, now grateful that she'd actually called a car in time to cover her foolishness. "It's here. Since we're going the same way, we can share," she said, then stopped herself and looked at him. "That guy is gone now though. You don't have to leave the club. I'm fine getting back home from here. It's such a short ride. I could practically walk it."

She went to let go of his hand then, but he squeezed hers tighter. "No, you were right. We are going the same way. At least for tonight."

The car ride was short—too short—and they were pulling up onto their block when she realized they'd held hands for the entire four-minute ride and didn't even get all weird about it. Was she out of her mind? Did she just want to be casually touched by any man after having not been for so long, or did she want to be touched by him? Why did she let him hold her hand so easily, and why did she go all half-cocked dancing with him in the first place, leaning on him, grinding on him? Melting into him so easily and seamlessly.

Syd looked around and saw the interior lights of Scrubs shining brightly. Mr. Bill was most likely on, or maybe their long shot, Glen. When she got out of the car with Lucas, the news would be back to her grandfather as soon as he was within earshot.

"Um, could you stop on the far corner?" she said to the driver so that he wouldn't stop directly in front of Scrubs.

"So after all this time you still don't want to be seen in public with me."

Syd snatched her hand free of Lucas's and looked his way. "You really are ridiculous."

Lucas laughed. "Am I? I guess that's why you're getting so bent out of shape about me mentioning it then and why you are all 'stop on the far corner.' But don't worry, beauty, I wasn't going to try and steal your hand from you. I'd have given it back when you asked," he said.

That's what I'm worried about, Sydney thought, but just shook her head in answer as the driver stopped.

She thanked him, tapped for a five-star rating and hefty tip, and was about to say good night and head her way when Lucas opened his mouth again.

"I still owe you that drink. And your knitting lesson."

Her insides went all wavy. Dammit. Tenacious Bastard.

Syd smiled and turned. Tenacious B. Legendary L. Both fit him. The Lucas she knew and loved never gave up no matter how many times she took his small acts of kindness and either ignored them or slung them back in his face. He kept offering more and more. She looked at him. Though they were a few doors down, the light from inside Scrubs shone on his face and he seemed to glow. Shiny and bright, eclipsing the moonlight. A breeze kicked up, still warm with only a hint of autumn cool as it blew his hair, tousling it and giving him a boyish charm that he hadn't shown earlier that evening. She shivered, the moment feeling like one of those daydreams she used to have about him but never thought she'd actually live in real life.

For a second Syd wondered if that was why she was so angry all the time and specifically why she was angry at him. Was it more a regret over the life she could have had? One full of more laughter than tears? Was she being unfairly resentful of the love and joy she'd run away from and taking it out on him instead of the life and the man she'd settled on?

She shook her head. "I don't think drinks and a knitting lesson go together so well."

He grinned wider and his eyes sparked with a glint of fire. "You'd be surprised then if I told you that they mesh perfectly."

Go upstairs, Sydney. Be good. Walk away. This has been nice, but just go the fuck upstairs.

"I don't think I could handle all of that," she said and saw the disappointment wash over him.

"But maybe one thing at a time," she added. "How about we start with the drink first?"

12

HE COULDN'T BELIEVE she was still with him. But she was. Syd's acquiescence on the drink had left him dumbstruck, but only for a moment, as his mind reeled over where to go and how to make her happy.

"Okay," Lucas said. "Where do you want to go? You can come up to my place. I have liquor. I even have food. Though I'm sorry to say I can't guarantee us privacy."

He knew Jesse was staying over at Kerry's tonight, but damn fate to all hell—Noah *would* choose now to come back. Shit, he'd missed his younger brother like crazy, but just another couple of nights on the road would have been perfect.

He saw her eyes shift. "How about a club?" he asked. "I know a nice little one not too far uptown in the Heights."

She nibbled at her bottom lip and then looked up at him. Her face went all shy, but then suddenly there was a spark of fire in her eyes. "This is nuts, huh. Look at us. Two adults and not a private spot between us."

He shook his head. "Yeah, look at us." Lucas frowned, then looked back at her, his eyes wide with questions. For a second it felt like that dream was coming back again. "You're going to have to make it plain for me, Sydney. You accused me of not making things clear, and now here you are talking about a private spot. Just what are you saying? I need to know, because I've had feelings for you for way too long. If you don't want this or at least don't want this right now tonight, that's cool. I just need to know. You tell me what's up and set me straight."

She grinned. "Nice to hear you finally say what's on your mind. For once I don't feel like I'm going out of my mind wondering what you think."

Lucas shook his head. "Seriously, woman? All this time?" He took her hand. "Come on."

She pulled back for a moment. "Where are we going?"

"Just trust me. We're going somewhere private so that I can show you exactly what I think."

THE FIRST HOTEL was a bust. There was no way he was taking her to some by-the-hour spot. Fucking Flex and his shitty recs. He should have known. After looking at the Love Express and its flashing sign, he texted his brother Damian for a recommendation. Damian was the most persnickety person he'd ever met about where he'd lay his naked ass. You'd think his skin was as precious as a new-born babe's, the way he went on about thread counts and shit.

> Lucas: I need a quick hotel rec stat.

> Damian: Do you know what time it is?

> Lucas: Which is why I need it stat.

Damian: Who do you think you are? Jesse?

                              Lucas: Old Jesse.

Damian: It's the really old Jesse. Kerry knows
better which is why she hasn't said yes yet.

                    Lucas: Just give him a chance Dame.

Damian: There you go always babying him.

There was a cough from by his side. What the fuck. Why was
he arguing with Damian about Jesse when the woman he'd been
dreaming about was right the hell next to him in his car?

                  Lucas: I'm going to destroy you. You're about to
                  fuck this up for me. A hotel/motel or whatever.
                                     I need the rec.

Damian: Give me a name.

                              Lucas: None Your

Damian: What?

                         Lucas: None Your Business

Silence. And it was long and drawn out. Lucas could practically
feel Syd's mind changing as he battled with Dame.

Lucas: Shit. Ok but it stays here. Sydney Harris.

> Damian: You idiot! Why the hell didn't you say so
> in the first place. The Blue Mountain off 119. I'll
> text you directions. Ask for the prestige package.
> Executive Suite. It's fantastic. Or will be to you.
> Forget it. I'll call ahead and make you a
> reservation. Do not fuck this up and please
> finally get your head on straight.

A moment later the address and directions were coming through to his phone. Lucas sighed with relief.

"How is your older brother anyway?" Sydney asked.

"He's fine. A total pain in the ass, but fine."

The drive to the Blue Mountain was short, and on the way they got wine and takeout for the hotel.

There was a little too much quiet after the text session with Dame, and Lucas was starting to feel like Sydney was having second thoughts. The hotel was getting close, and at a red light he turned to her. "Hey, it's okay if you want to go back. We can finish the food in the car. It's no rush."

Suddenly she was on him. Hands firmly on both sides of his cheeks while her lips pressed softly against his with a light and almost hesitant pressure that was so lethal it might as well have been a sledgehammer hitting him square in the face.

But just as quickly as she was on him, she then eased back into the passenger seat. "I suggest you do rush. The night isn't getting any younger, and we're about to lose this light if you don't go now."

Lucas looked up from his shock as she smoothly relatched the seat belt he hadn't seen her unbuckle. He pressed the gas—too fast, and she laughed. It was deep and throaty and sexy as hell. He suddenly wanted to hear it again, but coming from her on her back. He wondered if she'd sound different from that position. Lucas swallowed and willed himself not to fuck up and get pulled over before they made it to the hotel.

THE HOTEL WAS just as he expected, it being a Damian Strong rec and all. Clean, classy—and when he went to check in, he found it was also discounted. His brother had hooked him up with some insidery, Groupon-type deal he had. Lucas was thankful for Damian's nonstop frugalness, if not for the fact that the clerk on duty chose to not hide said discount from Syd by blurting it out.

She raised a brow. "Come here often, do you?"

"Damian made the reservation."

She frowned. "He's a frequent guest?"

Lucas shrugged and gestured for her to walk ahead of him by waving their takeout bag in front of him as they headed toward the elevators that would take them to the top floor and the promised Executive Suite that Damian had raved about in his text. The casualness of the gesture and the fact that he was doing it with Syd wasn't lost on him.

Would they even eat? Dammit, they should have just eaten in the car, or he should have done something better than sorry-assed takeout. Takeout and a late-night hotel. If this didn't scream one-night stand, he didn't know what did. But why should that bother him now? Because Sydney, of course. He'd been dodging anything permanent for so long, but in the back of his mind it had always been Syd. And now here she was, and he was making less effort with her than he had with any woman in he didn't know how long.

Was he intentionally trying to push her away while trying to pull her in at the same time?

"I don't know. But with Damian, I do know he wouldn't rec a place unless it was clean and safe. So I trust it. As for the rest, he's a hard one to crack."

She nodded and pursed her lips as he pressed the button for their floor. "He's not the only one."

Lucas laughed. "You should talk."

The lurch of the elevator coming to an abrupt stop on their floor let them know this was definitely not the five-star Dame claimed it to be. But a person can't have everything when it's a late-night quick stop.

This felt all wrong! Why was she even still here with him? And why was he so nervous? It took a minute before he even realized that he was standing in front of their door with the key in hand.

"Don't tell me you're nervous."

Lucas looked at Sydney. How could she appear so calm and act so cool after they'd spent so many years of on-and-off flirting that he barely knew which way was up?

Suddenly her lips were on his. Again. She had him up against the doorjamb, pressing in hard while she was soft and lush, and he was just about ready to melt into a puddle on the hallway floor.

Get it together, Lucas!

He reached around her, trying to be smooth with it. The take-out bag crinkled when he shifted the key card in his fingers and simultaneously pulled her in even closer, and damn, her ass was fine as hell. Lucas moaned as he deepened their kiss and dropped the bag and key card. He hoped he hadn't ruined their already crap meal, but he also didn't really care, and he pulled her in tighter so her body was flush with his.

KNOT AGAIN   153

This was it. Everything. Sweet heaven, she fit perfectly even in the imperfect position. Syd's lips melded to his as their tongues urgently intertwined. He let his mind go and swore he could taste the years of longing she might have had too, mixed in with the sweetness of the cocktail she'd had earlier.

He inhaled and pulled away, licking at her full bottom lip, and she moaned. Lucas sighed. Or did he whimper?

"If we don't get this door open fast it's very likely one or both of us is going to embarrass ourselves right here in this hallway."

Syd blinked, then swallowed. "Then let's get that door open."

Once inside the room, Lucas flipped on the light as he went to place the food on the dresser, making a quick assessment as he noted the room's sprinkler system and calculated how far the room was from the emergency stairway, as was his habit. It was a nice room. Damian hadn't lied about that. Except for the fact that you could hear the grinding of the elevator, it was quiet. Maybe too quiet.

He looked over at Syd. "I'm being weird, aren't I?"

She nodded. "A little." But then she smiled. Great. Now she was going to laugh at him. Laugh at him and then leave. Leave and go back to her life. The perfect life that was of course better for her. Oh well—at least he'd had the kiss.

"I thought it would only be me that thought this was strange," she said. "Look, I understand if you don't want to. I mean." Sydney bit at her bottom lip then. She blinked. Fast, like she was blinking back tears. But she let out a short, hard breath and looked more like her fierce self as she looked him in the eye again.

Lucas's heart began to race. He didn't know what he feared more—an angry Syd or a scared Syd. Angry he understood. Scared just scared him.

She continued. "I mean. I get it. Being here. Sleeping with me— I mean, why would you? You essentially had your pick of women at that club tonight. Messing with a broke-down single mother I'm sure was not high on your list."

She might as well have punched him. And for a moment it felt like she had. What the hell was she talking about?

Lucas stared at Sydney. Stunned.

Was this the same woman he'd been in love with? Okay, so he'd never admitted to being in love with her, at least not out loud, but fuck it. IN LOVE with for most of his life, and here she was talking about herself as if she was a form of someone he didn't even know?

He didn't know how to comprehend it.

But she was still talking, he guessed to fill the air of his stupid silence and the noisy-ass elevator.

"I know I was maybe a little shitty to you when we were young. Not catching your signals. And emotionally taking way more than I gave." She paused and sucked in a breath before continuing as she lowered her eyes. "Which was practically nothing."

Lucas fought the lump in his throat. He'd be damned if he screwed up this night by crying all over this woman and losing an erection that was practically one for the record books. No fucking way. He leaned in and kissed her quick. "No, no. Don't you realize you gave me plenty? We were young. Young and stupid." When she stilled, he spoke quickly. His words tumbled over one another. "Me way more the stupider one. Wayyy!"

Syd gave him a small smile but shook her head. She was stepping back now, farther out of his reach physically, and he could somehow feel her invisible wall being built. Brick by tiny brick. "No. I didn't give enough. Even up until, well, the other day. Tonight. And I'm sorry about that. But I am grateful for you getting me away from the jerks outside the club and humoring me with bringing me here. Whatever happens or doesn't, you don't have to feel like it's going further than tonight or that I'll try and cling to you. I know that I'm not—"

Hold it a fucking minute!

He was back across the room to her in two steps, lifting her by her thighs, forcing her to wrap her legs around him. "Not another word, Sydney Harris. We've both talked enough."

She looked at him with wide eyes full of shock. He leaned forward and nipped at her nose, then grinned when her brows scrunched up as she smiled. "What is wrong with you?" she said. "I'm trying to be serious!"

Lucas shook his head. He was an idiot. "I don't know what it is, but you always bring back memories for me and it's like when I first met you. I'll do anything just to get you to notice me."

"Well, don't you think it's time we both grew up? Why don't we just face facts and realize we're not kids anymore? Like I was saying, I'm—"

He kissed her then. Kissed her hard. He would kiss her until whatever words she was about to say were long forgotten in the desire about to be unleashed.

When he finally pulled away, Syd's eyes were glassy and her lips shone with the proof of their shared passion. Lucas sucked in a breath as he fought to control the thumping of his heart. "I swear you're like an angel," he said without thought as his mouth came down on hers once again, this time more reverently, tasting her, breathing her in. Trying his best to absorb as much of the essence that was this wonderful woman as he could.

Bringing them over toward the bed, he swung Syd in a slow circle before sitting down on the edge with her perfectly positioned on his lap. Once again Lucas couldn't help but wonder if this was real.

"Stop looking at me like that," she said, as if reading his thoughts. "This is real. At least for now. So now that you've distracted me, what do you say you take it all the way and really shut me up?"

13

LUCAS SEARCHED SYD'S eyes to see if there was actually real truth behind her words, uttered with so much bravado.

"Why are you looking at me like that?"

For a second Lucas thought he may have glimpsed some of her false bravado falter, as her voice caught in a little hitch on the last word. But she snapped back fast. "Listen, we've only got so much time. If you're just gonna play games with me like you normally do, we can just eat our food, reminisce a little bit about the old days and go home. It's already been a pretty long night."

Lucas laughed. "Woman, you don't know long yet," he said.

Syd's eyes went skyward as she let out a sigh.

"Okay, that was probably about eighty-five percent terrible, and I'm sorry." Lucas swallowed as he worried at his lip, not quite knowing what to say. He looked her straight in the eye once again. "Every time I'm anywhere near you, I always flip back into the past and resort to the same old stupid quips and jokes. I should be beyond that, and yet somehow I'm not." Lucas sighed, embarrassed by his disappointment in himself and suddenly feeling like it was a mistake bringing her here.

Sydney nodded, seeming to agree with him. "I know," she said. "It's like I've been stuck in a perpetual state of stunted adolescence. Stalled at the starting gate forever." She let out a disappointed sigh as she made a move to get up. Instinctively, Lucas's hands tightened on her hips.

She looked back up at him as her eyes widened, and she sucked in a breath. Instantly, the air between them was charged, and all he wanted to do was have her. It was all he'd ever wanted. Lucas's lips were on hers again as he flipped her over and was on top of her, with her leg still blessedly hooked behind his back.

He looked her in the eye. "Tell me to stop now. If you do, I'll never ask you again."

She bit at her lip. "You say that like it's a threat."

He shook his head. "I'd never give you a threat, Syd. Only promises."

She closed her eyes for a moment and turned away. Lucas let out a breath, trying his best to push away at his disappointment as he moved to get up. But her legs tightened around him as she looked back up and brought her hands to his face. Her fingers gently stroked his furrowed brow. "Promise me that for the next couple of hours you'll do your best to make me forget everything about my past and only think of you, this room and this bed."

Once again, the worlds of dream and reality collided. He brought his lips to her neck, tipping his tongue out to taste her sweet skin again. "I can't control the way your mind works, Ms. Harris. I never could, but I can promise I'll do my very best."

LUCAS WAS LOOKING at Syd as if he wanted to make love to her in the most desperate way, and that realization shocked her in a way that it probably shouldn't have—but it did. The fact that the feelings were new and exciting, and also terrifying, would probably seem sad to most people, especially coming out of a marriage with Redmon of more than ten years, but it was the truth. The past few years—hell, almost all of her years with Redmon—making love with him felt more like just having sex. Most of the time, Sydney felt like she was just going through the motions, a step-by-step of what she knew Redmon liked in order to get himself off as quickly as possible.

It wasn't that hard, really: kiss a bit, move down to his chest, lick his left nipple, then move to his right . . . while her hand stroked his cock, played with his balls—never forget to play with his balls—wait for the cue when he pushed her head down toward his crotch.

But never in those moments had Redmon looked at Sydney with such admiration as Lucas was looking at her with right now. In this moment, Lucas was looking at her as if he was really trying to see her, as if she was the one he wanted to make love to more than anyone else in the world. For the first time in a long time, Syd didn't feel like just a body that was easily replaced by anybody else. A lump formed in her throat as finally feeling like a whole person hit her deep in her soul. Suddenly all her nerve endings exploded at the same time. Her lips pulsed and her nipples peaked, and moisture flooded between her legs. She wanted this man, wanted him inside her and around her all at the same time, even if it wasn't for more than tonight. Just for tonight, she wanted her and Lucas to feel like forever.

"Please stop looking at me like that, Lucas Strong," she whispered. "Because if you don't, I may not be able to come back from this night."

But being Lucas, he didn't listen; he just continued to stare at her as his mouth came down on hers again, taking her, his tongue intertwining with hers, stealing her breath away. Capturing that bit of a heart she'd been stubbornly holding on to all these years.

Lucas leaned back, and the air between them quickly chilled, but her body heated up as he pulled his T-shirt over his head. She sucked in a quick breath as she got a look at his finely muscled chest and broad shoulders.

Holy fuck! He'd always been well put together, but the years . . . shit, the years had filled him out in amazing ways. If having to tote around heavy hoses and climb ladders was what did this to a man, then they all should be doing it. His shoulders were so broad that part of her wanted to pull out one of those big old Craftsman tape measures just to know the difference between his shoulders and his finely tapered waist. Broad shoulders, a wide chest, then bam, bam, bam, bam, bam, bam, all those fucking abs peppered with the most gorgeous wispy black hairs . . . suddenly Sydney's mouth watered. She let out a breath and swallowed as she pushed at him.

"Little hot in here, isn't it?" she said, making her way to get off the bed, not knowing if she was relieved or not when he swung his legs over and gave her the air and space that she needed.

Sydney jumped up and went over to the thermostat on the opposite wall, only half pretending to study it, then trying to hide her embarrassment when the temperature gauge read a cool 68 degrees. Syd turned around, expecting to see Lucas still spread out on the bed. She jumped when she found him right behind her, big, broad and oh so close.

Words stilled in her throat as he leaned down and kissed the edge of her jaw, then tipped his tongue out, slightly at first, then more, dragging it slowly along her bottom lip. She moaned as Lucas dropped to his knees. Holy hell!

"What are you doing?"

"Following my heart."

Sydney looked down at his sleek dark hair and broad shoulders, and her hands nearly hurt with wanting to reach out and place her fingers through his hair and pull him close to her. "I have a hard time believing it's your heart you're following, Mr. Strong," she said, trying her best to keep her voice steady.

He looked up at her then, his dark eyes connecting with hers in a way that took her back to the past, when she used to believe in a thing called trust. "Then you don't know my heart at all."

Sydney felt like she was breaking apart and being pulled back together all at the same time and she couldn't stop her hands from doing what they wanted to do. She reached out and grabbed at his hair and pulled him in close to her center. They both moaned at the same time. Sydney pulled her top over her head, and Lucas pulled her pants down over her hips toward her ankles. As she balanced on his shoulder with one hand, she stepped out of her jeans. When she started to tip over, he easily caught her, lifting her over one shoulder and carrying her, one leg still stuck inside her jeans, back toward the bed.

He dropped her unceremoniously on the mattress but was gentle as he pulled the other pant leg off, kissing her ankles. "God, even your ankles are beautiful."

His eyes slowly roamed over the rest of her body, sending each bit of flesh that they grazed, ankles to knees to thighs, tingling. The next fit of heat she felt was right at the center of her tummy, then her breasts, then her lips, then her cheeks. Sydney put her hands up and covered her face. "How is it that you make me feel so shy?"

He was on top of her again, taking one hand, then the other, holding them apart and pinning her to the bed. "How is it that you make me feel so bold?" Suddenly Lucas's mouth was all over her. On her mouth, her neck and shoulders. Sydney arched as he kissed her through her bra, tonguing at her nipples until the fabric was wet and the hard points were almost painful. She was ready to come. He stopped, leaving her panting on the blissful edge of ecstasy as he lifted first one breast then the other from her bra, pushing them together. He began to suck one then the other as if he'd been starving for this just as long as she had. His hands went to her center at the same time as hers went to his. She strained to reach down into his jeans, and he got easy access into her panties as she spread her legs. "No fair," she half whined. "You got a head start on me."

Lucas groaned, kicking off his sneakers, shedding his jeans and underwear faster than she thought possible. Damn, his dick was huge. And getting huger by the moment. She let out a breath, bracing herself, licking her lips in anticipation of having it in her mouth. In her.

It had been so long since she had actually looked forward to sex, she didn't quite know what to do with the emotion. But she didn't have long to think about it. Suddenly Lucas was there again, grabbing her hips and pulling her closer to the edge of the bed. He dropped to his knees and began to pleasure her, not with that huge dick but with his mouth pressed tight between her legs.

Sydney gasped as he secured one leg over his shoulder and with one hand held her ankle wide. With his other he gently stroked

along her belly and inner thigh while his tongue played at her intimate center. She was right on the edge, fighting against the impossible pleasure of it all when she heard his voice. A low, soothing
moan. "Don't think, just feel. I've got you."

He lowered his head again, kissing one thigh, then the other,
letting his breath whisper past her center before lowering his head
and teasing her at first back and forth, then in slow . . . slow . . .
slow circles until he got increasingly faster and faster, deeper, longer, going toward the middle, tongue now all the way inside her.
Her back arched until finally she could take it no more and broke
apart in what felt like a million sparkling crystals. "Fuck! Lucas
Strong, what the hell have you done to me?"

Once again Sydney covered her face in embarrassment. A woman
shouldn't say such things out loud, a woman was supposed to come
quietly or at least come more elegantly, with much better words.
She opened her eyes and there he was, smiling. "Ms. Harris, I'm just
getting started."

She watched as he slipped a condom from the pocket of his dis-
carded jeans. He reached out and grabbed his length as she spread
her legs and opened herself to him.

"Now," she said. "Lucas, I need you now."

Her words were barely out before he was inside her. Plunging
into her and at the same time kissing her, and it was completely different than any time she'd ever had sex before. A whole lifetime
was exploding into this one moment. It all collided in ridiculous
fireworks behind her eyes. Their past, present and future she didn't
dare to believe in.

This, this was everything. Lucas going deep inside her felt like
he was taking hold of her entire being in a way she could fully get

behind, over, under. Just whatever the hell he wanted. As long as he was doing it.

At least for tonight. For tonight he could take and she would too. They both had waited way past long enough to enjoy this moment. Whatever it was or didn't turn out to be.

14

IF HE WASN'T half-unconscious, Lucas would've been surprised to find himself drifting off into blissful sleep after making love to Sydney. He couldn't quite remember when he had felt so relaxed. So satisfied both physically and emotionally. So purely content and at peace.

His rational mind kept telling him that the feeling wasn't real. That it was just the aftereffects of their lovemaking. The pheromones still buzzing throughout his body. *But what if it could be real?* he dared to imagine for a second. What if this terrific moment with Sydney in his arms, soft, pliant, fitting his body perfectly, could truly be something that was in his life all the time? Lucas let out a long breath as he stroked Sydney's back and brought his hands up to her curls, reveling in the springy softness.

The low rumble of a snore that came from Syd surprised Lucas, and he couldn't help but laugh. He'd thought the snoring that woke him was his own, and he was shocked that he'd fallen asleep at all.

He must have finally hit that wall he'd feared was coming—

that or it was the rounds of mind-blowing sex. Any other thought, like *forever* or *happiness*, was too scary to think about.

Sydney let out a quick snort, and it vibrated through both their naked bodies, the feeling utterly delicious, though it seemed to wake her with a start.

"What?" She looked at him in confusion as she pushed her upper body off his chest, her nipples tickling his skin and her eyes going wide in shock over he could only guess what. Either her nakedness or the fact that she was naked with him. Probably both.

"No, you're not dreaming." Lucas cupped the sweet area where Syd's thigh met the curve of her behind and pulled her in closer to his returning erection.

The swat to his shoulder shouldn't have come as a surprise, but it did. "Dreaming, my ass. How could you have let me fall asleep?"

"Don't worry, we only dozed off for a few moments."

She shook her head. Then let out a long breath. "What am I doing?"

"You? I think it was both of us."

"You, me, us? What does it matter? I'm a freaking mother. I have a daughter, a hu—" She stopped, the air between them suddenly charged with tension.

Lucas felt her shiver despite their warmth. He raised a brow. Would they really talk about that? She wouldn't dare speak his name while he still had her in his arms, would she? "You still have a what?" he asked, fighting to keep his voice low, steady and even, not knowing who he was trying to challenge more, her or himself.

She closed her eyes for a moment, then opened them, meeting his own. Letting out the breath she'd been holding. "I have a daughter, and a grandfather who will be up at five no matter what. I have responsibilities. I don't need to be falling asleep in some Westchester hotel room with a hot firefighter."

Lucas felt the corner of his lip quirk up at her half-hearted speech, which would have been quite righteous if her nipples weren't still tickling him and distracting him so. "So you're finally admitting you think I'm hot?"

Syd cocked her head to the side and gave him a deadly stare. "Does now really seem like the time to fuck with me, Lucas Strong?"

He let his hand travel upward a little bit and caress the smooth brown skin on her ass. "Now seems like the absolute perfect time to fuck with you, Sydney Harris," he said.

He leaned forward and let himself once again nuzzle at the sweet, heady area beneath her chin and down toward her collarbone. He slipped out his tongue and tasted her skin, slightly salty from the intense physical exertion. Despite her talk of where she should or shouldn't be, she tilted her head back, giving him wider access as she arched her back and he pushed his pelvis forward. Another round coming up.

But no. There was an abrupt stop as Sydney's hands came up against his chest and she moved away. Lucas blinked and was half-surprised to see her already up and heading toward the hotel's bathroom. She was beautiful, shapely and gorgeous, all her curves highlighted perfectly by the bathroom light. She turned to him, her body soft and pliant-looking, but her eyes very much his usual no-nonsense Sydney.

"Going to be in and out of the shower in three minutes, if you want to shower yourself before we go. I'm giving you two and a half, and then we're outta here. I need to be back home before my grandfather is up and ready to take over the morning shift from Mr. Bill."

Lucas jumped up, flipping the sheet away from his body. "So how about we combine our showers? Your three minutes plus my two and a half . . . that's five and a half minutes of pure bliss. What do you say? Wanna get a little dirty while we clean up?"

Even after the past couple of hours together, for some reason Lucas still expected Syd to say no; her eyes, her posture, everything about her in this moment, despite her nakedness, made him feel like she was gonna say no. But then those soulful eyes of hers softened for a moment and she looked sweet and vulnerable, and he saw a small hint of the young and fragile girl who used to play at being brave back when they were in high school. The girl who wanted so badly to come out and play with him, get into a little bit of mischief. She reached up and ran her hand across his brow where his scar was. Lucas closed his eyes, reveling in the feel of her soft fingertips as she came forward and kissed him. Her touch was like a healing balm in a way no other's ever had been. Then she swatted him on his naked behind as he opened his eyes and met her saucy grin.

"Make it four and a half and you've got a deal," she said.

He looked at her, mouth open for a moment, dumbstruck with both love and terror.

15

Y OU KNOW I called you last night. Multiple times."

"I know. I was out." Sydney had seen that Red had called when she was at the club, but she hadn't been about to let him and his mood ruin her night.

"So you're just letting my daughter go and stay out at anybody's house now?"

She sighed, then laughed to herself. He didn't matter. What he said didn't matter. Not anymore. It was just Red barking like Red. But then she frowned.

"How did you know that Remi was out?"

"Because I called the house and spoke to your grandfather when I couldn't get you."

This jerk. "What did you do that for? He has a schedule to keep, and you know he's not in the best health. Why did you go bothering him? Was it urgent? Is something wrong?"

"No, but I have a right to call." Syd felt heat start to lick at the back of her neck. She knew that at any moment her ears would be on fire too.

"A right? I don't think so. Any rights you think you may have have henceforth been terminated." *Henceforth?* She didn't know where that had come from, but it sounded final enough.

"'Henceforth'?" He chuckled.

Dickhead.

"Anyway, I'd like to know what it is you told him. He used to be so cordial. The old geezer was downright rude last night."

"Oh no. Did you get your little feelings hurt?" Syd mocked, then was immediately annoyed at herself for falling into the muck-hole of a conversation with Red. "I didn't tell him anything he didn't already know."

"What does that mean?"

"You think about it," she snapped. "Now, why are you getting up in arms about Remi going to a friend's house?" She needed to be done with this conversation. Redmon calling her this morning was ruining her mood. "She went over to Kat's place for a sleepover with her friend Aisha. There is absolutely nothing wrong with that. And there's absolutely no reason for me to explain anything about my whereabouts to you either. Besides, you of all people should know about sleepovers at friends' houses."

"I don't know what you're talking about, Sydney."

"Bullshit, Red, you know exactly what I'm talking about. But you know what, it doesn't matter, because I really don't care. Now, was there a specific reason you were trying to get in touch with me?"

"Does your man have to have a specific reason to hear your voice?"

"I'm hanging up."

"Okay, okay. My God, can't you even take a joke, Sydney?"

"I took you, didn't I?"

"Ha. Very funny," Red said, though judging by the simmering

anger she heard laced in the undertone of his voice, he wasn't amused. She had to admit she felt good about getting that small dig in. But she didn't have time to deal anymore.

"Seriously, Red," she said, "I'm hanging up now. I have things to do, and I'm sure you do too."

"Actually, I do have things to do, which is why I'm calling. I need a favor from you, Syd."

Sydney tried to find some patience. This fool was really asking her for a favor? A favor was not snipping off his balls when they were flapping happily between the thighs of that woman with whiny moans and stand-up breasts. She shuddered against the repulsive image. "I don't do favors, Redmon, not anymore. I'm clear out of favors for you. Now, if this is an issue directly related to Remi, fine. If not, I'm done talking. I need to get on with my day. I have work to do."

"Well, it is about work, and in that way, it's about Remi," Red said quickly.

She was just about to click him off, but of course in perfect Red style he knew just what to do to grab her attention. "What is it?" she said.

"I know you don't want to make a big deal about our divorce, and frankly neither do I, at least not right now and not with the people at my firm. Honestly, with the way things are and jobs being what they are, reputations and all, we do whatever we can to hold on to our positions in the hierarchy of things—me as well as you. You know as well as I do that it's not easy for a Black couple to make it to where we did. I may be foolish, Syd, but I'm not dumb enough to think I did it all on my own."

Sydney was having a hard time trying to figure out what the hell Redmon was talking about, but she was shocked as hell over his small acknowledgment of her contribution to his career. But *repu-*

tations? *Our positions*? What the hell kind of trouble had he gotten himself into at his job, and what kind of trouble would that get her into when it came to her monthly settlement? She shook her head. Either way, it was his problem, and she didn't want to get entangled with it.

"I don't know what you're talking about, Red, and I don't know how I can help y—"

"No matter," he said, cutting her off in that way he had a thousand times before. "We'll talk about it when I see you."

See me!

"What are you talking about, see me?"

"What? Did you think I was going to stay in DC forever and not come and see my daughter?"

"Well, I would think you'd actually schedule a time to come and see your daughter and not just show up, so I hope this phone call is to schedule a time."

"Schedule? Who has the time for schedules? Not me. As a matter of fact, I'm running late as it is. I'll have to talk to you about this later. But like I said, I do need your help." His voice lowered a bit and slowed to hold the chilly threat of a warning. "It's not like you don't get the idea of needing help, Syd. Weren't you just hounding me about needing financial help for Remi?"

Fucking bastard. Remi's future depended on the finances they got from Red, and he knew it. Not for the first time, Syd wondered if that had been his plan all the times he'd dissuaded her from working outside the home and using her art degree. She thought about the times he put down her jewelry designs. Not flat out put them down, of course, but just talked about them in an offhanded, condescending kind of way. "Oh sure, honey," he'd say. "Those earrings are cute for being homemade." Then when she'd bring up taking some of her sets to boutiques, instead of encouragement, he'd shrug and give suggestions like the PTA or Junior League bazaars. "Those aren't the types of things for a society mother like you. You don't have to worry about working; I've got you." He would always say *I've got you*. It was that thought about *I've got you* that brought the night with Lucas back to her mind, and a shudder ran through her body. *I've got you*.

It had been the first time in years that Sydney had heard those words out of a man's mouth and actually felt relief instead of some sort of weird sense of ominous threat. She let out a sigh. "Well, I'll let you know, Red. Seems we both have a lot to do today."

With that she hung up. It didn't feel right thinking about Lucas while she was on the phone with Redmon. Not like it was a betrayal to Redmon, and not that she owed Lucas anything, but it just didn't sit right with her for some reason. Some reason she wasn't in the mood to sort out right now.

When she hung up with Red, it took more than a few minutes for Sydney to clear her head and get herself back to some sense of normalcy. But what was normal when it came to her anyway? She was still getting used to the idea of being divorced, and her body was deliciously sore from a night in bed with a man she'd dreamt of spending the night with for longer than she dared admit.

Sydney shook her head. But that couldn't happen again. And she'd told Lucas those exact words, multiple times. She remembered saying *This can't happen again* as her hand went for his erection a second time, and then she said it again when she encouraged his head down between her legs in the shower. But she was dead serious when he dropped her off at home at four a.m. and kissed her so passionately that she damn near chased him across the street as he went back to Strong Knits.

"This can't happen again," she'd told him. Her voice was steady, and he nodded in agreement in that devilish way that let her know he didn't believe a word she was saying. Her eyes had gone toward her bedroom window and in the direction of Strong Knits across the street. "You dummy," she had mumbled to herself. "You could have had a rebound affair with anybody, but you go and choose the literal boy across the street."

16

A CROSS THE STREET, Lucas didn't get much sleep, but still he woke with a renewed energy that he hadn't felt in a long time. It was an odd, heady feeling that he longed to hold on to, but it quickly faded when he made his way down the back stairs to the main room of Strong Knits and found all three of his brothers turning to stare at him as soon as he hit the main floor.

"So, our very own Magic Mike is finally up," Jesse said from where he was arranging some wool and cotton blends in a basket by the window.

Noah smiled at him as he got up from where he was sitting on the windowsill. He undulated his body in an exaggerated S-curve roll, which Lucas was sure was supposed to be considered sexy, and gave his brother a wink. "Did you do some of the moves I taught you at the club last night? I bet you did. If I was there too, we could have done one of our old routines."

Lucas shook his head. "You're a nut. We're not kids anymore."

"So what? We would have been awesome." Noah slid over to and around Lucas in three smooth steps, mimicking an old dance routine they used to practice that had some early pop-lock moves.

Lucas grinned. "You never change."

"And you love me for it. You know you remember. We would have killed there last night."

There was a loud snort from Lucas's left as Damian let his presence be known. "From what I hear, it was something, all right."

Lucas shot Damian a look of warning. He'd already texted his thanks but had also told him to keep things hush about Syd. One look in his eyes this morning let him know Damian was practically itching to spill his secret to his other brothers. All for one and one for four was how they rolled, and there was no changing it.

Currently Damian, the most troublesome of the four, was at the farmhouse table scowling as his fingers raced, flipping and twisting an expensive gray, cream and gold cashmere yarn that he was working for what would undoubtedly be one of the most complicated and expensive scarves known to man. It was so very Damian: overdone and overworked, when he could have easily chosen something simple.

"What are you doing here so early in the morning?" Lucas said to Damian. "Don't you have a haircut appointment or sample sale to get to or something?"

He saw what might've been hurt flash for the barest millisecond behind his brother's eyes, and instantly Lucas felt guilty. It wasn't fair. He knew he'd been an asshole for the past few months, and he knew being an asshole was out of his usual character, so it was probably putting his brothers on edge. He needed to be better. But being better wasn't in him. At least not right now.

Damian put his needles down on the table, and they landed with a loud snap. "You know what, Boy Scout?" he said as he pushed his chair back with more force than was needed or, knowing Damian, probably intended. "I've been tired of your hot and cold attitude for a while now. And it's way too early in the day for you to be starting with me. I didn't come here to see you or hear about your supposed strip show for charity. You ever think for a moment that my visit may have something to do with the fact that Noah is back home and that not everything is about you, your mood swings or your late-night pickup sessions?"

Pickup sessions? Lucas glared at Damian as his blood started to boil. As if Syd were nothing more than a woman he was just picking up. Lucas looked down and was surprised to find his hand fisting and his chest heaving as he fought to control his breath.

"Gobble, gobble," Damian teased, then smirked.

Lucas tensed up, ready to lunge across the table when both Jesse and Noah chuckled over the exchange.

But Lucas found himself blinking in surprise when he felt the cooling pat of Kerry's fingers on his bicep. He hadn't even noticed she'd entered the room. "Why don't you relax with all that flexing there, Lucas? You know he's just trying to get a rise out of you." She tilted her head Damian's way and gave him a hard stare. "Be nice, you," she warned, then tapped Lucas again and touched the tight muscle that had knotted up on the side of his neck. It was the exact spot Mama Joy always went for. Lucas jumped. He hadn't let his brothers or anyone rile him up in years. He needed to get his shit together.

"Jeez. You are tense," she said. "I'm surprised, after spending the night with Syd."

"I'll say. What, my rec didn't work out? Always is a clincher for me," Damian teased.

Lucas let out a long sigh before slowly leveling his gaze on his brother. "I'm gonna kick your ass. Just know this."

"Stop. As if he had to tell me. I don't know who you think you're fooling. The quicker you get that in your head, the calmer you'll all be," Kerry said.

"She's not lying there," Jesse chimed in.

"Seriously, you should stop babying him, Kerry," Damian said, with a fully babyish pout that didn't match his large frame, dark eyes and masculine features.

"And you shouldn't act so defensive because she calls you on your insistent bullying," Lucas said.

"And you both need to stop fighting over my woman and get your own," Jesse said, coming over to stand between Lucas and Kerry. He made a big show of removing her hand from Lucas's shoulder, and Lucas loved seeing Kerry's slight blush over the attention.

Lucas was still amazed by the change in their youngest brother this past year since Mama Joy's death. Though none of them had fully healed or come to terms with her sudden passing, it seemed as though Jesse, the one they thought would handle it the worst, had turned out to be the one handling it the best. And it was all surprisingly due to Kerry. Or maybe not so surprisingly. She was everything that Jesse needed and kept him from falling off the ledge that he'd been teetering on for way too long.

She gave Jesse a teasing glance and waved her hand in his face. "I don't see no rings on these fingers."

He pulled her into a tight hug and nuzzled at her neck before he pulled back. "You really know how to kick a man when he is down, woman," Jesse said. "Just how many proposals is it gonna take from me before you finally say yes?"

Kerry shrugged nonchalantly and gave him a flirty look. "Who knows? How many licks does it take to get to the center of a Tootsie Pop?"

There was a collective sound as Lucas, Noah and Damian all gasped. "Kerry Girl!" they cried out in unison.

She looked at them and shook her head. "I thought we'd come to an agreement on that name?"

"Did we?" Noah asked. "Because I didn't get the memo."

She smiled. "You're fine, Noah. I'll give you a pass since you've spent so much time away from home." She looked at Damian and Lucas. "But not either of you."

There was the sound of hand-clapping as the shop's front door opened and Kerry's friend Valencia Gibson walked in. "That's my girl," Val said as she strutted to the center of the room, turning the small shop into her very own runway, her late-summer Harlem style a blue batik print sundress showing off her brown skin, dark hair and curves to the best advantage. "Look at you go. I should be jealous, but for some reason I just love watching you take control of your little male harem here."

"What are you talking about, 'male harem'? The only male in her harem is me, thank you very much," Jesse said.

Val cocked one of her perfectly arched brows and gave him a skeptical look. "Okay, if you say so, player." She looked around, making eye contact with each of them. "But why would she settle for one when you look so good as a collective?"

Damian growled, and Jesse shook his head.

"Val, stop teasing," Kerry said before leaning forward and giving Jesse a playful kiss on the cheek.

"Fine." Val shrugged. "But if you're gonna act like that, you might as well go ahead and put the poor man out of his misery. And me too, by letting me be your maid of honor."

"Now you're talking, Val," Jesse said. "You want some coffee?"

She shook her head. "Nah, I'm off caffeine this week. Doing a cleanse."

Damian shook his head. "I saw you over at Larry's Rib House the night before last."

"And today is Sunday, Mr. Minding My Goddammed Business. I said I was on a cleanse THIS week. Damn, you're nosy as hell for someone so fine." She turned away from him then and looked at Noah. "Speaking of fine, it's good to see you back, Noah. Not that we were expecting you, but it's good. I'm dying to hear all that went on with Hathaway. You have got to spill."

Noah shook his head. "I wish I could. But there is confidentiality and all."

Val's eyes narrowed. "Ugh. Not even if I buy you drinks and buy one of your expensive yarn packages?"

Noah made a face like he was thinking the offer over before sighing. "Not even over drinks, but I'll gift you some yarn and teach you the pattern."

Val nodded. "Good enough. You're easy. I'll get you to spill eventually."

He shook his head. "You won't. But I will say most of what you heard about our diva Hath is true."

"This is the type of mess I got up early for." She turned her attention to Lucas then and gave him a knowing look. "Speaking of mess—I hear you got into quite a bit last night yourself, my sweet little lifesaver."

Lucas hoped more than anything that Val was talking about what went on at the club and the women bidding over him, but the sudden prickling at the back of his neck and the stutter of his heart told him different.

"What you talking about? I didn't get up to anything last night."

Val's eyes shifted from Lucas to Damian and back as if somehow she knew that Lucas had texted Damian and asked him for a hotel recommendation in the middle of the night.

"Didn't you, now?" she asked. "So, you don't know anything about your little bidding war? Or the fact that you ended up leaving with a certain newly divorced woman who just so happens to be back in town and happens to be someone you used to go to school with?"

The "Oh fuck" was on the tip of Lucas's tongue. "I just gave her a ride home," he said.

"I guess y'all took the scenic route. I mean, it doesn't normally take four hours to drive, what is it, ten blocks between here and the club?"

"What are you doing?" Lucas started. "Trying to get your honorary membership in the OKGs? You have to be a woman of a certain age to get in."

"Listen, don't you go disparaging the OKGs. Those women are legendary," Val said.

"I'm not saying that they're not," Lucas said. "I'm just saying they're also really into everybody else's business."

"Jeez. You all are a testy bunch this morning. You'd think all being back together"—she made this declaration to Noah—"and you being semi-famous and getting all sorts of women throwing ass your way"—this was directed to Lucas—"and you . . ." She paused when she got to Damian. "Well, you are you!" She tossed her long hair over her shoulder in such an exaggerated way that Lucas couldn't help but smile.

It brought him back to his moment of joy from the night before, and suddenly he wanted more than anything to see Sydney again. He was sure she wanted to see him too, though at the same time he was just as sure that she didn't. She was probably over at Scrubs having a panic attack and saying a prayer that he'd stay away.

The mixed feelings were battling in his mind when Jesse spoke up. "This has been fun, but we need to get set up for the first class of the day."

The class. Lucas still had Syd's certificate, and he could use that as an excuse to go over there and make her an offer she couldn't refuse.

17

SYDNEY DIDN'T WANT Lucas to come in, she told herself. At the same time, she was staring at the door of Scrubs and hoping against the fluttering of her stuttering heart that he would walk through. Business was surprisingly light for a Sunday morning, and she guessed it had to do with the brightness of the day, folks not wanting to be stuck inside the laundromat when the weather was so nice. Still, she found herself watching the door, even though she knew he was probably out doing what the rest of the city seemed to be doing and enjoying the fresh air and sunshine. Besides, she'd essentially freed him last night—multiple times—just like he'd freed her.

Once again, though, she quickly glanced at the door when it opened, hoping to see Lucas but expecting to see another customer or Remi, who was due back home soon. The real surprise came when instead it was Redmon who walked in.

Shit.

She couldn't believe him. She'd hung up only a couple of hours before, but of course she should've known from his stupid hints that he was already in town and on the path to ruin the little bit of peace she was on her way to finding.

"Schedules, Redmon, and setting times," she said as she stomped forward and put her finger in front of his face. "Do you not get the concept?"

Red swatted her finger away and walked fully into the laundromat, looking around as if he owned the place and was taking a quick inventory.

"And do you not get the concept of a favor?" he said. Then he turned back with a look that said he was serious. "Or the fact that I am here to see my daughter? Did you stop to think even for a second that she might be missing me or that I might be missing her?"

Sydney sighed and mumbled. "Well, you had plenty of time to see her when she was back home and you were spending your nights . . . working."

His jaw tightened and he looked down at her. "One has nothing to do with the other, Syd."

She cocked her brow. "And yet we're here."

Sydney folded her arms across her chest and stared at Red. She knew that. Of course she knew that. She'd explained it to their daughter numerous times. Not in those words, mind you, but she'd explained that the fact that she and Redmon were not together had nothing to do with Remi and that she should have no guilt and no feelings leaning in that direction. No, this was about Redmon's lack of feelings for Syd. And because of that, she needed to get it straight in her own mind and realize that she couldn't do more to damage Remi's relationship with her father.

Just because their marriage failed didn't mean her daughter had to have an estranged relationship with her father. Syd didn't want that for her. It would be the worst thing she could do. It would hardly punish Red and in the end could potentially ruin Remi. Syd didn't need to make a total and complete failure of everything and fuck up her daughter too. Not any more than she already had. She let out a breath and tried her hardest to see things from a different perspective. To once again give Red the benefit of the doubt and push aside all the times he'd lied to her, cheated on her and failed to fulfill his promises to her.

"You're right, Red. Let's keep that out of this." She looked over Red's shoulder when she saw the door open, and her heart began to race. Just great. Of course *now* he showed up. Sydney tried her best to act cool and not give herself away as she slid her gaze back to Redmon. "Either way, Remi's not home yet. She's still out with friends. So you just have to call me, like I said, and come see her later."

She tried her best to keep her focus on Redmon and at the same time watch as Lucas walked in with a small bag of clothes clutched in one hand and a bottle of detergent in the other. Syd was giving Red a challenging stare but could feel Lucas's hesitation as he slowed his steps toward her and stilled just three machines away. What a contrast they were. There was Redmon with his perfectly pressed linen shorts, Coach loafers, no socks, linen camp shirt, Ray-Bans perched on his sharp nose and a freshly lined haircut. She noticed he'd gotten his mustache and beard lined up too.

Then there was Lucas. Today it looked like the most expensive things he was wearing were his immaculately clean Jordans. He'd paired them with gray sweat shorts that hit just above his knees and hugged his ass in a way that made her want to push Red aside and run over to cop a feel. And he had the nerve to top it with yet another black tank, which she was sure he probably got three to a pack but should still be illegal for a guy like him to buy. The way the ribbed fabric hugged his six-pack and the way the lack of sleeves defined his wide shoulders . . . all she could do was remember how her legs had been hooked around those shoulders the night before.

"Sydney, are you paying attention to me?" Red said. "I'll just stay here and wait for Remi. I'm sure she'd want to see me. Call your friend and tell her to bring her back now, and while we wait we can talk about what I wanted to talk to you about on the phone earlier."

She looked up at him. As if she wanted to discuss him and his favors in the middle of Scrubs and in front of Lucas Strong. "How about I don't go calling Kat and have her upend her plans just because you showed up without warning? Remi was excited about being with a friend today, so you can wait. Everything is not always about you, Redmon. Just like I have work to do and don't have the luxury of stopping it just because you decided to show up. Like I told you before, there is such a thing as scheduling. And you need to learn about it. Call me later and we will discuss things."

Red's jaw tightened, and he pulled his glasses off the top of his head, running his hands over his scalp in frustration. "Listen, Syd, I don't know why you're not getting this, but I'm serious." He reached out as if to grab the top of her arm, and Sydney took a step back. At the same time, Lucas walked over and stood right behind Red, holding up his laundry card.

"Yo, Syd," he said, giving her an easy smile that was way too relaxed. He had to have overheard, and he had to know who she was talking to. What the hell was he doing? "Can you help me with my card? I thought I had money on it, but the machine isn't reading it for some reason." He did that cute little pout thing he used to do back in high school when he was trying to distract her from a boring lecture. Sydney felt her cheeks heat, and she feared they were reddening in front of Lucas's eyes. Dammit, she probably was blushing, judging from the way his own eyes were sparkling in return. Smug bastard.

Red shifted and looked over at Lucas like he was a puppy who'd just come over and pissed on his shoe. "Do you see we're talking here?"

Lucas leaned back and put his hands up, shrugging. "Oh, I apologize, man. No offense at all. It just seemed like you were going on for a while, so I took my chance to get in where I could fit in."

Sydney snorted to herself and would have laughed out loud at Lucas's double entendre if she wasn't the butt of it.

Lucas continued, "I mean, I really need to get my wash started. This place can go from quiet one minute to being packed the next, and I wouldn't want to lose my spot in line and miss my chance." He locked eyes with Sydney once again, and she felt her face heat up for a moment before he turned back to Red and gave him an easy smile. "At getting the dryers, of course."

Lord save her. She watched as Lucas did his quirky best to come to her rescue, and the whole display was sexy as hell. She didn't think her nerves could take it. But more than anything, she didn't need any type of scene with Red today. And there would be one, because in that moment Remi came bouncing in full of excitement and running into her arms.

"Mom, I had so much fun!"

Syd hugged her daughter tightly, sniffed at her hair and rubbed at her back. It felt good to have Remi back in her arms. Though she was only gone for one night, and though Syd had spent that night in the arms of Lucas, it had still been strange not having Remi near this morning. She'd grown even more fiercely protective of her daughter over the past year. She knew she was probably overreacting, but for some reason, with all they'd been through, it felt like all she had was Remi. "I'm so glad you did, sweetie. That's fantastic. I knew you'd have fun hanging out with your friend."

"Don't you all look like the perfect happy family?" Kat said as she walked up behind Redmon.

"Don't we, though?" Redmon said, answering Kat's question.

Kat gave him a look of surprise. "Oh, Red, are you in town? I didn't even notice you there."

Red gave her a confused look. "I see you're still as charming as ever, Kat," he said, stone-faced. He'd long given up on being nice with Kat, since he knew she was Syd's true confidant.

"Daddy!" It was at the sound of his voice that Remi noticed her father for the first time.

Kat looked at her, then Lucas, then Red and grinned. "Aren't I?"

Syd was just about to break out into a cold sweat. If Kat said anything about her leaving the club with Lucas last night, that was it. They were through as friends. Kat suddenly gave her an "I got you" look. "Though I'd love to stay, Aisha is in the car with my sister, and we are double-parked." She blew a kiss to Remi. "Bye, sweetness. I'll see you next week, okay?"

Remi nodded. "Thanks, Aunt Kat. Tell Aisha I'll call her. On her cell phone."

Now Syd leveled Kat with another long look. "Hey, it wasn't me," Kat said.

Syd watched for a moment as Kat headed to the door, then she looked back at Remi. Just great. Remi would be begging for a phone next. She had the tablet, and now it would be her own phone bill. How was Syd going to handle it all? She started to feel the familiar stirrings of panic over money and how she was going to survive without a true safety net.

Add that to the fact that there was no denying the way Remi was clinging to Red, and Syd's heart sank with guilt. That was it—she was officially the worst mother ever. She must have secretly, despite her bullshit talk about co-parenting and all that crap, wanted her kid to hate her ex just as much as she did.

Still, Syd couldn't help being a little surprised by Remi's reaction to seeing her father, the way she ran to him and put her arms around his waist. When they left DC, she'd barely been mentioning Red. Their relationship had been one that had her resorting to whispers and walking on eggshells. Was this change what missing him had done to her?

Syd didn't know what she had expected, but it wasn't for her daughter's eyes to well with tears and for her to feel like her heart was being ripped out by something reaching into her throat and pulling it out that way.

"Told ya," Red said smugly, jolting Syd back to reality.

She looked at Remi, then remembered that Lucas was right there and felt heat lick up to her cheeks once again. "You two catch up. I've got work to do."

This was suddenly about as too much as too much could get. What Sydney really wanted to do was grab Lucas and give him an earful about coming in today when she'd specifically told him not to, even if she *had* secretly wanted him to. No, scratch that. What she really wanted to do was grab him by those delicious biceps of his and haul his ass to his car so he could drive them both back to Westchester for a repeat of last night. But that particular pleasure was completely off the table.

Instead, she tapped him on the arm, indicating he should follow her over to his machine so that she could check his card.

When she did, though, Remi looked over. "Hi, Mr. Strong. I've been practicing with the yarn I got! I think I've already gotten the hang of it."

Lucas gave Remi an easy smile. "That's great, Remi. And you can call me Lucas. There are way too many Mr. Strongs, and besides, when you say it, it makes me feel old. Like my oldest brother." He gave an exaggerated shudder and Remi giggled.

"Is he very old?" she asked.

"With his curmudgeon ways, at times you'd think he was." Lucas grinned again then. "But I'm just teasing. Don't forget that you're welcome for a class or just to come by and ask a question anytime you get stuck." He gave a pointed look to Syd. "I know Ms. Kerry would be happy to have you."

Redmon put a protective hand on Remi's shoulder. Syd watched as Lucas's eyes followed his hand and darkened. He seemed to take it as his cue to head back over toward his machine. Syd started to follow to ask him about the card when she heard Red talking to Remi. "You'll have to tell me all about these classes, Remi. I thought you were interested in piano. That's what we were talking about when you left."

Syd noticed Remi's expression and her immediate disappointment. Her daughter had about as much interest in piano as Syd had when she was a kid and her mother tried to force it down her throat: none. "How about we discuss it over pizza and ice cream? I was hoping to go with you *and* your mother, but she seems to be busy."

Remi looked between them, and Syd could see her wheels starting to turn. She hated that at this young age her daughter felt she had to be so calculating. She smiled up at her father, and Syd could see the hint of falsehood behind that smile. "Just take me, Dad. I miss you. It's been so long since it's been just the two of us. Okay?"

When Red gave Syd another triumphant look, she knew that her daughter had indeed seen and learned too much over the last few years of their broken marriage. Whatever it was he was about to try to hang over her head, she couldn't bite. She had to find a way they could co-parent from a distance and keep Remi from getting damaged in the process.

She looked over toward Lucas and saw him taking the clothes he had put in the machine back out and shoving them into his duffel bag once again. She walked over to where he was standing, hoping that Red was now busy enough with Remi to not pay her any attention.

"What are you doing?" she asked Lucas in as nonchalant a voice as she could as he put his clothes back in the bag. "I came over to check on your card. I thought you were here to do your laundry."

He paused suddenly and looked at her. "Did you really?" he said, his eyes full of unspoken challenge. It was then she noticed that he'd been holding tight, very tight, to his composure for the past few moments and was about ready to blow. She'd rarely seen him like this. Honestly, only once, many years ago—and to some it might be scary, but with her, a lump formed in her throat and it broke her heart. She wanted so badly to reach out and touch him. To console him. As he had consoled her when she'd needed it. Hell, she wanted to tell him she definitely wasn't one he should be getting so damned worked up about. But she couldn't. Not with Red and Remi nearby.

She took the bag from his hand and snatched his card. "Come, let's move to this machine," she said, walking to the other side of Scrubs and forcing him to follow. As she stuffed his clothes inside the machine, she noticed their clean fragrance. She looked at him, her brows drawn, and shook her head.

"Don't say it," he warned.

She slipped a glance toward Red and Remi. "You're so lucky I can't right now."

After inserting his card, she slammed the machine closed and added a tiny bit of detergent. "Come back in twenty-two minutes." She let out a breath as she looked over at Red and Remi again. Her grandfather had come down and was now talking with them both. Two other patrons came in, each with shopping carts, going for the triple loaders. Just perfect.

Suddenly Lucas spoke up. "How about I leave these and pick them up another time? It's not like I don't have anything else to wear." He was about to turn away when he pulled something out of his back pocket. "Oh, and there's this. Now that your daughter's becoming an expert at knitting, you wouldn't want her to show you up, would you?"

He placed the certificate Kat had won for her the night before in her hand and walked out the door. When she opened the certificate to read it, she saw he'd scrawled his cell number in that almost illegible scratch that he called handwriting underneath the lovely penmanship of the person who'd written "Free One-Hour Knitting Class." She could still hardly read his writing and had to squint to make out the numbers and the fact that it said "redeemable anytime—day or night."

18

"WELL, THAT DIDN'T take long at all," Sister Purnell shouted as soon as Lucas walked back into Strong Knits. She and some of the other OKGs, Ms. Watkins and Mrs. Hamilton, were all sitting around the table working on their usual gifts, getting an early start for this Christmas's Angel Tree drive, the charity that Ms. Cherry spearheaded for community outreach for children of incarcerated parents. Strong Knits donated much of the yarn or gave it to the OKGs at a discount, since they flat out wouldn't take a straight donation. Not that they should pay anything for the yarn, since the women were small-share silent partners in Strong Knits, along with the rest of the community, having bailed them out after Mama Joy passed away last year.

And they were the best sort of silent partners, never once hitting the guys up for their money. They seemed to consider it more of a donation, with the stipulation that Strong Knits stay open for get-togethers for the elderly and for the kids in the community. As long as the brothers continued to keep the yarn shop as a sort of sanctuary and private, safe place to gossip, the ladies were good. Though happy to honor that commitment, Lucas had to admit there were times the gossip part did start to get under his skin. Sure, having been raised by Mama Joy and the whole "it takes a village" way of thinking, he knew it came out of love and genuine caring, but goodness, these women took it too far at times. Still, he loved this group of ladies. Respected them too. He also knew they needed the shop and each other now more than ever. On top of Mama Joy being gone, they'd lost another of their dear friends, Ms. June—or Junie B, as they called her. He and his brothers missed Ms. June too, as did so many in the neighborhood. She had been a kind woman who would do anything for her fellow neighbor, be it offering childcare or food if a person was in need or knocking a head or two if someone was getting out of hand. When she got ill last year and then died so suddenly, it had been a rough blow to them all.

Logically, of course, Lucas knew that was how these things went. He'd lost one mother back when he and Noah were young. He'd come to terms with the reason for it too: he wasn't where he should have been. If he'd just stayed put, not gone out, listened to what his mother had told him, there wouldn't have been a problem and maybe she would still be here, instead of having gone back into the building to look for them after the space heater in their apartment tipped over.

Yes, they said it wasn't his fault. That he'd had no choice but to leave. Even Mama Joy and the therapists she'd made him see had told him so, but still he didn't buy it. Not then, and not now. If he hadn't gone out to run down to the store for chips for himself and Noah it would have all been fine. He would have heard the heater as soon as it fell and not gotten there too late. Not have only been able to get Noah out.

But he wasn't even able to save the damn cat.

And then there was Mama Joy. He was her own son. One she'd chosen. Educated and put faith in. The person with the skills to save her. And he was just not there when she'd needed him. If only he'd been home that day. Seen that she wasn't feeling well when she called a car to take herself to the hospital, then went into cardiac arrest on the way. Maybe, just maybe, he could have done something, and she would still be here too.

He could only imagine what Mama Joy's last hour must have been like. Her scare, the car ride. Then cardiac arrest. The fact that she didn't call him still baffled him to this day. He always wondered if she had known the truth—that he didn't have the power and, in reality, like with his birth mother, he couldn't save her at all.

Lucas looked at the women around Mama Joy's table. Here he was again, faced with a whole gaggle of meddlesome mothers, all with eyes in the back of their heads. How long before he lost them too?

"Good day to you ladies," Lucas said, plastering on his well-trained, cordial smile.

"Don't give us that 'good day' crap," Ms. Watkins said, which was surprisingly uncharacteristic of her, being that she was normally one of the more demure OKGs—if you could use "demure" to describe a small gang of senior women who met as a knitting circle and prayed together but also drank, gossiped and ran tabs on the neighborhood's comings and goings with better precision than most upper-level crime bosses.

"Oh, stop being coy, Lucas Strong. Coy is not cute on a man," Ms. Watkins said. "We all know you went over there chasing after Sydney Harris. What got you back so quickly? Did she run you off?"

"Oh, I beg to differ, Peach," Ms. Diaz said, pausing in her current project, an intricate pair of slippers with top cables. He hoped the receiver would appreciate the loving handcraftedness that went into them and not treat them like a pair of mass-produced booties from a by-the-register bin at Gap. These were true, one-of-a-kind heirlooms.

Ms. Diaz continued, "Don't you remember Reginald Tretone? He was so cute and would act coy all the time."

Ms. Watkins gave her friend a hard look over her needles. "Really?" she said. "You're using old Reggie T who used to hang down at Nipsy's on 126th?" She let out a huff.

Ms. Diaz shrugged. "Well, he was cute and coy."

"Yes, with all the boys."

"Well, that's neither here nor there, is it? It wasn't criteria for the conversation, Peach."

Ms. Watkins sighed as Lucas squelched back a laugh. This was how conversations usually went with them. He was about to head upstairs, thinking he'd gotten away, when Ms. Diaz spoke up again. "Or was she just too worn-out to deal with any more of you after your long night together?" she said, giving him a surprisingly saucy wink.

Holy hell. How have they descended this far this fast?

"Well, if she needs a tag-in, just you let me know. I'm still young enough to know what's good."

"Be quiet with all that talk, Elena," Sister Purnell admonished. "Your old ass could knock a hip out of joint just thinking too hard about him. I swear. We might need to get you checked out. Going from talk of old Reggie T to scaring poor Lucas here. Whew. You need me to pray over you? Lord. You keep up that talk and Joy's spirit gon' come right back in this shop and beat your old ass but good."

Ms. Diaz shook her head. "Oh, me and the Lord are just fine. You can keep that one in reserve for emergencies." She said it but still gave a quick look around as if the spirit of Mama Joy just might sneak up and whack her one from behind.

"Come on now, Sister Purnell, don't go getting on Ms. Diaz. Besides, there is nothing wrong with thinking," Lucas said to her teasingly, hoping to deflect the conversation away from Sydney by flirting with the ladies. He walked over and picked up the tail end of a scarf Sister Purnell was quickly knitting—her old, knobby hands seemed to have a mind of their own as they flipped and twisted the yarn on autopilot. He ran the scarf back and forth across his chest and did a little shimmy. She swatted at him in feigned admonishment.

"Cut it out, you! Don't let that little calendar persona go to your head. You just stay sweet now, boy. All that dancing and gyrating." She shook her head, then stopped abruptly, popping her head up and looking at him accusingly. "Wait, was it her stuck-up mama?" she asked. "Don't go letting her deter you. She's just mad because that man she was with all these years ain't never made things honest with her."

"Sister!" Ms. Cherry chided. "That's a lot even for you."

Sister Purnell rolled her eyes, then shrugged, suddenly looking a lot more girlish than her seventy-something years. "It is what it is. Evangeline always had her nose way too up in the air. Her daddy would be over there slaving away, and she come over from Long Island how much? Putting on airs like she's some grand dame out there in Huntington. As if that's something when we all know the deal. As if she went and did something so great getting her daughter married to that jackass." She looked over at Lucas and smiled. "Like the good book says. For everything there is a season." She looked at Ms. Cherry then and gave a quick nod. "Besides, we all know she ain't never liked our Joy worth a damn. You know how she was."

Lucas looked around the table. Sister Purnell nodded at Ms. Cherry, Ms. Cherry at Sister Purnell then at Ms. Diaz, then Ms. Diaz at Ms. Watkins. It was all quickly, silently done. Lucas caught a chill. It was as if a Mafia-like pact had suddenly been made.

Lucas nodded, confused, but he was going with it. Did the good Sister really just give him the okay for going ahead with Sydney on the full-court press, deeming him worthy, despite her being newly divorced and him being not in her rich league and not anywhere near dad material? He looked around the table as the rest of the women nodded and mumbled their agreements.

Just then Jesse came from out of the back room with the serving tray and the ladies' preferred mugs of tea and coffee. He looked surprised to see Lucas. "That was quick. What, she didn't want to see you?" Lucas gave his younger brother the side-eye and shook his head.

"Once again, I don't know what you're talking about. Who said anything about anybody seeing me? I'm going to the gym to work out. After today's interrogation, I might as well get back to work and forget having the day off."

LUCAS KNEW THAT Sydney didn't want him coming over, so it wasn't like he was hiding. More like following directives. Or like his phone wasn't working. And by all means, it wasn't like he was sitting at home waiting on her either. He'd gone to the gym, where he worked out poorly, distracted on account of the fact that he kept checking the time on his cell, the wall clock, then his cell again to see if they matched up.

They didn't, but they were only off by a minute, so no biggie there. But still for some reason he felt like writing a complaint email to somebody. Anybody. The bureau of This Woman Is Savage

And Has Got Me Twisted All The Fucking Way Out. Stuck on the clock situation, Lucas didn't realize his mistake until it was too late: Michelle was at the gym too, on the elliptical not too far away from the wall clock. Talk about a poor time to have this particular line-of-sight issue. He was getting off his machine, and she hopped off hers and headed his way.

"Hey there, firecracker. Saw you checking me out."

Lucas frowned.

She chuckled and did the lashes thing.

"Hi, Michelle. I didn't see you. I was actually checking the time. How's that sock yarn coming?"

"The what?"

"The yarn—how are you doing with it?"

She made a face as she put the yarn and his question together. He knew she'd not touched it. "Oh, it's coming fine. Though it would be a lot better if I had something to fill it with. It keeps getting terribly tangled. I could maybe use a little help."

He nodded, and she perked up. "Why don't you come by the shop on Wednesday night. Say, six thirty?" She grinned wide. "Someone will be happy to help you out."

Her grin quickly turned to a grimace. "Someone? You mean not you?"

"I mean someone. Most likely Kerry. I believe that's her open-knit night. She loves helping beginners that night, and she's a real wiz with that yarn. It's a great group. You should stop by."

Michelle continued to frown, but he could tell she was trying to rebound. She shrugged. "Fine. Maybe I will," she said before walking away.

Lucas didn't know whether to take that as a threat or not. Instead, he looked down at his phone again. The messages were blank.

"Fine," he said as he walked out of the gym.

Later that night he fumbled with his own sock yarn, getting tangled in the thin threads as he tried the simplest cast on. He thought of Michelle and karma and how Syd never called. Like his number was kept in her mental break-glass-in-case-of-emergency box. And she'd broken it the night of the auction, he'd put out the fire, and now all was clear. Emergency over.

Not that he blamed her, coming off a failed relationship. And not that he'd given her a reason to trust him. He never did. But how was this fair? How did she get to be the only one to break the glass?

Lucas groaned. Maybe he should just go over to Scrubs. He did have laundry to pick up, but his twenty-two minutes were long past, and now he'd just make an ass of himself. Or more of an ass. He should have just stayed. Done his own fucking laundry despite the husband and left with his goddammed clothes.

But then he'd have had to watch her and her daughter be perfect together with her jerk of a husband. That didn't seem weird at all.

For the thousandth time that day Lucas stalked around the shop and wondered if she was still there.

"You're going to be the one refinishing that floor when it gets all dull," Jesse said.

Lucas ignored his brother and stomped over to the window. Surely her ex-husband wouldn't still be there. He couldn't be, could he?

Of course he could. He'd want to spend as much time with Remi as possible while in town. And Syd was his ex-wife, but exes were still family, and family was forever.

Fuck. Not knowing was making him crazy. All it took was a nanosecond and it was high school all over again. He was confused and sweaty and didn't have a clue what to do, when his whole schtick was always being the go-to guy who knew exactly what to do in any situation.

So damn close, but an eternity away. He let out a frustrated grunt and had started to turn away from the window just as a car pulled up in front of Scrubs and he saw Sydney step out. Remi got out after her and waved back into the car happily. He noticed Syd had changed out of her casual clothes from earlier and was now wearing a flowy black sundress with strappy sandals, and her usually down hair was twisted and pinned up. She turned from the car and headed into Scrubs, but her steps were slowed. He could tell she was tired, and for some reason she seemed to him to look torn between going inside Scrubs and the life and the work ahead and back toward Red and the ease and comfort of that car.

Lucas ached. He could see the pain on her from her head down to her feet. She deserved more. She deserved her steps to be so much lighter. To not have to make these choices.

It wasn't like what he could offer her was so much better. What could he offer but a chance to move away from home, clear to the other side of the street? And if they left the neighborhood, where would they live on his salary—a plush convertible two-bedroom with a hellish commute out in Long Island City? He knew that lifestyle wasn't for her. Nor was it for him. She was about to go inside Scrubs when her ex jumped out of the car. He handed her a small bag, then touched her arm and leaned down to kiss her before she turned away. The kiss didn't linger and it wasn't like she kissed him back, but still it was a kiss.

Lucas seethed. *Man, fuck those clothes.* They could stay over there until Syd was good and ready to tell him to come and get them, or they walked back across the street on their own.

19

"DAMMIT, STRONG. IF you don't get your head in the game, I'm going to beat your ass!"

Lucas glanced down at the card table to see that there were two hearts and a ten of spades, and he'd just thrown out a jack of spades. He looked across at Dee with wide, apologetic eyes. "Shit, I'm sorry, Dee."

"Did you really just cut above me?"

"Hey, no talking to your partner across the board!" Flex yelled. "You want to have to give up three books?" He reached his hand out as if to take some of their books from in front of Dee. She shot him a look.

"You want to lose three fingers?"

He quickly pulled his hand back. "No, ma'am."

Tim, Flex's partner, gave him a warning glance. Not that Flex didn't need it, and not that Lucas wasn't taking heed of it either. Just like with every other part of her life, Dee did not like anyone losing focus, and she didn't like to lose. He'd better get himself together. They were on their break enjoying what should have been a relaxing game of Spades—if a game of Spades could ever be called relaxing. But there he was, head in the clouds . . . well, head on Sydney Harris and the fact that he hadn't heard from her and was now back to work and about to get his ass beat by Dee for cutting over her book and possibly losing the game for them. He gave himself a mental shake and forced himself to pay attention to the cards. He couldn't waste any more time thinking about Sydney. She'd come around or she wouldn't, and the way things were looking, she was definitely heading in the "wouldn't" direction.

He didn't know what had happened after he left, but he could clearly see that though the guy was an ass, the little girl loved him. He might not be all Sydney wanted, but he couldn't be all that bad if he had such a wonderful daughter.

They got to the final book, and the cards were played. Once again, dammit, Lucas hadn't been paying attention. Shit, who threw out what? Oh well, it didn't matter; he only had one card to play, so it was going to be what it was going to be, and all he could do was hope that Tim coming behind him didn't have a spade higher than his sorry-ass six. He threw down his six of spades and held his breath for a moment as he waited. Tim gave him a look and shocked him by throwing out the three of clubs.

"Ahh, you got lucky there, Strong," Tim said. "For a minute I thought I had you."

"Luck? What are you talking about, luck?" Dee said. "Our team is unstoppable. We deal with skill, not luck. You'd better ask somebody."

Lucas laughed to himself as he thought about her words. Luck or skill—which was it when it came to winning, losing and things that were never meant to be?

SYDNEY LOOKED OVER the knitting certificate one more time, study-ing Lucas's handwriting in his "day or night" invitation. It was currently night. Late at night. Pops and Remi both had gone to bed, but she was wide-awake, while Mr. Bill was manning the shop downstairs. Her phone buzzed, and for a moment hope bloomed, but that quickly turned to anger. It was Red again. She couldn't believe what he'd pulled after having a perfectly benign dinner the other night, almost lulling her into a false sense of comfort, think-ing maybe they could make this multistate co-parenting thing a go.

They were almost back home and Remi was dozing when he started going on about the laundromat not being a place suitable enough for his daughter. As if he'd somehow pulled her from the slums or some such mess. It wasn't like Red came from much of anything besides the middle of middle class his damned self. He coasted on the incredible gift of his father's innate salesmanship, which was passed to him. Bullshittery ran in the family. But she'd been too tired to argue then. And who knew? Maybe it was a hint of PTSD that brought back some of her old behaviors of going along to get along. But she'd just let it go, hoping to have a peaceful night for Remi. Still, out of the situation and Red's orbit, she knew she needed to stay smart. Be alert. Get out of the fog she was in regard-ing Red—and even Lucas too, especially when it came to her over-active hormones playing a teenage rewind game.

Even so, after her night all she could think about was Lucas's invitation and the clothes that he never came to pick up. So, what? Was he never going to come back to get them?

Was he just gonna disappear, pretend their night never happened? And pretend he didn't have a whole bag of mismatched sheets, towels and T-shirts taking up space on her shelves? The thought of it was starting to annoy her so much that after a good thirty minutes of it, she dialed his number and impulsively hit the video call button instead of just making a regular call.

Lucas's sexy face filled the screen. He was obviously awake and lying in his bed—she could tell by the pillows in the background—and Sydney pulled the phone away in shock, crossing her legs in a sort of sexual reaction that he automatically elicited from her. She brought the phone closer and stared into his eyes as he stared back at her.

"Why answer so fast?" she asked. "Were you waiting for a special call?"

"I was waiting for you to call," he answered without hesitation.

"And how did you know it was me?"

"I've always had your number, Sydney."

Sydney blinked. "Since when and why?"

Lucas didn't answer, just stared at her in that way that made her feel vulnerable as well as nervous, like he was seeing her in a way that nobody else seemed to see her. She watched as he bit at his bottom lip and continued to stare. Damn him. Not talking, just looking and making her feel more alive than she had in the ten years of her marriage.

"Answer me, Lucas—how do you have my number? The last time we did a video over social media. So you wouldn't have gotten it that way."

He continued to stare at her seriously before he opened his

mouth. "Is how the real question, or is why I never used it the real question, Syd?"

Sydney sucked in a breath. So very like him to go straight to the heart of things. He could simply have answered the question, but he had to read into her soul and go straight to what was really bothering her. "Fine—if you had my number, why didn't you use it in all this time? Though I still want to know how you got it and how long you've had it."

Lucas nodded. "That's fair." He seemed to hesitate, then he looked down before looking up. "I've had it for a couple of years now. From when your grandfather first started showing signs of feeling a little run-down. Mama Joy gave it to me. She knew we'd been friends. And I don't know if she knew that your grandfather was feeling unwell, but she passed it on to me, saying to keep it handy in case it was needed." He shrugged then. "So, I kept it handy."

"Why do I feel like there's more to the story?" She stared at the screen like there had to be something more when it came to him having her number or like she knew what Mama Joy knew, but thankfully, she didn't push it more. "Eventually your grandfather gave me your number too, when I started hanging around the shop checking in on him when I'd go over and do my laundry there. I guess he just wanted me to have it too. But he told me not to call you and bother you unless it was truly necessary. I'm sorry. I couldn't go against his wishes."

Sydney was both shocked and dismayed and maybe a little annoyed over the fact that Lucas had had her number and never used it to call and tell her how sick her grandfather was. She opened her mouth, but he interrupted her.

"Before you jump on me, know that I did consider calling you to tell you how your grandfather was faring here on his own. But I knew that if I did, I'd probably never be welcome in Scrubs again after betraying his trust. I figured the best way to handle things was to let them go the way they were going. He'd stay in touch, and if there was a real emergency, I'd call you. There was no other reason for me to call. You made it clear after the one time we spoke that there was no room for us to be any kind of informal chat buddies. So I was following your wishes too."

Sydney was quiet as she took in the way things were and the way he'd been thinking of her while she was back in DC living her life as Mrs. Redmon Hughes. She blinked quickly, tears threatening to overflow from her eyes and fall down her cheeks. "Fuck fuck fuck fuck fuck fuck! I hate all this."

"I'm sorry. So sorry. I should have told you." He paused then, and Sydney blinked back her tears. "I wasn't being a good friend to you because I was . . . I don't know." He sighed. "Pissed off because I couldn't be what I really want to be to you, Syd. All we had was the call that night, and then you went back to your life."

Syd felt the heat of shame rush up her cheeks, this time not because of her grandfather but because of what she'd done to Lucas. "I'm sorry. I shouldn't have called you that night."

He shook his head. "I answered, didn't I? I could have chosen not to."

She paused. She'd never thought of that part.

Lucas continued. "Honestly, I'm still pissed because I still can't be what I want to be to you. I never will. And I don't know where or how to carve out the space so that we can be friends." He laughed at himself. A wry laugh that held no joy. The hollowness of the sound made Sydney do the same.

"Yeah, we are pretty fucked," she said.

"Woman, you've got to stop using that word, because every time you do it takes me so much further away from the friend zone, where you keep telling me I need to be, and it puts me right back in that hotel room—your lips on mine, my hands all over your body—and it drives me wild."

Sydney felt her nipples harden. "Well, fuck, you can't say that and think we'll get anywhere different either."

He licked his lips, then stared at her. "What words can I use?" he asked as she watched him settle deeper into his pillow. Goodness, if this man didn't tempt her. She swallowed.

"Listen, I've got to go, it's late. I need to get some sleep, and you should too."

Lucas frowned. "Sleep? I don't know how to sleep anymore. The last good sleep I got was the half hour that I was holding you. That's it. Before that, it hasn't been since before Mama Joy passed away."

"That's not good, Lucas," Sydney said, the worry clear in her tone. "You're going to drive yourself insane, not sleeping."

"I know it," he said. "Don't think I haven't tried. My mind wanders too much. To the past year, to the losses, and I just can't calm it down. Oddly enough, when I wasn't sleeping, I found a bit of peace coming into Scrubs and just sitting and knitting, and then your grandfather and I got close," he said. "When I'm there and I'm knitting, I always feel slightly anonymous. The white noise of the machines, just me and my needles and no one else to bother me, and your grandfather's late-night cool company was always perfect for my sensibilities. And when he was chatty, the subject was always you, so I never really minded it. He'd talk about his sweet Sydney, and before I knew it, time would just seem to flow, and I'd always leave the laundromat feeling like I'd had a good eight hours of sleep."

Suddenly Syd got it. She understood his being there and why he had probably been there that night when she'd yelled at him in front of Remi. Looking back, she had probably been way harsh about that.

It made sense. It was the same reason she'd headed back home. Scrubs was her refuge, and it was that for him right now too. There was something comforting about being in Scrubs.

Sydney gave him one of her no-nonsense looks. "Well, you might think it's weird, but I get it," she said. "Anyway, we veered off topic. That's not the reason I called you tonight. What I called you about was redeeming my certificate. Pick out some yarn for me and we can have our first session the night after tomorrow. We'll do it in Scrubs. I'm supposed to work the late-night shift anyway, so we can do it there after I get Remi and Grandpa to bed."

She could tell Lucas was shocked by the way his eyebrow went up. She knew he was trying to play it cool, but he couldn't help the smile that tugged at the corner of his lips and then went into a full-blown flash of gorgeous white teeth and sparkling dark eyes.

"Really?" he said. "But I don't want to pick out yarn for you. Yarn is very personal and something you're going to be working with for a while. How about we have our first lesson over at the shop? Come by on a night you are not working, after you get Remi settled down. You tell me when and I'll be waiting. Is that okay?"

It was such a small thing, yet it felt so big and so good. Sydney nodded. "Is tomorrow night too soon?" she asked.

"Cut to me wishing that tomorrow night was already here," Lucas said.

Sydney smiled. "Good night, Lucas."

"It is now, Sydney," he said and clicked off.

20

SYDNEY SPRINTED ACROSS the street to Strong Knits, her eyes darting back and forth, trying to look inconspicuous and knowing she was anything but. Here it was almost eleven at night, and though she wasn't really dressed up, she'd still taken extra time with her accessories . . . and yeah, maybe a little extra time with her hair and makeup.

Of course, neither Remi nor her grandfather had any intentions of turning in at a decent hour, and when she left the house, they had both been wide-awake and watching TV, giving her "Well, where are you tipping off to?" eyes.

She looked guilty as hell but just couldn't wait any longer to see Lucas. "I'm, um, heading over to Strong Knits to see some of the old gang. They're having a late-night knit-up, so I thought I'd see who's by." She hoped like hell her voice didn't sound as sketchy as she guessed it probably did. "Do you mind watching Remi, Pop? Just another half hour of TV and then bed."

"Of course I don't mind. This is the stuff I live for. Who knew cartoons even stayed on at this hour?"

Syd sighed and paused. "You really don't have to. I can just stay home. This isn't important."

He waved his hand, shooing her away, and his voice got serious. "Go on, girl. Knit you up some fun. I've got everything under control here. I've been sticking to schedules way too much anyway. I think we all have."

Sydney's eyes went wide as her cheeks started to burn. And there she was again, back to being sixteen. Did anything get past the old man, and did he really hate Redmon that much?

Her grandfather chuckled. "The answers are no and yes," he said. "Now go. But don't be out too late. You've got a shift in the morning. Oh, and on your way, can you stop and grab that bag of clothes for the customer across the street who seems to keep forgetting to pick up his order? Thanks, sweetie." He turned away from her, his attention now back on Remi. "All right, so what you have me watching? I hope it's not anything scary. I can take a lot, but I can't take anything scary. Or too romantic. I don't go in for that sort of thing," he said with clearly fake gruffness.

As Syd got closer to Strong Knits, she looked back at Scrubs, its awning lights still on but the inside lights dimmed for the new night hours she'd gotten her grandfather to agree to. For overnights they would do drop-offs only at the new window, where people would also be able to pick up again at eight a.m., when the shop was back fully open. That way it was a lighter shift and a lot safer. She and Mr. Bill agreed to trade off on those hours so that she could accompany her grandfather to any doctor's appointments and be able to help with Remi once school started. It felt good to have at least one thing settled. If you could call it that.

But then there was Red with his old bullshit.

Unbidden, the thought of Red had her recalling the day she told

Lucas about her scholarship and how heartbroken she'd been when his only reaction was to say congratulations, and for the first time ever she had felt that his smile was not genuine. She didn't know until that very moment how much she wanted him to say more. How much she longed for him to, yes, congratulate her, but if not ask her to stay, at least say he'd miss her. That he'd write, stay in touch. Dare she wish, come and see her.

If he'd given her any bit more, she would have held on to it for dear life. But that was it. Just congratulations.

The thought almost made her turn back.

But then again, how could she ever think her decision was wrong when the outcome of it was her precious Remi? She felt horrible for even imagining a life that was all about herself. What kind of woman did that make her? What sort of mother?

Syd sighed. Jumbled in her thoughts. At war with her body and mind, her heart and her obligations. And now she was here, standing outside the door of Strong Knits in a semipanic, a bag of laundry in hand, looking like an overdressed delivery gal. She pulled her cell phone out to tell Lucas she had changed her mind. She was just about to send the text when he opened the door and she looked once again into the depths of his sparkling brown eyes. He licked his lips and gave her a smile, and she put her cell back into her crossbody bag and reached out to hand him his laundry. *What kind of woman indeed?*

An orgasm-starved, horny-assed divorcée who was now about to use the guise of learning to knit as foreplay to hopefully screw the hell out of a fine-assed man. That was what kind.

"YOU LOOK GOOD."

Sydney turned from where she was admiring the rich mahogany shelves overflowing with colorful skeins of yarn. She was surprised by how excited the homey environment made her. When Lucas had opened the door to let her in, it took all she had not to pounce on him. She'd channeled her best old Syddie from The Gate in that moment so as not to jump him, but she knew she would hold out for only so long. She continued to look around as her heart thumped hard against her chest wall in a way it hadn't in years. She was either as horny as she'd been at seventeen or about to have a true emergency. Lord, she hoped it was horny and not her heart.

They were alone in the shop, as it was past closing. Lucas had told Sydney that Jesse was staying with Kerry, and Noah was visiting a friend in Brooklyn for the night. It was mighty convenient. Not that she'd look a gift horse and all.

Still, she couldn't help feeling anxious about being there. For one, there was her grandfather and not being able to hide a thing like this from him, no matter how casual she tried to keep it with Lucas. The block was just too tight-knit. And with the way news spread, how long could they keep up appearances in front of Remi?

She let out a breath.

"Just get through tonight, Syd," she mumbled. "Just tonight."

Shit. But what if tonight led to more? What if she couldn't stop it? Honestly, she hoped she'd be able to keep Remi in the dark for a good long time—until this, whatever it was, ran its course. She didn't need her daughter more confused or anxious than she already was.

Of course, she herself was a totally confused mess. A mess who was all atingle just because her old crush told her she looked good.

He was leaning against the back shelf staring at her with a ball of yarn under his arm while casually twisting the yarn over two

needles at an easy pace, as if the yarn and needles were an exten-
sion of his fingers and the movement somehow as easy to him as
breathing. She thought about Mama Joy and how she'd raised him
and his brothers here and felt nothing but regret. She'd missed out
on a lot with Mama Joy and Strong Knits. She'd only been in the
shop once or twice that she remembered, because her mother never
let her go in and "waste her time," as she called it, fiddling with
yarn. It wouldn't get her a decent husband, or a high-paying job.
Turned out the path her mother had chosen for her didn't get her
those either.

"You don't look so bad yourself," she replied to Lucas.

He gave her a half smile with a shrug. "If you say so."

She walked toward him, touching yarn as she went to keep her
hands occupied, because she wanted to touch him so badly, and she
hoped that this would stave off the impulse. At least for a while. She
got about two feet away, then leaned against the table. "You say that as
if it's not true and as if you don't hear it all the time. Hell, I was there—
I saw you on that stage, saw how the women were going wild over
you. You're practically an icon in the city now."

He came forward and stood right in front of her, so close that
she thought he might lean forward and kiss her. But in the end, he
only put his work on the table and walked around her. Sydney let
out a breath.

"I wouldn't say an icon," he said. "More like the flavor of the
month. Any attention I have now will be gone with the new year
and the next FDNY calendar."

Sydney stared at him. He seemed so different than he had during their video call the night before. His mood had shifted, and she
could see his guard was firmly in place. She wondered what had
changed. "What makes you think that?" she asked. "I mean, it's not

like you were starving for companionship even before you were in the calendar."

He looked at her with surprise. "How would you know what I was starving for? You weren't here."

Lucas's words hit her with the heavy weight of their accusation. Instantly she felt she should go on the defensive. "What are you saying, that I should have been?" She stared at him long and hard. "Why? Tell me why, when there was never any solid reason for me to do so." She and Lucas stared at each other for long minutes before he finally broke the tension by turning to the big wall of yarn, pulling out skein after skein.

He worked quickly, first going down low and picking out a pretty gray heathered wool. Then he moved to the left and picked out a sunny yellow skein, then some white cotton, before he moved over again and picked out a blue yarn. Syd's eyes could barely keep up as he reached to the left of that and chose a cobalt ball, but then he changed his mind and went for a periwinkle one, tossing it on the table more roughly than the sweet yarn deserved. He turned and she got distracted by his fine back muscles and how they stretched out his tee, and she had to force herself to focus as he moved back over to the right and went for a vibrant orange wool, then, seemingly ignoring her, he went to another wall and picked out a multicolored twisted yarn and threw that in the growing pile on the table.

Sydney frowned. What was he doing? It was like he was in his own little world and completely ignoring her. "You planning on letting me in on what you're doing, or is this design something for you to know and me to find out? A surprise ugly sweater, perhaps? And what does all this yarn have to do with my knitting lesson?"

Lucas looked up at her. At first, he didn't answer, then he

looked down at the array of yarn and back up at her again. "Tell me what you like," he said.

Sydney blinked in confusion. "Why are you asking me what I like? You're supposed to teach me, so how would I know?"

Lucas tilted his head to the side, and Syd needed to take a breath. She closed her eyes then and opened them back up only to be met with the same quizzical look from him. Why did he always do this? Why did he always insist on leaving things up to her, forcing her to make decisions? Didn't he know she sucked at it?

"Of course you know what you like, Sydney," Lucas said, his voice smooth and steady. He ran his hand across the gray yarn, and her eyes followed. It looked so enticing, so sensual, the way his fingers gently trailed over the furry cloud. "How about this?" he said. "Even if you don't know what you like, you definitely know what you want or want to try."

Sydney swallowed, and she felt a low tightening deep within her core. She looked from him to the yarns and back up. "I want you to teach me how to create something new," she said, her voice soft, and in a way she hoped that he didn't even hear her. But she continued, this time slightly louder. "I want you to teach me how to make something for myself and no one else."

Lucas nodded but said nothing. She was grateful to him for that. She knew that if she said those same words to Redmon, the outcome would be very different. Instead, all Lucas did was nod and watch as she came forward and looked over the yarns on the table. She ended up dismissing them all and instead turned back to the wall and chose a beautiful sky blue yarn, so soft it made her think of clouds full of dreams. When she picked it, he smiled and went to grab a couple of needles for her.

"That's gonna be fantastic," he said. "Now follow me upstairs and I'll show you where the real magic happens."

Sydney couldn't suppress the snort that came out. It seemed the old Lucas couldn't help but rear his silly little head. "I bet you say that to all the girls, Lucas Strong."

He shook his head and grabbed her hand. The feeling of his touch was electric, and he pulled her toward the stairs at the back of the shop. She was breathless from the sensation of being so near him and the realization of what that meant and what they could and should not get up to in the time they were together. Two steps up, Syd following blindly with one hand in his and the other full of yarn, he paused and turned back to look at her.

He raked his free hand through his hair, narrowed his eyes and bit at his bottom lip in that way that made her feel like he was taking a bite of her flesh. "I may have said it to a few, Sydney Harris, but you need to know I truly mean it with you."

Bullshit.

That's what her mind told her. But still, Sydney dropped her yarn and was on him in a flash. Mouth eager, body on fire. She needed him. Wanted to taste and feel him and breathe him in just to make sure what she was experiencing in this moment was real. She felt in a way still ridiculously inexperienced. How dumb was that? Old—well, not that fucking old—but divorced mother that she was, and she was feeling inexperienced. She knew her kisses were probably too sloppy, urgent and wet, but shit, what did it matter when his tongue felt so good stroking against hers?

There was a moan, and she didn't know whose mouth it came from, but it was she who spoke. "God, your kiss is my heaven," she said as she pulled her head back slightly and licked the tip of his sweet tongue. He pulled her in closer, wrapping one arm around her, the other caressing her behind as he leaned back on the stairs and she placed her hands on his chest.

She continued to kiss him as he caressed her, and they fell into a hazy sexual swirl on the narrow staircase. She ground her center against his thickening erection, and her breath started to hitch in shallow gasps. She wanted to feel more of him. She needed to feel all of him. Suddenly greedy—well, greedier—Sydney let her hand go under Lucas's tee to rub at his bare skin. When her fingertip ran across his nipple and he drew in a quick breath of pleasure, hearing it again was all she wanted. She pulled up his shirt slightly, then looked at him, their gazes locking in a seemingly foggy mist. Lucas quickly pulled off his shirt at the same time that she pulled off hers. She bent to lick at his nipple, and he sucked in a low, whispery breath that filled her with more joy than she had felt in a long while. But then he turned the tables and reached forward to stroke at her tender breasts and she just about tumbled back down the stairs.

"Is this enough for you? Should I continue?"

"Is it for you? And should we continue?" she countered.

"I asked first." Lucas raised that cute brow, his little moles rising with it.

Syd leaned forward, her hard nipples pushing urgently against his palms as she reached out and ran a thumb along the length of his almost impossibly hard erection. "I think we both know what we're doing right now is not nearly enough for either of us."

Lucas grinned and for a moment, in just a blink, his eyes went from seductive to serious. "No, it isn't, is it?"

Syd let out a sigh, knowing immediately that in that moment it wasn't just his hard-on talking. That his words, sweet and seductive and full of promise of so much more than just sex, were what dreams were made of. But those weren't the types of dreams she dreamt. Not anymore. Lucas wanted a relationship and all that came with that. It was something she couldn't give. Not now. Maybe not ever. She felt her body tense.

Lucas leaned down and ran his tongue gently along the shell of her ear. "I'm sorry. I didn't mean to press. Relax. Just think of tonight. Only tonight. Now, do you want me to stop?"

She narrowed her eyes and pulled back, reality slowly making its way back in. She looked at him now. Sexy, half-naked, sprawled out on his late mama's back stairs. "Why aren't you asking me the right question, Lucas?"

"Because I won't. That's not a question I'm going to ask you."

"But it's one I should ask myself."

Lucas shook his head. "Well, you do that. You've been doing it long enough, and you've got plenty of practice with it. So go ahead. Ask yourself what you should be doing. But as for me, I'll always ask what you want. Because that's all that matters to me."

Sydney let out a snort and moved to get up. She was a mother. She couldn't play these games. It wasn't just her who could get hurt.

Lucas didn't reach out to stop her. But then again, she had known he wouldn't. It wasn't Lucas's way. "Are you really leaving?" he asked.

She shook her head and picked up her top, then her yarn and needles. "No. I came for my lesson, and that's what I'm going to get." She walked past him on the stairs with as much dignity as her shaky legs would allow her. "You asked me what I wanted. Well, I want what's owed to me, and right now, it's one knitting lesson. I'd like you to pay up."

IT'S HIS SHOULDERS. *It has always been his shoulders,* Sydney thought as she followed Lucas into his room. He'd given her a proper house tour and now they'd finally made it to his bedroom on the top floor. She tried to relax and keep up the cool divorcée bravado she had going, but then she went right back to thinking of Lucas's other fine attributes. She stared at the back of him again. Maybe his neck. That little space between his freshly cut hair and T-shirt collar that always looked so soft, inviting and kissable. Even back when they were at school she'd see him in the hall from behind and just want to reach out and touch him. This time she did.

Lucas jumped, turning around. "How is it you constantly surprise me?"

"I could say the same about you."

He looked around. She saw his cheeks redden. "I'm sorry my room is such a mess. That I'm such a mess. I know this is not what you're used to."

Syd stared at him. "What?"

He stepped back, and for the first time, she really looked around. Took in the neat but modest room with the full sized bed that prob ably barely accommodated his large, muscular frame. The dark paneled walls, desk, computer, gaming system, the weights in the corner, the folded clothes on the small chair by the window. The Scrubs laundry bag hanging on the back of the door. Somehow it was what she'd imagined his room to be. Neat, basic, masculine, with an immediate feeling of home. "Do you mean that mess over there?" She pointed to the folded clothes and took in his slight blush.

He shook his head. "Now you're making fun of me. I thought I was supposed to be teaching you to knit."

Syd came forward then, running a hand across his shoulders and tossing the balls of yarn she had in her other hand on his bed. She jumped on the bed after them, feeling more daring than she had in years. She pulled out a long strand of yarn and ran it suggestively through her fingers. "Fine. Show me again how you cast on. I just can't seem to get it."

Lucas laughed. That deep, throaty, sexy laugh that made her want to cross and uncross her legs. "Oh, I'll show you, all right, Ms. Harris. And by the time I'm done, you'll be a whole-ass expert. I guarantee it."

21

W HAT THE HELL are you doing?" Lucas looked over at Noah, then pointed his finger at Damian, who was inspecting his room as if they'd stashed D. B. Cooper in there or something.

"Do you know what his problem is?" Lucas asked Noah.

Noah shrugged while tightening the towel around his waist. He gave Damian wide eyes but still managed to keep his usual laid-back demeanor. He turned toward Lucas. "You know him—it could be just about anything. He's always up in arms about something."

"What are you implying?" Damian said, moving away from the bed where he'd been staring ultra hard at the immaculately spread comforter. Lucas wouldn't be surprised if he pulled out a black light.

He walked up to Lucas and stared him straight in the eye. "How am I supposed to trust you"—he turned to Noah—"or you either, Mr. Just Back Home Off The Road?" He turned back to Lucas again. "But definitely how am I supposed to trust you after hearing that Sydney was over here last night? None of you guys know how to respect my room or property, it seems, with all these women around the house. As if it's my fault you all keep your rooms looking like trash bins."

"Just because none of us have freaking color-coordinated bed sets with matching duvets doesn't mean we keep our rooms like trash bins," Noah said.

"And what would make you think I would put Sydney in your bed anyway? Or anybody's bed? I mean, why accuse me?" Lucas said. "Jesse was the one who was using your room as his personal sex parlor. Bother him." Just then Jesse came out of the kitchen and into the hall.

"Listen, all that is in the past, but once again, you all still throw it in my face," he said. "I only did it because you had the best sheets. I've since learned the error of my ways and gotten sheets of my own. Now, I'd appreciate it if you'd shut the fuck up about it and get over the whole thing."

Kerry walked by on her way from Jesse's room. She stopped and looked at all of them with a questioning eye. "What are you all talking about?" she asked. "What is it, Damian? You look upset. Don't tell me you're mad because Lucas had a date over last night?" She reached out and tapped Damian on his chest twice reassuringly.

He let out a breath, seeming to be swayed by her sweet temperament and easy words.

She grinned. "It's not like it's a big deal. He already changed the sheets with a replacement set that I picked up from HomeGoods for when me and Jesse like to switch things up."

When Damian growled and turned to Lucas, Kerry tapped him one more time before turning on her heel to walk away. She gave

Lucas a quick wink and headed down the hall. "Jesse, can you hurry up and help me with some of the inventory in the storeroom before it's time to open and I have to go work at the center?"

"She's just fucking with me or something, right?" Damian asked.

"Is she?" Lucas said before he walked away.

Noah laughed as he headed down the hall toward his room. "Like you said, it's something, bro."

Damian yelled after all of them, "I swear, you all going to keep screwing with me and I'm going to move back in here."

"Oh, we're so very scared!" Jesse yelled from downstairs.

"Gasp! The horror," Noah yelled from his room.

Lucas laughed to himself hearing so much commotion in the house. For a moment it sounded like old times, and if he let himself imagine just a little longer he could almost hear Mama Joy's voice in the background too. Things had been so quiet for so long. She was there one minute, the next moment gone. Just like his birth mother. No buildup and no goodbye.

He told himself early in life he was used to quick exits, but he was a liar. He'd never said goodbye to Syd, and he'd regretted it for so long. And now she was back, but until when?

He knew she was divorced, but how final was a divorce when there was a kid and a man who clearly still wanted both his kid and his wife back? This time when Syd left, would he be strong enough to say the goodbye he should have said the first time?

He thought of the night before. Their make-out session on the stairs; their much-more-than-make-out session in his bedroom. Her wants versus what she thought she needed to do. Hell, maybe she was right. What right did he have to tell her what to do with her life? The fact was, he had none. And the way she had flipped the switch from the woman on the stairs to the model knitting student to the sex goddess in his bedroom last night let him know she'd had things well in control. She was so cool, so poised, while she learned to cast on and get the basic knit stitch that one would never know her tongue had been down his throat just moments before or that his tongue had explored just about every intimate spot on her body.

Lucas felt his body responding now. Damned Sydney and her maturity. He let out a breath as the overwhelming desire to see her again came over him. He looked around for something to wash but came up empty. He couldn't make a fool of himself with clean clothes again.

Suddenly a fully dressed Noah was at his door. "Hey, you want to go get some breakfast?"

"Ahh, Noah!" he said, a light bulb switching on in his head. "No, I don't, but I do want to do some laundry. What happened to the towel you were using earlier?"

Noah looked at him. His normally quick-to-smile brother grew serious. "Laundry again?"

Lucas sighed. "Not you too."

Noah leaned nonchalantly against the doorjamb. He shook his head. "What? Only Jesse can give advice because he's Mr. Stable Relationship Man now? And Damian is, well—" He shrugged.

"Damian," they said in unison.

"Exactly," Noah said. He stalked to his room, then came back with not only his towel but a whole duffel bag of laundry. He shoved it at Lucas.

"What the hell? How do you have so much?"

Noah shrugged. "I've been away a long time. I'm doing it in bits and pieces."

Lucas stared. "Or you mean you're giving it to me to do in bits and pieces. I think I'm getting scammed."

Once again Noah grew serious. "Speaking of . . ."

"Watch it."

"I want you to watch it," Noah said, his tone low. "I'm not just looking out for you here, brother, but for her as well. Take it slow."

"We've known each other for fifteen years."

"And been committed for how many?"

Lucas was silent.

"I know it's been hard. You've been my rock and my literal keeper since our mother died. You've been our rock since Mama Joy died. But who's been yours? I know you. You fix. You use fixing or what you think is fixing as your therapy. But have she and her daughter asked to be fixed? Just take it slow, okay?"

Lucas frowned. He heard Noah's words but didn't want to fully let them in.

"I'm here. Dame and Jesse are here. You can call someone if you want to. But if you love her, don't ask her to be your therapy. Just love her."

Lucas let out a breath, then cut Noah a look. "Are you done?"

Noah shrugged. "Yeah, I'm done."

"Okay, fine."

"You still going over?"

He nodded.

"Well then, take my damned laundry."

Lucas shook his head and took the bag. He loved his brothers, but they could really be pains in his ass at times.

"WELL, WELL. IF this isn't just the cutest thing."

It was as if time stopped in a whole villainous-record-scratch moment at the sound of Sydney's mom's sarcastic quip.

Syd paused in her struggle to knit and stared at her mom taking in the scene in front of her. She looked good, her mother. Hair smooth, dyed jet-black and pulled back into a tight, low bun. She was wearing a white flowy top and printed capris with sandals and wide Jackie O–style glasses when she sauntered into Scrubs. The way her blouse flowed, you would think she brought her own fan. Even though Syd knew the visit wouldn't go well, she couldn't help but smile over her mother's entrance. Besides, it wasn't like her mother was wrong—it really was kind of the cutest thing. The laundry was quiet this afternoon, with only a couple of patrons doing their wash. Meanwhile, the "cutest thing" that her mother was dryly referring to was her grandfather enjoying a good laugh while watching Lucas send Remi into fits of laughter as he spun her around in one of the clothing carts.

"Dad, I can't believe you are letting them brandish the carts in such a reckless way," Evangeline said. "Do you know how expensive they are?"

Her grandfather let out an annoyed huff. "As if I don't, Lenny," he said, knowing how much Syd's mother hated the shortened name. "Which is why you should be thanking Lucas for fixing the faulty wheel on this one."

Evangeline turned and gave Lucas a dismissive up-and-down. "Well, aren't you just handy in all sorts of ways. Fighting fires and good with a wrench. So very blue-collar."

Syd cocked her head at that one. All sorts of ways. What was her mother getting at there?

"You want to ride too, Grandma?" Remi said.

Syd's mother shook her head. "Of course I don't, sweetheart. And you shouldn't either."

She turned to Syd. "I swear. This is why a child shouldn't be stuck hanging around a laundry all day. They start to think things like this are substitutes for actual activities and the arts."

Syd frowned. She'd just heard once more from Red about how the inside of a laundromat for hours on end wasn't the "type of environment for his daughter." The little bit of space and time apart had given Sydney some much-needed perspective to see his manipulative dickery for what it was—not to mention his elitism. It was clear to see why her mom had been so quickly taken by him. He was just her type.

"She gets plenty of cultural exposure, Mom," Syd said.

Evangeline looked at Lucas with another critical up-and-down. "I bet."

He smiled at her. Syd was glad he wasn't taking the bait, but she could detect a slight hint of tension around the edges of his lips. Just moments before he had been talking with her grandfather in an easy, relaxed way, like he was one of his old and cherished friends. And he was good with Remi too, giving her his undivided attention and a kind of patience that was surprising.

"Good to see you again too, Ms. Harris. You're looking lovely as always."

She responded with a frosty nod. "And you're looking surprisingly clothed."

Goodness. For a lifelong mistress, her mother sure had her nose in the air.

Lucas grinned wider. "You saw that?" he questioned. "I didn't expect you to be the pinup calendar type. What's your favorite month? I can have it autographed for you." He put his hands up. "No, don't tell me. Let me guess. Is it February? That is Trev Parks. The way they placed those hearts made him a fan favorite."

Evangeline let out a huff then and walked over to Syd, picking her knitting up from where she'd placed it on the counter. She glanced at it and then dropped it back down as if it offended her.

"You see there," she said, not even bothering to lower her voice. "That right there is exactly why I encouraged you to go to GW. This could have been your life for the past ten years. Never leaving this block, worrying over who's ogling your man's calendar photo."

Lucas had pushed Remi over to where Pops was in the waiting area and they were helping him with the rest of the refills, but Syd wondered if he'd overheard.

"Compared with what I ended up with in DC, it doesn't seem like a bad option at all, Ma."

Her mother rolled her eyes, then looked down at Syd's knitting. She fingered it once more, then shrugged. "Looks like you dropped a stitch right here, honey," she said. "You know if you don't get that sewn up and that hole fixed quickly, your whole scarf will be ruined before you've even had a chance to show it off."

Syd stared at her mother, then looked down to where she was pointing. Dammit. How had she missed that big gaping hole? If that wasn't a metaphor for her life, she didn't know what was. Just then her phone rang. "Oh look, it's Redmon," Evangeline said oh so loudly. Loud enough for Lucas and the rest of Scrubs to surely hear.

Syd picked up her phone and swiped it quickly. "What is it, Red?"

"Remi, it's your dad," her mother yelled. Dammit. Was this

woman serious? "Be sure to give him my love when you speak with him. Tell him we'll get together real soon."

"Pipe down, Lenny," she heard her pops say just as Red mumbled something about an upcoming gala. "Don't you have a train to catch?"

22

THE FINAL WEEKS of summer went by in a blur. Tonight the laundry was empty save for Syd and the night washing. She was glad to have the customers out and Remi upstairs in bed and beginning to settle into her new normal. The school year had finally started, and Remi was miraculously in the same class as Aisha and only seemed to hate her new life seventy-five percent. And she was such a sweet kid that she told Syd there were moments it only felt like fifty.

Though Syd could not be more grateful, she couldn't help but worry. Worry about Remi, the school year, and, selfishly, where she herself would go from here.

Could this really be it? Would her life be this? Syd shrugged. "Screw it. There are worse things than not having dinner at the best restaurants or being able to shop for what you want whenever you want."

She thought of Remi and the fact that her daughter was sleeping in her old bed. And the fact that she was sleeping in her mom's. The old folks would shake their heads and mumble about generational curses. But she had fucked up and made some pretty poor decisions, was all. Gone left when she should have gone right. Said yes when she should have said no.

In her head, Syd ran over her options—or her lack thereof. Either way, Pops needed care and the shop needed running. There was no way around that. Also, Remi needed her to be there for her as much as she could.

But, Syd thought as machine number 37 buzzed, calling for her to flip Mr. Cruz's things over to the dryer, where did that leave her? Had she really left her life in DC, what little life there was anyway, to make Scrubs her everything?

Syd looked down at her wrist and twisted it back and forth. Her little trio of silver bracelets jangled. It was a little family set she'd made back when she was pregnant with Remi. She had thought of only wearing two after everything with Red, but breaking the set somehow felt petty. Besides, putting them on was an old habit. Sort of like her wedding set—and she wasn't done wearing that yet either. She sighed.

Still, the bracelets were pretty, at least to her, and she liked their little jangle. Once again the idea of her own jewelry line flirted around in her head. *Silly*. She hated how that was always the first word that came to mind when she thought of her art and her dreams.

She had a small amount of money socked away, but using it to make pieces to sell felt selfish right now. She should be using that money for something more practical. Something for Remi, something that would further her college chances, perhaps a pre-pre-SAT course or some sort of art, a music or language enrichment class that the local public school didn't offer. She paused, wondering if she was hearing her voice or her mother's in her head. Her daughter was only nine.

But still, she wasn't done with worrying. Red had proven himself to be unreliable, first agreeing to the bare minimum settlement and now trying to backtrack to get her under his thumb again. How could she count on him to pay for college and anything else Remi needed? At this point she had to figure out something for herself, because health care alone was going to cost her a fortune now. She suddenly felt sick. Sick, angry and scared. These were the things that had kept her tethered to Red for so fucking long. She shook her head and shoved her hand into the machine to grab the wash and pull it out.

The sheets were tangled, twisted inside each other. Frustrated, Syd pulled hard, too hard, and her heart stopped when she heard a snap. *Shit!*

One of her bracelets broke, and her resolve with it. The tears came before she could stop them, and then she was wiping her snot on Mr. Cruz's sheets.

Syd looked down and threw the pile back in the wash, rerunning the load on hot. *Dammit!* Emotions were for crap.

Some time later, Syd once again found her finger hovering over the video call button on her phone. It was almost two in the morning. Mr. Cruz's clothes were in the dryer, along with a load from the local club. She was caught up with the rest of the day's wash, so things should be light for her grandfather in the morning. But Red's bullshit and the whole bracelet thing, which should have been nothing, were still bugging her. Hence her hovering finger. Lucas probably didn't want to hear from her. *Finger, move! Away from the damned button! Don't make an ass of us both.*

Too late; she tapped down.

Lucas's face filled her screen. He looked tired and was in bed, but despite the late hour, it was clear he wasn't sleeping because he picked up so quickly. His bedside light was on, giving his skin a soft, creamy glow that made her want to lick the screen and had her forgetting why she had even called.

"Why do you always pick up when I call?"

Lucas ran his hand across his face and did that half lip bite thing before looking back at the screen. "Why do you always call if you don't want me to pick up?" His voice was raspy and vibrated through her.

"You're really annoying, you know that?"

"Am I supposed to answer that question, Syd?"

"It would be nice if you answered some questions," she said. "Said something, showed some part of yourself and stopped letting this . . . whatever be so one-sided." He was sexy as hell, but she didn't understand how he could still at times be closed off. Something didn't sit right. Didn't he care at all about what had happened today with Red? It had made her uncomfortable; didn't it bother him? Or did he really not care? She looked down at her wrist and the two bracelets and blinked, fighting back tears.

"What is it, Syd? What's wrong? You're not really mad at me right now, are you?"

Sydney looked at him. "Congratulations."

He blinked. "What?"

She shook her head. *Fuck. Why did I go and say that? Anything but that. Please don't let it have registered.* "Nothing. Just forget it, okay?" She attempted a smile that wouldn't quite connect. "Look, forget I called. I'm sorry. This is not your problem. I'm not your problem."

Once again, she willed her finger to work. *Hit the fucking button, finger. Do your damn job.*

"Don't hang up, Syd," Lucas said.

"It's best if I do," she said, and, like a savior from the laundry gods, Mr. Cruz's dryer buzzed. She looked back at the screen. "I have to go anyway. Sorry again. Good night."

IF THERE WAS ever a stronger-willed, more infuriating woman, Lucas had never met her. And his own mother and Mama Joy had been strong contenders. Lucas paused in the middle of pulling up his sweats. He almost sat back down on his bed as the thought of his biological mother and Mama Joy and how they all meshed together hit him. He wasn't prepared for how the grief came at him so suddenly. How it mixed with thoughts of Syd—frustration but not so much pain. That part was scary too. And it felt like it, strangely, should be. With Syd, there was a comfort in him not being too comfortable. Like, so what? He was still okay anyway. Like he'd still be okay. But he knew he needed it to keep his distance and make sure she stayed unharmed.

Just then, Noah's warning came back at him. *Don't ask her to be your therapy.* Fuck! He really hated it when one of his brothers called him out.

Maybe he should take some time. Really talk to somebody.

But the moment for that wasn't now. Not when Syd's tear-filled image came flooding back to him. Her wobbly lips before she'd hung up on him made his heart beat extra fast. Getting to her was all that mattered right now.

Within three minutes he was across the street. He hesitated only a moment as he watched her folding clothes in the dimness of the half lights, and though he knew the doors were locked tight, the only communication with the outside at this time of night through the safety of the night window and security glass, he still felt protective and didn't like her working that shift. He rang the bell, and Syd looked up at him, her eyes flat, devoid of surprise.

She dropped the sheet she was folding on the counter, and he could almost hear the breath she let out.

"I thought I told you to go to sleep," she said, hitting the touch pad on the far side of the wall, then unlocking the door.

Lucas didn't want to reveal how grateful he was to be let in, but the breath he released was telling. It also made him wonder: Was he there for her, or was this for him? "You know I have insomnia," he said.

She rolled her eyes, then locked the door behind him. "I know you don't listen worth shit," Syd said and went toward the back of the laundry and her folding. She still looked gorgeous and sexy as hell even this late, in black leggings that hugged tight to her curves and a loose V-neck that hinted at all the best parts he remembered so well. He followed behind her like a puppy. When she quickly turned and looked at him, he stopped short and pulled back.

"Why are you here, Lucas?" she asked accusingly. "You didn't want to talk on the phone, and as you can see, I have work to do now." She picked up the sheet, so he picked up the other end.

"I can help you."

She glared at him and tried to yank the sheet from his hand. "I've got it. I didn't ask for your help."

He pulled her toward him. "You never do, Ms. Independent. So I'm offering. All you do is push yourself and act all strong, like you've got everything together, instead of coming out and saying what you want outright."

They were close now, and if he put his arm out or just leaned down the tiniest bit he could have her. Taste her lips once again. She looked up at him. Her eyes gleamed. Her lips pulsed. That little point on her neck throbbed as her pulse quickened, and he got a distinct pull in his groin as his dick hardened.

"Why should I? It's not as if you ever made a move. Ever!" She took a step back. It was small, but it might as well have been a mile. Make a move? And what move was he supposed to make? The thought of Mama Joy came back just then, but this time so did the old fears.

Lucas stared at her. He saw her not as she was now but as she had been all those years ago when they were kids in high school: perfect and always just a little out of his reach. So he kept her in his orbit by teasing, as if what he felt for her was something to laugh at, make jokes of, because he knew even back then that if he let it get too serious it would end in his heartbreak.

Even in the moment she'd stuck the dagger in and twisted it with Kat when she said she couldn't wait to go and would only miss her best friend—even then he couldn't be mad. She'd earned her full ride. She'd earned living rich, comfortable and happy. Just like what her mother always wanted for her. He remembered his own mother and the few photos she'd cherished. The stories she used to whisper to him over their kitchen table when she was sad and scared and hungry after working yet another shift in the bar she used to work at a couple of blocks down from their old apartment. Indulging herself in a drink while dividing her brought-home dinner between him and Noah, she'd tell him how he was made to be a better man than his and Noah's fathers ever were. "Don't make promises you can't keep, Lucas. Lying to one who loves you is the greatest sin."

He remembered putting his arms around her too-thin frame and lying to her not a moment later. "Don't be sad, Umma. It's going to be okay. I'll grow up and make you proud. I'll take care of you always."

When he heard about Sydney getting a scholarship to George Washington in DC, even though she'd already been accepted to Hunter and had gotten a City College scholarship, he knew he had to just congratulate her and send her on her way to George Washington.

He knew the first moment he saw her that their goodbye was inevitable. That she was meant for things bigger than he could ever give her and that he could never sin and promise her more than that.

Syd's frustrated sigh brought Lucas back to the present and he blinked, regretting his words to her that day but knowing he'd still say the same thing given a second chance: "Congratulations. They are going to be lucky to have you."

She shook her head. "Like I said, you never make a move. Ever. I don't understand why you're here." Once again, she tried to pull the sheet from him.

Something in him broke then and he grasped it harder, his anger and desperation so strong they were practically bubbling to the surface of his skin. "I don't know either," he finally said. "But shit, Syd. You called me! Why did you do that?"

She stared.

"Fuck. You call. I answer. I just can't help it. If you're near, I'm there. I don't get it, and I never did, but it's like the damned song, I guess. I wanna be where you are. Okay? Can you just let me do that? Can I just help you fold this damned sheet?"

They were silent, staring at each other for more than a few moments. Finally, Syd spoke. "Fine. Just don't mess up with the corners."

Lucas smiled. "Of course not. I'm a damned firefighter. I can save lives, and I know how to work with a sheet."

They folded in silence, and he was grateful. When they were done, they sat together on the little cot in the employee area in the back. It was late. So late that morning would come faster rather than slower. He dreaded that. "Are you tired?" he asked her.

"I am, but I'm kind of used to it now. I'll get some sleep when Rem goes to school. The rest I'll figure out."

He worried for a moment about *the rest* but didn't know if now was the time to ask. Didn't know if he dared ask.

"What about you? Don't you have to work today?"

Lucas shook his head. "Not today. Day after tomorrow I'm back on shift again. But yeah, like you, I'm used to it, being tired."

He stared at her. But for some reason held himself back. The idea of returning to work, fall coming so quick, and once again things changing had put him in a mood. "I'm sorry," he suddenly blurted out. "I wish I could go back and change my answer from back then."

When Syd looked at him with confusion, he continued. "When you told me you got into George Washington and I said congratulations. I'm sorry. I wish I said more and I wish I could go back and change my answer, but the fact was, I really was happy for you and wanted to congratulate you. It was all I could say to you then, and it's all I still can say to you."

"Why?" Her voice was soft, but he could tell she was holding tight to her emotions.

"How could I ask you to hold back on what was surely a better opportunity than me? I wasn't the best for you then and am still not anywhere near what you need and deserve now."

Her brows drew together. "What the hell are you talking about?

Have I asked you for anything now? Shit, did I ask you for anything then?"

Lucas blinked. "But you wanted me to ask you to stay, right? Isn't that why you've been so angry with me all these years?"

Syd let out a harsh breath. "Yeah . . . well, fuck."

Lucas laughed, and she nailed him with a glare that had him coughing it back. "I'm sorry."

"You'd better be," she said. "One more laugh out of you, and it may be your last."

He sobered quickly as he caught her expression. "But come on, Syd. What if I had confessed? What if I had asked you to stay? Are you telling me you would have?"

Syd was quiet, and in that quiet he knew he had his answer. And he leaned forward and kissed her. Her lips were soft and sweet, and he wanted to fall into them to dream in bliss forever. When he tipped his tongue out to taste her, the tang of salty tears surprised him. Lucas pulled back and smiled into her glassy eyes. "See, that's what you avoided. Useless tears, heartache and eventual pain all because of a bum like me. Just ask my mom, or Mama Joy." He tilted his head. "Oh, you can't though, because they're not here."

Syd sucked in a breath. "Oh, Lucas. I'm sorry. I didn't mean to bring you pain. You know you shouldn't think that way."

"Don't say that. You are not supposed to be sorry." He started to get up, and she pulled him back. Pulled him back and held him close. He didn't resist—not her pulling him back, not the kiss when she started on his cheeks, his eyelids and his brow—but still he was confused.

"I am sorry," she said. "I was a coward. I shouldn't have put all that pressure on you by bringing up the past so much. Pressure you didn't deserve. I was using you to deflect my own responsibility."

He shook his head. "No, you weren't. And it was fine. I should have known what you needed. I should have been there for you."

"Why?" she asked.

He was still.

"Why?"

Her eyes were serious, and it seemed like she really wanted him to answer. "Why should you have known what I was thinking and what I wanted from you?"

Lucas thought hard back to that time. He hadn't had anything to go on except his feelings for her. He'd wished he'd been honest with her, told her how he felt, but he didn't know if she felt the same way. He'd hoped, but hope had failed him so many times.

"I don't know."

"Exactly," she said. "It was my decision, not yours. I was a fool. You had made it clear enough, even with your silly adolescent teasing, how you felt about me. But I didn't tell you how I felt about you. I put too much on you. You were a good friend to me, Lucas, and I suspect you were a great son to both your mothers too."

He shook his head. He blinked. Blinked quickly. Because he would not cry. Not now. He couldn't let all this in. "No," he said. "You did right."

She nodded. "Well, I have my Remi, and I'll never regret that, so yeah, I guess I did.

"Still, I always missed you. And all this talk about me turning out like your mother or Mama Joy . . ." She sighed. "I know you're hurting, and I don't know about tomorrow and I can't predict the future, but I don't plan on going anytime soon. You're putting a lot on both nine-year-old you and—what is it, thirty-one-year-old you now?"

Lucas felt like a fool. "You're making me sound nuts, Syd."

"Maybe we're both a little bit nuts, Lucas. Or maybe we're just scared. I don't know."

Suddenly he was tired. That was the only thing he did know for sure. And when Syd pulled his head down to her lap, he let her. He enjoyed her gentle hands as they threaded through his hair and went across his brow. The next thing he knew, it was five in the morning and her grandfather was waking them up.

23

ONCE AGAIN LUCAS couldn't sleep. Or maybe it was that he couldn't stay asleep. He was back on shift at the firehouse, and of course that meant he couldn't slip over to Scrubs, so he spent an inordinate amount of time between midnight and five a.m. when not on a call wondering what Syd was doing.

"Just call her if you're that damned thirsty," Dee said over his shoulder.

He jumped from where he was standing in the kitchen and staring at his phone. "Call who?"

She tilted her head and stared. "I've known you too long for these games. The woman who's got you twisted. The one who's making you not be able to sleep but putting that dumbass grin on your face. That one. Little Miss Laundry."

Lucas frowned. "I swear I can't with this neighborhood. People know too damned much."

Dee laughed, then sobered. "So is it serious?"

He shrugged.

"I mean to her. I know it is to you. I can see it all over you. But what about her? She's got a kid, right?"

"Remi," Lucas said. "And I hope so. Or . . . I don't know. It's too soon. Maybe it is; maybe it's not. I don't know if I'm the kid-having, serious-family-man type."

Dee gasped. "So now you're trying to play me?" She raised her hand, then looked up at the security cameras that were all over the station. "I swear if we weren't in this station house I'd beat your ass for flat out lying. I should go find her and ask her the same question."

"Don't you dare."

Dee narrowed her eyes, then started in with a small but steady stream of curses. "Not family material? I cannot with men! I cannot with you. And you're supposed to be my friend. I thought I taught you better to at least not lie to yourself."

"What are you getting so mad about?"

Flex walked in. "What's wrong, Lieutenant?"

She turned to him, all seriousness. "Out of all the guys here, who do you think is most ready to be a husband and a father?"

Flex looked her up and down. "Is this a trick question? Is somebody pregnant? Who's getting fired? I swear I didn't do nothing."

Dee rolled her eyes. "Answer the question."

Flex shrugged. "Strong here. But he didn't get nobody on the team pregnant." He smiled at Lucas. "Hey, are you getting married to that girl you're secretly seeing who runs that laundromat? You think you can get me a discount?"

Lucas let out a sigh. "This fucking neighborhood. Might as well take out a freaking bus ad." It was going to be a long week.

LUCAS WAS FINALLY back home, in his room, and he couldn't be more uncomfortable. The air conditioner was droning on but over the past week had finally decided that enough was enough and wasn't doing much cooling. It was early morning, and he'd just gotten home a half hour ago. Once again he'd been awakened by Syd's grandfather. Lucas was glad he and Syd were doing nothing more than sleeping—a thirty-one-year-old couple suddenly caught and feeling like wayward teens. But still, it hadn't felt quite right when he'd gone running back across the street, avoiding the glances of the slowly waking neighborhood and, he knew, narrowly missing Syd's daughter. He was definitely going to have to do something. Come up with a better way. Rent a freaking room.

He knew it wouldn't be right if Remi saw them, not with her parents newly divorced and Sydney not having made things official with them. His mind raced whenever he thought about them settling down. Syd still seemed to want to keep him firmly in the friend / boy toy zone. He'd wanted to ask his brothers for advice about it but was beyond embarrassed to do so.

Lucas and Syd had only talked, just as they usually did, and though they felt closer, nothing was any more solidified between the two of them. He for one still felt the same. He wanted to be with her, but how secure was that? Could he really be there for her? And did she really want him anyway? The fact remained that she was on the rebound, and from their first encounter onward, she had said she wasn't in it with him for a relationship.

Hell, this should be good news. Very good news. His logical brain told him it was. But everything in his emotional and, as it turned out, completely fucked-up and illogical mind and uncontrollable heart was telling him it wasn't. He was on an out-of-control mental hamster wheel, and he didn't know how to get off. "Shit!"

And here he was thinking he was just starting to feel like himself and get actual rest—and he was afraid it was all because of her.

"Yo, boy, who got you cursing like that?"

Lucas looked up to see Noah peeking his head through his bedroom door. Now that Noah was back, Lucas needed to remember to close it, since he no longer had the top floor to himself. "What are you going on about over there?" he ground out.

Noah shook his head as he made his way into Lucas's room, making himself comfortable in his gaming chair. "Nothing, just a TikTok meme that everybody was into last year." He waved his hand. "You wouldn't know anything about it."

Lucas felt his eyes roll back on their own. "Am I that old?"

"Do you want me to really answer that?" Noah countered.

Now it was Lucas shaking his head.

"But really, what's got you breaking out in random curses?" Noah asked, his usual smile gone and uncharacteristic seriousness in his dark brown eyes.

"Nothing," Lucas said quickly. "Or nothing worth you worrying about. I'm fine."

Noah let out a breath, then reached his long legs out and let his sneakered foot kick at Lucas's bare foot hanging off the edge of the bed. "Cut the shit. That's what you always say. 'Nothing for me to worry about.' I wish you'd stop treating me like your kid and start treating me like your brother for once."

Lucas felt his brows pull together, along with the tightening of his chest. "My kid?"

Noah stared at him. "Yes, your kid. Aren't you tired? You've been doing it forever. Ever since Umma died."

"And whose fault was that?" Lucas murmured.

Noah's head shot up. "Whose? Not the fuck yours." There was an edge of anger in his voice that Lucas rarely ever heard. He stared at his brother for a long time.

"Okay. Fine. I won't go there."

"Fine. You won't, because I won't let you. And I hope that's not part of what's giving you a hard time. I know you're broken up about Mama Joy. Shit. We all are. I'm hurting every day. But she wouldn't want to see you not being you. And you know she'd definitely be pissed the hell off to see you not fully giving it your all for a chance at happiness."

Lucas looked at Noah in confusion. "What are you talking about?"

"Come on. You know what I'm talking about. With Syd across the street. I know you're beating yourself up, coming up with just as many excuses about why you shouldn't be with her as there are for reasons why you should. Just stop and do what you need to do. Give yourself some fucking peace for a change."

"You don't know all you think you know, little brother," Lucas said, his tone low.

Noah shrugged, then nodded and uncurled his long body from the chair. "Okay, fine. I don't know what I know. But I do know that it's late and you're in bed cursing the air for some reason. I'll just leave it at that."

He left the room and Lucas let out a sigh and closed his eyes. "Knit one, purl two," he said aloud, starting the familiar chant.

"But before I go—" It was Noah again. "You want this closed all the way? I do need my rest, and I don't know what you'll be calling out next late at night."

It was Lucas's flying pillow that ultimately closed the door behind Noah's raucous laughter.

But as it turned out, as if called by some silent beacon, Lucas once again found himself back at Scrubs. He let out a long sigh, Noah's laughter still practically ringing in his ears as he looked down at this night's bag full of excuse laundry. Scrubs was definitely named especially for him, he thought, as he walked inside, Damian's fresh sheets in one hand and his knitting in the other, his dignity nowhere to be found.

SYDNEY HADN'T EXPECTED to be working tonight, but when Mr. Bill called out sick, what else could she do? She thought of how many times her grandfather must've run into the same situation for the past several years and handled it all by himself while continuing to run his body into the ground and never once asking her or her mother for help. She also worried more and more for his health. The new schedule helped, but even with it, he kept a little too busy for her liking, and when he thought she wasn't watching, she could see signs of fatigue.

Sydney knew help would never come from her mother, and they were going to have to run the business like a business, with some stable outside help, at least for the night wash, or they had to eliminate it altogether. The thought brought an ache to her chest as she thought of Lucas and their nightly talks. Her grandfather would put on an annoyed face, but she could see he was playing both sides. He wanted her to make a decision about Lucas, but his sleeping over on the cot was not it.

It wasn't good for either of them, no matter how soothing it was for them both, or how right it felt. She couldn't use this area as her own personal cut-out-the-world blanket fort. It wasn't what adults did.

Not for the first time she wished she could turn to her mother for help. She knew her mother was never going to come back to the shop and help with the business. Evangeline hated it, and that was fine. But if only Syd could talk to her about what to do. How to manage her grandfather, Remi, Red, Lucas. But her mother would just say the answer was to sell the shop, put Pops in a home, get back with Red and go along to get along. It was her mother's way. Syd could hate her for it, and would if she genuinely thought her mother said these awful things from anyplace other than love. For her, money was security. Money took away struggle, and more than anything, Evangeline didn't want her or Remi to struggle.

Syd knew she could never do any of that. Despite her love for Remi, she couldn't sacrifice any of them, her grandfather included, for money. She would do all she could to make sure he lived the rest of his life however he wanted to. He'd worked for this, so it was his choice to make.

But she also now knew that though this was his life and he loved it, it couldn't be hers. Not entirely. She wasn't saying she wouldn't cherish Scrubs and keep up with her commitment to it and her grandfather, but now she knew that Scrubs couldn't be her one and only everything. Strangely enough, she had Lucas to thank for figuring that out. Lucas and Remi and their damned insistence that she learn how to knit.

Sydney looked down at the sketches in front of her and half smiled to herself. Lucas's skillful teaching and the emphasis he put on her finding out what she wanted had her really thinking about it for the first time in a long time. Not what she needed and not what was expected of her, but what she really wanted. And when she was knitting, what she wanted was for it to come to her as smoothly and easily as when she was sketching out jewelry designs.

No matter what Lucas did or how much of a patient teacher he was, it seemed like her fingers found nothing but frustration. Between the needles, the yarn, and keeping up the proper ends, she found herself cursing and throwing the perfectly innocent project across the floor.

But that's where the Universe got funny. The needles with the yarn, thrown as they were, landed in a beautiful twisted pattern, at least to Syd's eye. She quickly snapped a photo with her phone and silently thanked Lucas for the revelation in her frustration, then swapped her needles for a crochet hook and, before she knew it, was twisting yarn around her hook like an almost—well, sort of—semipro.

A few moments of surprising yarn bliss later, the door chimed.

"What are you doing here?"

"I could ask you the same thing."

"I work here."

"Well, I came to lay on your cot."

Syd frowned at the way her nipples responded to those unintentionally erotic words. "You have a perfectly good bed over at your house across the street. I know, because I tried it."

Lucas grinned. That cute-as-hell, pantie-melting grin that for some reason had her thinking that even if she didn't have Remi, damned Lucas "Mr. Perfect" Strong was deadly as hell and she may have ended up with who knew how many kids anyway if she'd stayed and hadn't been careful. His freaking smile alone made her ovaries flip. "You want to come over to my place and try it out again?"

It was Syd's turn to laugh now. "That offer is mighty tempting, but someone has to man the shop."

She could see her answer shocked him. He wasn't expecting her to be so direct. "Why are you surprised?"

He shrugged then, suddenly looking like the boy who would be gregarious one moment and then closed up the next. "I don't know. After our talk, I know I shouldn't be over here tonight." He bit his lip.

He was so damned cute. She'd laid down the law. No more cot overnights. They had to get things straight. Yet here he was.

"But you're here."

"I am."

She looked at the bag in his hand then. "And you brought laundry?"

"I did." He licked his lips.

"Well, come on in, then. Last wash starts now."

Lucas grinned and wrapped his strong arms around her waist. But she pulled back, pushing him out of reach as she closed the door behind him and flipped the lock, dimming the lights for the night. *One last time,* Sydney told herself. Then took a look at those strong shoulders. *Okay, maybe two more times. Might as well get him all out of my system.*

She let out a long breath. "You gonna put that load in the wash, or you want me to? If I do it, there's going to be a surcharge. House rules."

He looked at her. "You're mad at me, aren't you?"

She looked down and then back up at him. "I am. But maybe more at myself." Sydney took the bag from his hands. She was about to start throwing the laundry in a machine when he stopped her.

"I'll do it."

"I don't mind," she said. "I was just teasing about the surcharge."

But Lucas was already shoving the things in. "Well, I don't know if I can pay the price, teasing or not." He added a splash of detergent, then started the wash and stood. He looked back over to the counter at her knitting and let out a breath. "You want to sit with me and knit?"

"Do I have to?"

"Of course not. But I don't want you to think I only came for one—well, two things."

"The second isn't so bad."

He snorted. It was then that he spotted her sketches. Syd went to cover them but he leaned forward and moved her hand to stop her. "These are beautiful." His words stopped her more than his hands.

"They're nothing."

"You know they're plenty of something. You designed the earrings and bracelets and necklace you were wearing to the club the night we first got together too, didn't you?"

"How did you know?"

"The bracelets have this same tribal feel that you show here," he said, pointing to the wavy crimp she'd put in the shape of her necklace and bracelet design. "It's strong, but sexy. I like it."

Syd practically melted into a puddle right there. He couldn't have seduced her more if he'd been licking her spine from behind the counter. *Holy fuck, is this man talking about my sketches as if they have value?* She blinked.

"What's happening?" Lucas suddenly asked. "Shit. Did I screw up again? Whatever it is, I'm sorry, Syd. I seem to always do that."

Sydney shook her head. "No, you're fine. Just fine."

She picked up her knitting then, suddenly feeling the need to learn more. "Come on, let's sit. I think I was a little too hasty with this knitting thing."

24

LUCAS WOKE WITH a start, surprised by the bright overhead lights glaring in his eyes. But he was more surprised when the light shifted and Sydney came into his field of vision. "Please don't tell me your grandfather caught us again."

She shook her head. "No, he won't be down for a half hour at least. You're sweating, and then you started thrashing, so I woke you up."

He shook his head now, coming fully awake. "I'm sorry. That wasn't cool. Damn, these dreams are getting more and more realistic. I thought they had subsided. They had for years." He went silent then. "I don't know, it's just this year. It's been a lot. Now they come and go." He put on a smile then, as best he could. "I'll be fine. And now is when you kiss me, m'lady. Tell me none of it is real, that it's all just a dream."

Her eyes were soft and her lips softer. Her breath warmer than it was in his usual dreams. Lucas blinked.

"No, you're not dreaming, and sorry to say it was all very real,"

Sydney said. "As a matter of fact, you were having a nightmare. I had to shake my legs to get you to wake up."

Lucas frowned and sat up. Shit. Did he really fall asleep in Syd's lap again? "Hey, I'm sorry. Falling asleep on a date. That's hella rude."

She frowned. "Spending a night in this laundry and calling it a date is even more rude," she countered. "Now, what were you dreaming about? Exactly."

Lucas let his mind wander for a moment as his dream came back to him. Then he quickly tried to push it back. But the memory kept rushing to the surface of his mind. Always the same. Always the night of the fire and his mom. He was about to answer Syd, but Noah's words gave him caution. *Don't ask her to be your therapy.*

Noah was right; Syd didn't need his crap. "Don't worry; it was nothing."

She blinked and her nostrils flared and in a flash the soft eyes were gone. "Are you trying to piss me and my now immobilized leg off, Lucas Strong?"

"Why are you scary when you call me by both my names, Sydney Harris?"

"It's because when I became a mother, I got that superpower. Now answer my question."

"I dreamt about my mother," he said, not knowing why it came out so easily.

She nodded. "Mama Joy? I'm sorry. I know it must hurt."

He nodded. "Yes, her death still hurts like crazy. But no, I was dreaming of my other mother. She and Mama Joy must be looking down on me and comparing notes on how they both must regret me ever being born. Two women who I could have saved but was too much of a slacker to do so."

Sydney pulled back from him. Nostrils really flaring now.

"Okay, so now you're really trying to piss me off. Are you seriously telling me I gave up my night for this? What are you talking about? How are you a slacker? You're a whole lifesaving paramedic and firefighter who also just taught me how to knit tonight."

She looked over at her small swatch with more dropped than correct stitches. Lucas raised a brow.

"Well, you're teaching me, dammit."

"You're cute as hell," he said and pulled her in close.

Sydney pulled back. "No, Lucas, not now. Your shoulders, abs, thighs and tongue are not getting you out of this one."

"Really, not even my tongue?" He leaned forward, and she held up a hand.

Shit. Lucas ran a frustrated hand through his hair. "Fine, block me, but you'll know I'm right when you hear the story. My birth mother died in a fire that shouldn't have started—wouldn't have started if I'd been doing right and watching my brother as I should have. And Mama Joy has a heart attack, and where am I? Out on some bullshit-assed call that was a worthless false alarm while she lay dying."

She crossed her arms. "Explain."

"It was winter. I was eight and Noah was six. My mother worked in a kitchen in the back of a bar. Sometimes she'd pick up extra shifts doing front of the house. Anything to make ends meet. After school we had a sitter, a woman who lived in our building, right on our floor. Well, she couldn't watch us that day, because she had an emergency and had to go to the hospital for her own kid. I was eight—I could watch Noah. It was cold, and I knew I wasn't supposed to put on the space heater. My mother had told me plenty of times not to without her home. But I did it anyway."

He was talking fast now. He'd only told this story three times before: once to the fire marshals, once to his social worker and once to

Mama Joy. And he didn't know why he was spewing it out now, but spew he did. Like a freaking geyser, he just let go. "There was a spark. Then flames. I grabbed Noah and ran back out. When my mother and the rest of the bar staff heard the sirens, my mother saw where the fire was, and she ran in. She ran in for us and never came out. It was all because of me. Sure, they said it was a faulty wire, but I turned it on. It was my fault. She was all we had."

SYDNEY WAS STUNNED. Had he been traveling with this heavy guilt his whole life? He was just a kid when his mother died, yet he had blamed himself for all these years. And now he blamed himself for his second mother's death just because he was out doing his job. It was ridiculous. But she didn't know how to make him see that. She wondered if this guilt he'd been carrying had something to do with the two of them and why he'd never fully opened up to her. It was a presumptuous thought, but still she couldn't shake it. The worst and most vulnerable parts of ourselves tend to form pretty early and are usually the hardest to shake off.

She knew in her gut she was onto something, and it broke her heart.

She thought of Mama Joy then. How she'd died from a cardiac incident and Lucas had so much training in that area. She felt something shatter within herself as pieces of his puzzle came together.

Goodness, how ridiculous were they both? Two fools living completely guilt- and fear-based lives.

Sydney chuckled to herself and wiped at her now-wet face, and Lucas looked visibly shaken. "What the hell, Syd? Why are you crying, and more importantly, why are you laughing? Am I that much of a joke to you?"

She shook her head. "It's not you, but us. How is it we've lasted this long while trying to outrun these unseen fears? The both of us should have passed out from exhaustion by now."

She blinked and wiped at her face again. Then reached out and wiped at his. She let her hand linger on the scar she'd stared at ever since she'd known him. Now seeing it for the burn mark that she knew it was.

Lucas was crying. Syd didn't know if he even knew it. "Lucas, I don't know if or how I can make you see this, but it is not your fault. I suspect this is something that Mama Joy has probably told you and that you know deep within your soul too."

He snorted, and she shot him a hard stare. "Don't brush this off, Lucas Strong. I know she told you. That's how she was. And I know she wouldn't want you carrying whatever it is you're carrying about your mother or about her. A babysitter who was supposed to be watching two minor children left them alone without supervision and with a faulty heater. Take yourself out of it in any way you can and put other people's children there. It's a tragedy, but it's not your fault."

Lucas stared at her, and she could tell he was really trying to hear the words. She hoped with all her might that he was feeling them too. She knew she was right. Now if only she could take some of her own advice to heart. Lucas finally nodded as they suddenly heard her grandfather very loudly making his way down the back stairs.

Well, damn. Caught again.

Also, way to be covert with the eavesdropping, old man. Syd almost laughed.

25

SYD WAS GRATEFUL for the conversations she'd been having with Lucas at night. They were coming to a slow understanding of each other while giving no commitments, but still enjoying as much clandestine sex as possible. It was amazing how sturdy that little cot turned out to be. She wasn't ready for more than that and was happy he didn't pressure her, though sometimes she wondered just when she and he would be ready for more. Maybe when they had both done some more healing.

She was also grateful for the confidence he'd given her. On top of giving her more knitting lessons, he'd also taught her the basics of CPR and some special dos and don'ts about what to do in case an emergency situation came up with her grandfather. She was nervous and had told Lucas so. So one night their knitting session turned into a special CPR class, with more mouth-to-mouth than actual technique. But still, she felt a little more empowered, and for that she was grateful. For all his flirtations and playing around, when it came down to actually being serious, Lucas was an amazing instructor. She saw that with Remi and the kids when she sat in on one of the knitting classes that Remi attended. Even though the girls were way more taken with the little helper and knitting phenom, Errol—and the other moms watching the class with Lucas—she still caught on to how great a teacher he was. He stayed patient and focused and had a natural rapport with the kids. Remi already had a hat completed, plus half a scarf. Syd wasn't much past the swatch phase, but learning was half the fun in her private lessons.

Whether knitting or CPR, when Lucas was in, he was in for it all. He didn't half-ass things. He'd taught her so much that she now felt much more secure being in the home and being a help to her grandfather, even though she hoped to never have to use the techniques. It all seemed so scary but at the same time made her feel so much more empowered.

"Empowered." It was a good word for the way Lucas had made her feel. Though they'd been shaky and were still working things out, they were getting stronger each day. Which was why tonight she felt anything but. She should have just told Lucas about tonight. She'd end up telling him anyway. Her stupid justifications for why she had not sounded hollow to her own mind now that she was standing next to Red, teetering on uncomfortable heels.

Once again Redmon was in town, and she had agreed to come with him to his work party, just to keep up appearances one last time—but really this was for her to finally get a glimpse of what was happening with his job security and therefore Remi's future financial security.

She'd spent a good chunk of money redecorating her old room for Remi to get her ready for school, which made Remi happy, but at the same time gave her a strong realization. "We're not going back, are we, Mom?" Remi had asked most awkwardly after an afternoon visit from Lucas. He'd dropped off a lamp he'd picked up from Target that she'd mentioned she wanted. It was probably overstepping, and he'd immediately known his mistake.

She was totally screwing up the single-mom dating thing and for a moment wondered if Redmon had it right, at least with the just-screwing-on-the-side part. What was she supposed to do? How was she supposed to navigate when her new boo was right across the damned street?

It wasn't like either of them could easily get out of each other's hair. She couldn't move Scrubs, and he couldn't move the firehouse or Strong Knits.

"No, we're not going back, honey," she told her. "Are you upset with me about that?"

Remi was quiet for a while, then shrugged. "No, Daddy was a real jerk," she finally said, surprising Syd with her forwardness. "I know it, and I'm not happy with his behavior. I'm gonna tell him I need a new bed set for my room here. And a set of fairy lights too."

"Rem! That is not nice. You should not call your father a jerk," Syd admonished. Then she hugged her daughter. "But yes, I think a new bed set and fairy lights is totally appropriate."

Syd praised God for Remi's snapback and the fact that Kat had friends at the school. She knew her bestie must have pulled some strings to be able to get Remi in the same class as Aisha. It was one of the few things giving her daughter a smile, and Syd prayed their friendship could make it through the volatile tween years. She was enjoying her classes at Strong Knits, but she still needed something else. She wanted her daughter to be able to pursue her joy, and lately she'd been expressing interest in African dance classes, which would of course take money. So here she was about to put on another one-night-only performance of one of her Stepford wife specials.

One look at the sign in the hotel lobby though and Sydney knew disaster awaited. See what happened with dishonesty? An ass-biter every time, and not in the fun, sexy kind of way.

FDNY's Fireman's Honoree Gala. *Shit*. FDNY.

Syd wondered if Lucas would be there as her eyes quickly scanned the faces of the pictures of the honorees. But she already knew the answer; she'd known it as soon as she saw the sign. Red hadn't brought her to this particular event for nothing. But she needed confirmation. And then she saw him. Well, it was Red who'd spotted him first, or maybe he'd had his eye out for Lucas all along. She had her suspicions. He pointed. "Isn't that your little friend from across the street? The one with all the dirty laundry," he said way too gleefully.

Syd's blood began to heat. *This dickhead!* He had planned this out. Yes, his company was sponsoring the dinner, but of course he brought her here knowing that Lucas was being honored.

And then it hit her. Why didn't Lucas tell her he was being honored? Why didn't *he* ask her to come? She looked down at her left hand. The one that still wore Redmon's ring. Double pangs of hurt hit her as her original fears and shame came bubbling back to the surface. She felt exactly like she had when she'd first walked into that hotel room with Lucas. Like she wanted him but with all her baggage she wasn't good enough to be with him. Like she was no better than the women Red had slept with on the side. Like the countless women she and the other women at The Gate laughed about over the years. She was washed up, her best years behind her, when Lucas had barely made it out of the starting gate.

She could feel Red's triumph radiating off him next to her, and she shot him a side-eyed glance. "Yes, it is, and he's not little at all," she said before waving off his offered arm and starting into the hotel's ballroom.

26

THE BALLROOM WAS a crush of uniforms and suits with a mixture of expensive cocktail dresses sprinkled throughout. Sydney was a jumble of emotions as she scanned the crowd over her over-priced glass of cheap company-sponsored Chardonnay.

"Could you stop thinking about your little pinup boy toy for a while and remember our agreement, Sydney, for tonight at least? Be nice and we can discuss more specific financials tomorrow. Now, my bosses are on the way over. It's showtime. Remember your mission."

Sydney cut Red a sharp eye. "I'm always on my game, but maybe you should have thought of that before you tried to get so damned cute with this little stunt, bringing me to an event where you knew he'd be. You may be able to control me through Remi, but you can't control everyone."

"Well, if you know what's good, you'd better find a way to control your little crush," Red mumbled. "I don't know what you were thinking—or not thinking—stepping out on me with some civil servant who lives across the street. Right across from my daughter."

Sydney turned on him fully then. *Civil servant? Stepping out?*
The fact that he said these things with a straight face only proved
three things to her: he was a bigger elitist than she thought, she
had worse taste in men than she originally thought and this idiot
was maybe on the way from stupid to insane.

She was about to tell him those exact words when a couple of
the suits, with matching women in cocktail dresses on their arms,
descended on them, sending Sydney further into a mental tailspin
as so much more came into clarity.

Red immediately turned on the charm and started dancing for
his life. "Sydney, this is Chad Eveline, our new VP for PR and com-
munications, and his wife, Sophia."

Syd gave the blond couple, who looked so much alike it was
bordering on eerie, a pleasant-enough smile. Red must be pissed.
He'd wanted that VP job and had to be seething over this guy Chad
with the perfect veneers getting it. But it didn't matter to her.
Cheers to Chad and his lovely twin. She took a swig of her drink,
and her eyes went wide as the next couple came forward. Syd had
met the man before—he was Red's boss. But it was the woman on
his arm who really caught her attention. Yep. It was official. Red
was both stupid and insane, and though she'd been in their marriage too long, thank God she'd gotten out when she did. She
fought to keep steady. The whole moment went by as if in a dream.
All she could think of was the movie *Sleeping with the Enemy*.

"And you remember our CEO, Jeff Ackerman. This is his wife,
Tracy. I don't believe you two have met."

The fuck he didn't. Syd would know those breasts anywhere,
even if they were partially covered this time. A woman didn't forget someone she'd caught in her own bed with her husband.

"Haven't we?" she said. "Something about you seems familiar."

Tracy smiled. "I don't think so. I really don't get out much."

Syd narrowed her eyes. "Really? You look like you get out plenty."

"No, she really doesn't," Red's boss chimed in way too quickly, though something in his tone told Syd he knew good and well what his wife was up to, or at least suspected it. No wonder Red's job was in jeopardy and this Chad dude currently had his promotion.

Jeff put out his hand. "Good to see you again, Sydney. I was telling Redmon that it had been way too long since we were all together."

Syd let out a breath as she shook the man's hand. It was cool and parchment papery. She nodded. "Yes, a total inconvenience," she said dryly.

Red pulled Syd in by the waist, close to his body. She looked at him in confusion. It all faded away when she locked eyes with Lucas, who had walked up to their little party with an older uniformed man and a woman who was also in uniform. "You have got to be kidding me," Syd mumbled.

Both Lucas and the woman looked dashing—the only word she could think to describe it—in their uniforms. Lucas filled out his finely, and the woman, with her perfect proportions, made hers look both strong and sexy. Syd looked around at their little group and suddenly felt small and dirty.

Jeff turned. "Ah, Captain, thanks for having us."

The captain put a hand up. "Thank you for sponsoring us. With city budgets being what they are, we need all the donors we can get. I'd like you to meet two of our brightest young stars. They are our future."

Syd practically held her breath as the introductions were made. And the whole while Red kept his arm tight around her waist, even when she tried to pull away. She watched as the muscles in Lucas's jaw tightened and his nostrils flared as he tried to hold on to his composure. Finally, Red let her go, and she stepped back with relief. She was about to walk away and leave the whole situation when Red spoke up, addressing Chad's wife. "Sophia, I think you and Chad have a daughter around our Remi's age," he said, loud enough to be sure the whole group overheard. "Now that I'll be based here in New York, maybe we can get the girls together. I'd love for Remi to make some new friends as we establish ourselves as a family here."

Syd looked at him like he'd grown a third head. Based here? Since when? And suddenly she realized that Lucas had heard that particular bombshell at the same time that she had. She looked at him. His eyes were wide and full of pain as he looked from her to Red to her hand, which felt heavy and weighted by her rings. She was about to say something when Red's boss chimed in.

"That sounds fantastic. We'd love to have you all up."

This was madness. She needed out, and she needed out now.

"Fantastic, Jeff," Red said. "We'd love to come."

No fucking way. She turned to Red, about ready to open her mouth, when she heard her name, or a version of it. "Syddie, Red! I was hoping to see you while I was in New York. Who would expect that I'd run into you here? I was going to call you tomorrow, Syddie."

Oh, fantastic. The gang was all together. This should be fun.

Lucas's expression went from pain to rage, then to hatred as his ire aimed right at Red. But then the perfectly proportioned beauty put a hand on his arm and gave him two pats, and miraculously, he turned and walked away. Syd was shocked. WTF. Who was she and what sort of magic power did she have? Two taps. Syd couldn't get it out of her head as she watched Lucas walk away. His back was ramrod straight. He didn't turn back around. Zara was talking. Why was Zara, the Zara from her former life, here and talking?

It ended so quietly that Syd was stunned. She didn't know what she'd expected. Not an all-out brawl, of course, in the Peacock Ballroom of this hotel. But the quiet of it still was a shock. Or maybe it was the tap. No, two taps. What did it matter? It was over. She didn't care about any of these people. The one she did care about was hurt, had hurt her. Hell, they had hurt each other, and now he was gone. She might as well leave too. Syd turned to go, but Red grabbed her elbow. She looked at him with hard eyes.

"No." He let go, but Sophia's voice called her back.

"I'd love it," the woman said brightly. "Let's exchange numbers, Syd. That would be great. As it turns out, our club is looking for new members, and we think you all would be perfect. You'd be a shoo-in too, since I'm on the diversity and inclusion committee."

Syd stared at the woman a beat, then blinked. "I'm sure we would, but right now I'm not looking to have my daughter vetted for any type of inclusion." She put her drink on the nearest passing tray and went off to get an Uber and head home.

27

HOW COULD I *have been so dumb?* Lucas thought, then realized it was easy—he was always dumb when it came to Syd.

But still, this hit it at a new level. He was out on the terrace of the hotel's balcony in a far corner. Dee had followed him, but he shrugged her off. Told her he wanted to be alone. That he was fine. When he heard the click of heels, he knew she hadn't listened. It was so very Dee. "I said I'm fine, Dee. Leave me alone."

"Ah, so Dee is her name. She seems nice enough. Was kind enough to tell me she isn't your date and that you were out here sulking before saying something that I guess was supposed to be a threat about not hurting you. As if I was going to back down from that."

Lucas turned from the beautiful view of the city toward the deceptively beautiful view of Sydney and stared a moment as he bit the inside of his bottom lip. Finally, he spoke. "What do you care what her name is, you flat leaver?" He frowned. "Wait a minute—you stood up to Dee?"

"What's there to stand up to? Am I supposed to take threats from some woman when it comes to you? She's not your wife, right?"

He snorted. "No."

"Girlfriend?"

"No."

She shrugged. "So, I'm not taking any shit. I called dibs back in eighth grade."

Lucas wanted to laugh so bad, but he was too damned mad. "That's not funny, Syd. Don't joke with me."

"Well, I did, even if it was stupid and silently and only to myself, okay? And if you can be all immature and say dumb shit like 'flat leaver,' what's wrong with me calling dibs? What are you, fifteen?"

He shrugged. "Well, it's not like I'm wrong. If the name fits, why not use it?"

She shook her head. "I swear, you are so damned immature, Lucas. It's like with you we're stuck in a constant state of high school animation. It's ridiculous."

"Well, it's a good thing you are not stuck with me and you have the option—oh, no wait, it's a good thing you'll be settling back here with your husband and perfectly happy family."

Syd let out a sigh. She was slow with her words. "Did you actually believe the bullshit he was spouting back there?"

He wanted to not believe it, but everything suggested it was true. The arm around her waist and the fact that she was even out with him. "What's not to believe? Isn't he coming back here to work?"

Syd was quiet before she answered. "I don't know."

"Okay, so why didn't you tell me you were going out with him tonight?"

Again, she was quiet before answering. "I don't know. Why didn't you tell me you were coming here tonight? It looks like a big night—you're being honored. Am I not special enough to know?"

"I didn't think it was anything like this," he said. "During this dumb year I've been to at least six of these. My brothers won't even show anymore. Any corporation that wants to have a photo op does something and the calendar guys and gals have to show. It's part of our duty. I didn't think to ask you to it. All I could think of was getting through it and getting back to you."

Syd frowned, and Lucas let out a breath, still thinking of that ex who looked less and less like an ex with each passing day.

"Okay," he said. "Now maybe this one is a little bit easier. If you don't still have feelings for him or dreams of this perfect family, why is it you've never taken off that ring? Not once. Not even when we've made love?"

Sydney swallowed. She looked at him. Hated the ring, hated Red, hated the question and all taking it off symbolized. Her failure. When she took it off, she was no more. But she couldn't say that out loud. She looked down. That stupid ring was all the sparkle she had left. What was she without it?

She looked at him, then let out a long breath. "I don't know."

Lucas snorted. "Don't worry, Syd, this time you don't have to have any guilt about walking away. I'll be the one to say goodbye first."

28

SYD WAS EXHAUSTED when she made it back home. She kicked off her shoes in the front hall and started up the stairs. She'd noticed the night light on dim in Scrubs and Mr. Bill at the counter as her Uber passed and dropped her at the corner. She thought of waving but was just too exhausted to do so. She continued up the stairs to the residence, eager to get out of her cocktail dress. "Stupid Red. I can't believe I let him talk me into this shit," she mumbled. "Or wore this damn dress." She could still feel his arm wrapped possessively around her waist and Lucas's eyes hard and hurt as they narrowed in.

She was tired. Both mentally and physically. All she wanted was her bed. Well, not all she wanted. But she didn't want to put a name to the other thing she wanted, which, let's face it, already had a name—but he didn't want to speak to her right now. And it was probably best. Maybe tomorrow. Or who knew? Maybe not. She let out a weary breath. Men were fucking exhausting.

Well, there was one man, she thought as she hit the middle of the landing, who she was done letting exhaust her. Redmon. She was done with him and his stupid games. He'd had her spinning like a top for the past ten years, and she was fucking over it. Tired of being his puppet plaything, arm candy, housekeeper and all-around cheerful doormat. Tired of letting him pull her strings like his own little marionette. It was time to coolly and completely cut the strings. She paused, not quite enjoying the nonsensical imagery, but then again, what did it matter? Nothing made sense in her life anyway.

Still, it was time something, anything, did. She'd make sure of it. Get things on track once and for all. When she had been talking her big game to herself and making her plans to leave, however half-assed and far-fetched they were, she'd seemed to have it all together. Now that reality was at hand, she needed to still grab hold of that devil-may-care, fuck-it-all-to-the-wind thinking. And hey, surefire motivation was there when the devil himself was breathing down your neck.

The time had come. Red would pay up or pay the price. He was Remi's father, and for the privilege of being that and being in her life, he'd share in the responsibilities—not just the rewards when he felt he needed an ego boost. The bullshit stopped here. No longer was her child going to be a pawn in this ridiculous chess game.

He was paying up, paying on time and paying fairly, she decided, and if he wasn't, then he'd have to learn the hard way that she could fight just as dirty as he did.

Quickly, before better thinking or fear got to her, Syd pulled out her phone and texted Red. She let adrenaline and what she imagined her favorite real housewife would do in this situation be her guide as her fingers went to tapping.

> Sydney: The games are done. This is not a renegotiation. I will have my attorney draw up a

formal agreement letter for your lawyer with a
50% extra monthly spousal settlement plus full
college tuition for Remi deposited immediately
into a fund that I have custody of. Don't contact
me again for any galas, dinners or events. I will
only attend prearranged co-parenting meetings
with you for the benefit of Remi. You will,
pending signed agreement, still have the
prearranged visitations with Remi, of course,
and that is that. Rgrds, Sydney Harris.

Red texted back immediately:

Red: Cute but stop joking, Syddie. Is this about
your little fire boy getting upset? Don't worry.
He'll get over it. I'll stop by tomorrow and see
you and Remi before heading back to DC. You
were great tonight. Chad and Soph would love
to have us over. They can't wait for their
daughter to meet Remi. We'll just forget this
little outburst and let bygones be gone.

Syd let out a breath as she shook her head. This dumbass.

Sydney: Don't be stupid, Red. You can call Remi
in the morning. Say your goodbyes. Then you
will GET THE SETTLEMENT DONE. Tell your
colleagues what you will about our divorce but
make it clear because I will be announcing it on
my end. You have seven days to respond to the

modification of the settlement. I'm sure you don't
want this to have to go to mediation or beyond
or for witnesses to be called into court.
PS Fuck Chad and Soph.

She attached three texts. All were proof of his infidelities and his stupidity. All would clearly jeopardize his career and reputation. Especially the one that showed what were clearly his hands, birthmark and wedding ring included, on his boss's wife's bought-and-paid-for breasts. Sure, they would make Syd look like a fool too for being with a man who clearly cheated and still playing the role of loving wife to save face and all that. But she was now willing to go down with that ship. At this point she was just tired of being tired.

She put her cell back in her bag, not even interested in Red's reply. It didn't matter. Besides, something in her knew he'd back down. He had no choice. She added her wedding and engagement rings to the bag too, only for a moment marveling at how smoothly they came off her finger. Lucas's question had stung so much, and the revelation she'd had of the truth, of how much the answer wasn't about her daughter but about her own identity, had hit her worse than any blow. She should thank him for that. And she would. Just not tonight. Tonight she was hurt, and rightly so, and they both needed space.

Space to think and heal. Fuck, who wouldn't be over and done with Red's dumb ass showing out? But still, Lucas had to learn to trust her if they were ever going to find their way to this love they were playing on the edges of. Then she remembered the hurt in his eyes when he saw Red's arm around her waist. She didn't want Red's hands on her just as much as Lucas didn't. Red's little possessive husband show was nothing but a mind fuck, and Lucas, who'd been through so much, didn't deserve that. He had to know he could trust her to be there for him if they were ever going to make it.

Syd froze. For a moment she was barely able to breathe. Hold the phone. Make it? What was she thinking, and why was she even daring to think of a future when her present day was so screwed up?

She had been so upset when she thought Lucas hadn't invited her. That he was out with someone else. Even thinking back to the charity auction, she had been ready to go at it—with Kat, no less—when she had hardly even said boo to Lucas in years. Syd shook her head. She was a mess.

What about all the Miss Independent bullshit talk she'd been spouting to herself for the past few months? Dammit. For all of Lucas's talk, when it came down to it, he'd seemed to forget that part, and it turned out he could barely bring himself to trust her at all. Syd closed her eyes for a moment, wishing she could finally break down that barrier that had always been there with Lucas. Make it through one of those cracks she'd been so desperately chipping away at. For a moment jealousy stabbed at her as she wondered if anyone had. She hoped it was one of his brothers and not the woman who had ushered him away at the party. But she did hope it was someone. He deserved that. He didn't deserve to keep all his feelings, his pain, bottled up and twisting in his gut, his mind, for him to deal with alone.

Syd was still thinking of how to get through to Lucas when she entered the residence and was surprised to find her grandfather up and watching TV in the living room. "Pops, what are you still doing up?" she said.

When he didn't immediately answer, she knew something was

wrong but prayed that he was only asleep, despite the icy chill that ran along her spine. She ran over and shook him. "Pops!" He tilted to the side, and a scream lodged in her throat as adrenaline coursed through her body. Instantly a million thoughts ran through her head, but the loudest was Lucas's voice. *Don't panic, and follow these steps:*

Check his vitals. Shit. How to do that? Neck? Arm? She thought she felt a pulse in his neck.

Call 911.

The operator was speaking, but she was hearing Lucas's voice. *Clear his airways.*

Start chest compressions. Pops gasped. That was a good sign, right? Right? *Yes.* Was that her voice or Lucas's? It sounded like his, but how was he in her head? *Don't stop,* the voice told her. *Just don't stop.* This time it was her voice, and for the first time she felt a little surer of herself.

"Stay with me, Pops. We've got this. You've got this." The burning was going up her arm and into her throat as the tears ran down her cheeks.

Still, she heard Lucas on repeat. *Follow the steps. You'll be okay. He'll be okay. I believe in you, Syd. I've always believed in you.*

Just then Remi came rushing into the room. "Will he be all right, Mommy? Will he be all right, Mommy?"

"Yes, baby, he'll be all right."

Please, Lord, don't let me have just lied to my child. Make this one thing true. Give them more time. She needed more time.

Stay calm, Lucas's voice said. *Follow the steps.*

It was only a few minutes, but it felt like an eternity as she followed the steps and prayed to God that she hadn't lied, that her prayer would come true, that a miracle would arrive and God would forgive her and give back the wasted time. So much wasted time.

NOT FOR THE first time in the last half hour, Lucas wished he could kick himself in his own ass. But no, he'd leave that pleasure to Syd. Right after this stupid ceremony was over. "New York's Bravest." Yeah right. If he was brave, he wouldn't have walked away from her. Wouldn't have gone back into the banquet and let her leave. Wouldn't have watched while she was in a clearly uncomfortable situation with that ex of hers. But the whole time Red had had his hands on her, there he'd stood. Frozen. The thought of that ass's hands on her waist made Lucas want to kill. And he knew it made no sense, knew they had a history, would always have one that ran deep, maybe deeper than she and he would ever have. Frozen. Why was he always frozen when it came to her? Also late. Too late.

He'd wanted so badly to chase after her. To not let her go again. But like a fool who didn't learn, he was bound to let pain and history repeat and let her go, only to be faced with this alone. When he'd finally gotten back to the ballroom, he was once again too late and she was gone. And that jerko Red had no answers and seemed to not care a bit about where she had gone. He was such a phony, sitting back at their table smooth as could be with an empty place where Sydney should be, and he just talked over it, making small talk with the tan man and the twin-looking couple.

Red looked at Lucas once and attempted a smirk but then smartly thought better of it. Lucas should have left. Should have gone after her. But once again he'd lost out as he let his old fears and anxieties come up and grab hold of him. It was as if they were his own hidden vines that followed him, waiting underground to root him to the spot when it was time to make that critical move, to grab him by the ankles or wrap around his throat and cut off his breathing when all he needed to say was "No. Stay."

And now here he was, stuck at a table waiting for his name to be called for some crap award. Thank goodness they were nearing the end of this year and it was time for the next roster of pinups to be ushered in. This strange award-slash-handover ceremony was odd— one of this company's last hurrahs to show off how much they'd raised for the department in so-called goodwill. Currently there was a video highlighting a dunk tank that was only slightly cringe-worthy. Next up were awards for "Best Smile" and "Most Swoony."

Lucas's hands hovered over Syd's name on his phone. What to say? Maybe he should just go. Not text—just go over there now. She would be mad at a text anyway. She would be mad at a call. Would she answer either?

"Are you paying attention, Strong?" It was Dee, pulling his attention. "I know you're upset, but you need to focus. Yeah, you screwed up. But you'll fix it. She's a tough one, that woman. Don't worry—she won't bail on you that easy. Now get it together; they're talking about you."

Lucas frowned and shook his head. "Not yet. They must still be on someone else. I've got time." The captain was going on about accommodations and many lives saved, and then a woman yelled out about mouth-to-mouth. There was a chuckle from the crowd, and Captain Morgan tried his best to stay on script. Lucas could tell he wanted nothing more than to be out of there almost as much as he did. But then all of a sudden, his phone vibrated with a text from Jesse.

Jesse: 911.

Lucas's heart plummeted.

Jesse: I don't know exactly what's going on but
they had to take Mr. H to Harlem's ER. Syd went
with them in the ambulance, and we have
Remi here.

Fuck.

Once again, he wasn't there. He was here in some downtown hotel playing dress-up, and she was all the way uptown on the way to the hospital. Lucas knew he needed to move, but his feet were frozen. Once again. As always. Frozen. The woman he loved needed him, and he wasn't there.

"Strong. You need to move. They're calling your name."

He blinked. "Huh?"

Lucas looked at Dee. She patted his shoulder. "You need to move."

He nodded. "Yeah. I've got to go. It's 911. Tell the captain. Call my brother Jesse for the details."

Dee looked at him, then she nodded. "Do you need me?"

He shook his head. The adrenaline was pumping now. "No, just cover for me."

She nodded again. "Okay. Go. Hurry." After years of friendship, all it took was a look. She had him covered. Lucas heard his name being called from the podium, but he was already halfway out the banquet hall's door when he suddenly stopped. There was that asshole Redmon. He was focused on the big-breasted woman laughing it up while Syd and Remi were both going through so much. He should just go. Screw Redmon. He was a jerk, and they didn't need him in their lives. Lucas went for the door again, then paused and turned back toward the asshole that had gotten to spend way more years than he deserved with the woman that Lucas had loved with all his heart for all his life. Still, Redmon was Syd's past and Remi's forever, and it was his choice whether he'd step up or not.

Just fuck it all again! Lucas ran in and gave him a few quick words before running out of the hotel and, as quickly as he could, to Sydney.

WHEN LUCAS ARRIVED at the hospital, he all but expected Syd to kick him out. The car ride was so long he'd practically had to sit on his hands to keep from jumping out and driving himself. He was shocked beyond belief when instead of kicking him out or yelling, she melted into his arms and started to cry. Oh hell, this was worse than he thought. Mr. H must have taken a turn for the worse. Dammit! Suddenly it was all too much, and Lucas felt like he would break apart too.

"Are you all right?" he asked. "Are you all right?" He rubbed at her hair. Felt her tears through his shirt. It felt like they went right through to his heart. "Baby, I'm sorry. Syd, shit. I'm so sorry."

She sniffled loudly. "What are you sorry for?" she said, pulling back and wiping at the tears that were flowing from his cheeks. *Shit*. This woman was forever either wiping or kissing his face. When did he turn into such a crybaby?

"If I were there, you wouldn't have had to go through this. I could have helped with your grandfather. I could have saved him."

Syd hauled off and hit him in the arm. Hard AF!

"Ouch! Violence, woman! Do you know how hard you hit? Also, cameras." He pointed up. "I could bring charges against you."

She pulled him into a tighter hug. "Do it, you dummy. You really are the most beautiful but dumbest man in the world. I don't know why I love you so much, Lucas Strong, when you drive me this crazy."

"I'm dumb?"

Syd blinked, then let out a sigh. "You got that, but not the I love you? I swear, I don't know how you have the reputation you do. It must be your looks. You seriously have a one-track mind."

Lucas swallowed, then grinned. "Yeah, but that's why you love me."

"Yeah, you're dumb. You weren't there, but my grandfather is okay, or he will be, thanks to me saving him." She smiled a little, then fell into his chest once again. He could feel her exhaustion, and it felt so good to hold her. To be there for her. To let her sink into him. And in that moment, he let his body go and sank into her too.

Lucas led Syd to a nearby set of fused-together chairs that had seen better days. His adrenaline had been so high but he was starting to come down, and it felt like he'd just finished a marathon. He could only imagine how Syd felt. She was still in her cocktail dress from earlier, and if she had performed CPR, her chest and arms would be sore as hell come tomorrow, if they weren't already.

Mentally and physically, she must be wiped out. He looked at her and marveled for a moment. She'd been through so much, had been going through so much for long enough, and there he was almost nightly coming and sleeping on her cot like some affection-starved waif. Lucas realized then that he owed her an apology. A big one.

He'd wanted to be there for her, but on his terms—as if she didn't have enough on her plate and enough to handle, he'd added on another one hundred ninety-five pounds of emotion.

Lucas went to put his arms around her then, but Syd stopped him and took his hands in hers. Her brown eyes were still glistening with tears, but he could see she was pulling herself together, getting that firm Sydney Harris set to her jaw. *Shit. Here it comes.* The kick out the door he had been preparing for all the way over here.

Not that he didn't deserve it. He'd fucked up. Many times. There was no reason for her to give him a chance and let him into her life, not again.

He closed his eyes for a moment. "Sydney, I'm sorry, please—" he started.

"Thank you."

Lucas opened his eyes.

She brought his hands up and kissed his fingers. His breath caught.

"You and these beautiful hands. I may not be so great with the needles," she said, "but it's thanks to you and what you taught me that Pops will make it. So I should be thanking you." She let out a breath.

"I don't understand."

Her eyes, which had softened, grew serious again. "Lucas, you have to let this go. You can't be everywhere all the time and stop all of life's tragedies. They are going to come no matter what you or me or anyone tries to do to stop them. Do you think I don't want to pull out some crystal ball and know all of Remi's life?" She frowned then, thinking for a moment. "Well, not all—but do you think I don't want to know all those points in her life that could be potential harms or dangers ahead of time so that I could be there to stop them? Of course I do."

Syd swallowed and looked away. When she looked at him again, her voice was softer. "Do you think I wouldn't have wanted to know my own, so that I could have avoided those?"

Lucas felt his heart race with what he dared think was hope. Please let her be talking about their past and hope.

"But we can't change the past," she said, as if reading his mind and sweeping away regrets. "All we can do is know we're doing our best and hope for a brighter future. There will be pain, just as there will be little pockets of unexpected joy. If we hadn't fought tonight and you hadn't walked away and I hadn't left the hotel early, then I may not have been in time to save my grandfather. Everything happens when it happens, Lucas Strong. It is what it is. So we have to make the best of what we have now."

He blinked and nodded. "You're right. I am dumb. But I'm sorry. Please just take this apology and know I mean it. I will try harder. Harder to fix myself."

Syd tilted her head to the side, as if to say "Told you." She smiled then. "There is nothing you have to fix, my Mr. November. You may have a one-track mind, but you're perfect to me. You always have been."

He grinned. "You'd better watch it, girl, talking like that. We're in public, but I'll find a private space."

She laughed. Then seemed to sober. "Also, thank you from Remi. I got a text from her and I spoke to Red. It was really big of you to let him know what was going on. It was great of Kerry to rush over when she heard the sirens and take her, but she felt better having Red. They are bringing her by with a change of clothes for me."

He swallowed.

She took his hand. "I know that was hard. But you did great."

Lucas looked down at her hand and her bare finger. He looked back up at her, afraid to ask the wrong question. "It wasn't you. But I'm thanking you for that too," she said. "I kept telling myself wearing the ring was for Remi, but really it was about keeping up appearances of an old life and not knowing my own identity. I think I'm getting closer to it now."

Lucas leaned down and kissed her finger. He knew it would be a while, maybe a long while, before she was ready to put another ring on that hand, but he also knew that when it was time, it would be his ring and that he would hold her hand forever, because this time he wasn't letting go.

Lucas tilted her chin up so he could look into her soft brown eyes. This was where he'd wanted to be. Lost in them. Lost in her. "You're right," he said. "I am dumb, but I was smart about one thing."

She blinked, and there they were again. Those challenging Syd eyes. Fine, he'd take those too. They were the same ones that had sent him into a tailspin over fifteen years before. He'd take her any way and every way.

"And what's that?" she said.

"Falling in love with you all those years ago," he said.

Syd pulled a face. "All those? How many?"

Lucas shook his head. "If I tell you, you're just gonna hit me in my arm again. Better to leave that one alone. I've been beat up enough for one day. Besides, what does it matter when I first fell for you? If it was when I saw you walking in the halls of our high school or walking down Seventh Avenue, or maybe the first day I looked across the street and saw you through the window of Scrubs helping your grandfather while the other kids played out on the sidewalk? Either way, I always saw you, and each time I did, from then until today, I fell in love with you all over again, and I'll do so forever."

Sydney shook her head, and this time he was the one wiping away her tears. "Lucas Strong. If I find out that during the past ten years you ever said this beautiful shit to anyone but me, I'm going to destroy you."

He smiled. "Good for me you won't have to do that. Now let's cut the tears. I'm here now. Let's get it together, love, and go in to check on your grandfather. He sees all this crying and I'm going to have to take a beatdown from him, and who knows what sort of hopped-up super drugs they put the old man on."

She laughed then. Her tears dried up, and Lucas kissed her— kissed her long and sweetly and tried his best to fill her with all the hope that he'd wanted to for so very long. He sealed the kiss in his mind. They were letting go of the past and christening a new beginning.

EPILOGUE

The launch of the SYNCED line of jewelry by Sydney Harris, her boutique collection, was a quiet affair, but anyone who was anyone in the tightly knit Harlem community wanted an invitation to Ms. Harris's trunk show. It was held during a Thursday-night Sip and Knit and hosted by Kerry Fuller and Jesse Strong. Sydney Harris sold out of all her pieces and has taken orders, giving her work clear up through the next six months. Her pieces are even being worn by megastars such as Jett Hathaway.

Ms. Harris's daughter, Remi Hughes, and her business partner, Aisha Bell, also launched their own line of knit headbands under the name Remi-Bell.

The party was a huge success and went late into the night.

OF COURSE, TWITTER went in another direction:

> Harlem still be humpin': The biggest non-secret of the
> night is what IT jewelry designer was out creeping

after her launch party with a hunky fireman who knows
how to twist things up right and tight. Have at it, you
two crazy kids! Keep it sudsy!

SYDNEY TOOK ONE last selfie wearing her fancy low-cut, cinched white dress, showing off her new earrings, necklace and ring set in front of the Scrubs dryers. She waved her fingers proudly. It had been over six months since she'd worn her wedding band. It was now in a safe-deposit box, and she'd probably sell it one day or repurpose it for Remi. Maybe make earrings for her. Either way, it was no longer a part of her life. And despite not being the perfect DC socialite, the Harlem mom and jewelry designer / laundress was doing just fine for herself with her rebranded IG page: JUSSYD.

For the first time in a long time, Sydney felt like she was really enjoying her life; putting the show behind her and thinking of all the plans she had in front of her didn't give her anxiety but filled her with joy.

What did give her fluttering butterflies, the best kind, was the silly anticipation of waiting for Lucas to come over and pick her up. It was ridiculous that he was coming across the street to the door of Scrubs only to walk her back across the street to his car, but that was Lucas. He was taking her away for a weekend vacation to the hotel and spa that Damian had hooked them up with on a Groupon deal way back when. She had to admit Damian really knew how to come through when it came to the deals. He was a fantastic resource for her new business too, sourcing materials and helping her with the books. And even though she was still all thumbs when knitting, surprisingly she had quite the aptitude with a crochet hook. Lucas would be so shocked when he received his new hat and scarf for Christmas.

She couldn't wait to get away with Lucas. The two of them were going out now and dating as much as possible, doing it all, as if they were making up for the time they'd missed when they were apart for all those years.

"You two are sickening, you know," Kat teased when Syd dropped Remi off for the weekend. "You both act like those old people who you read about on Facebook or something, off on their last hurrahs. You're only in your thirties." She leaned in and whispered in Syd's ear when Remi went to Aisha's room, "Seriously, is the dick that good?"

Syd pulled back and grinned. "Better! So much better."

"Grrr! I hate you. Why don't you just get married?"

Syd's eyes went wide, and she shook her head. "Not now. And I don't know when. Let me enjoy this. I need to enjoy this for a while."

Kat nodded her understanding. "Off with you, then. Don't break nothing."

Syd's grandfather was doing well, and they'd even given Glen a permanent part-time position at Scrubs so that Pops had to do no more than manage and oversee operations in the laundromat, working his allotted hours while still taking time out for his meals, medication, exercise and of course *Jeopardy!*

After her ultimatum—and it was sad that it had to come down to that, but of course it did—Red came through with an amendment to their spousal agreement, and the money was good and settled. Syd felt much more secure knowing that at least Remi's college tuition was safe and their monthly stipend would hold out as long as his employment did. It wasn't the most secure thing, knowing

Red and his proclivities for touching other people's things, but it was all she had. And so far, his position at his current firm seemed secure, but that was only because stupid Chad and his twin wife got caught in a threesome with old Jeff Ackerman, and Jeff's wife was one step ahead of him. Well, it was what it was. Lucky Red. As long as Syd's money stayed on time and he kept Remi out of any nonsense, she was fine.

Remi seemed happy—or as happy as she could be, having had her life turned inside out and flipped upside down. Sydney knew it wasn't easy for her daughter. But for some reason, the sullen gene hadn't stuck to her baby, and for that she was forever grateful. Most of the time she was just Remi, and the light that had threatened to dim was back and brighter than ever, which was something that gave Syd more and more strength each day. It gave her yet another reason to smile, just seeing her reflection in those beautiful brown eyes.

The night bell rang, and Syd's phone lit up. She flipped the screen so his face appeared. Lucas smiled. Not that sweet Boy Scout, boy-next-door, you-can-trust-me smile. No, this was the smile he only gave to her—the wicked one that made her knees weak and her legs cross. The one that she had seen glimpses of back in high school, the one that she would foolishly shy away from, then look back at when he thought she wasn't looking, but she was. She was always looking. He just never knew.

Syd reached down and pulled out the little box with the engagement ring she'd designed for him. She'd make damn sure he knew she was looking. Always and forever.

ACKNOWLEDGMENTS

With this book, as with all my books, it seems that writing the acknowledgments feels like the hardest part. I always worry that I'll leave someone out, someone who's touched me during the book's conception in some amazing way, and on account of my own fluttering mind, I'll inadvertently forget and not give them the thanks they are due.

First, I'd like to start with my husband, Will. Getting tangled up with you is the best thing I ever did.

I'd like to continue with a blanket (ha, how knitterly of me) thank-you to all of you who have supported me in the ways you know and in the ways you don't. You are truly a blessing. Next, though really this was the first in my heart, I'd like to thank God for the inspiration and for another chance to see another day and another story making it out into the world.

It's also a pleasure and an honor to thank my amazing editor, Kristine Swartz, for her patience and her tireless championing of the Strong brothers. I'd also like to say a huge thank-you to Michelle

Kasper, Mary Baker, Fareeda Bullert, Jessica Brock and Yazmine Hassan for all their tireless work with bringing *Knot Again* in front of people in the real world. Thank you all so much!

Next, I want to thank the Berkley art department and my cover artist, Farjana Yasmin, for my gorgeous *Knot Again* cover. I'm so grateful.

Now I must thank my amazing agent, Evan Marshall, for always being not just in my corner but by my side every step of the way with this series. Evan, you are a rock star! Also, thanks for always telling me how I'm "sooo young." You're brutally honest, but you do know when to fib just a little bit.

Destin Divas, thank you all for continuing to be the greatest friends that a writer could ever ask for.

To my Dear Twins, you know that you both are always my reason. I love you forever.

And to the rest of my family, thanks for always cheering me on.

I'd like to also take a moment to give thanks to all the first responders, especially those on the front lines, who have been working so tirelessly these past two-plus years. It's been hard. Harder than we've all ever imagined, and the sacrifices greater than we'll ever know. Thank you. Thank you. Thank you.

A huge thanks to the firefighters of Engine 69/Ladder 28/Battalion 16, aka the Harlem Hilton. This was the firehouse down the street from my own nana's house, where I grew up, and the one I had in my mind when I fictionalized Lucas's firehouse and home away from home. This firehouse is near and dear to my heart and to the community, as so many local firehouses are. I want to give them a special shout-out and a nod of thanks for their many years of service. I'd like to also give an extra-special thank-you to firefighter Eric Ruckdeschel for kindly answering my call for a bit of research clarity. Anything that's right, thank him; if there's something you consider wrong, we'll call it creative license.

I would also like to thank Mona Swanson and the staff of The Children's Village, Susan Watson and the other individuals who took time to share their stories and experiences with me. Your kindness and generosity have meant so much.

Now finally, I'd like to thank you, my dear readers, especially those original fans of the Strong brothers and of Jesse and Kerry from *Real Men Knit* who have been asking for each brother's story. I hope you enjoy *Knot Again* and Lucas's story, and I thank you so much for your devotion to Mama Joy's boys.

Love Strong,
Kwana

KNOT AGAIN

Kwana Jackson

QUESTIONS FOR DISCUSSION

1. Lucas is the second of the Strong brothers to express internal-
    ized guilt over Mama Joy's death. Do you think this is a way
    of coping for the brothers instead of dealing directly with her
    death?

2. In high school, Lucas had a crush on Sydney. Why do you
    think he didn't let Sydney know how he felt? Was it out of
    fear, or was it a sacrifice?

3. Did Sydney make the right initial decision to listen to her
    mother and leave Harlem?

4. Do you think Sydney's mother was intentionally pushing her
    daughter in the wrong direction or just trying to do what she
    thought was best for her?

5. What were Sydney's reasons for leaving her marriage and returning home? Do you agree with them?

6. Both Lucas and Sydney see themselves as loners when in reality they each have pretty strong support networks. How do their friends and family give them strength?

7. Do you believe in soul mates who are meant to find their way back to each other? Are Sydney and Lucas destined to be together?

8. A running theme the author explores is that love takes courage. How is this shown in the relationship between Sydney and Lucas and in their interactions with friends and family throughout the novel?

Keep reading for an excerpt from

REAL MEN
KNIT

by *USA Today* bestselling author Kwana Jackson,
available now from Berkley!

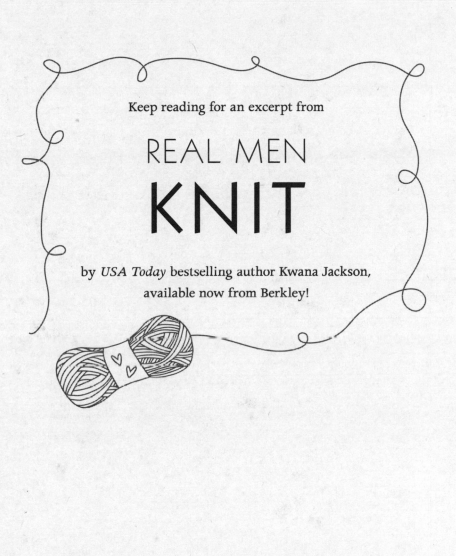

THERE WAS NOTHING cute about the first time Kerry Fuller met Jesse Strong.

He broke her glasses, she bloodied his nose and they both ended up in a tangle of yarn on the floor in the loft space of Strong Knits being scolded by Mama Joy.

What she wouldn't give to be scolded by the older woman just one more time, Kerry thought as she adjusted her dark-framed glasses and purposefully pushed aside the almost-long-forgotten childhood memory. She glanced over at the front window of Strong Knits, the Harlem yarn shop that had been so much a part of her life growing up.

Any other day Kerry would have loved walking through the door of Strong Knits. It had been that way since she had first stepped foot in the little knitting shop where she'd worked part-time for the better part of the last ten years and pretty much just hung out for most of her childhood years before that, making it her unlikely sanctuary. A place of calm in the midst of the chaos that was the concrete jungle of upper Manhattan. But this day was anything but normal. Despite the summer sun, warm and glinting off the freshly cleaned windows, showcasing the vintage baskets overflowing with color from the brand-new yarns that Mama Joy had gotten in barely two weeks before, Kerry still felt a chill run through her body that sent goose pimples rippling across her bare forearms.

Even the cute little display to the right of the baskets with fake ice-cream cones made of balls of finely spun cotton in creamy sherbet colors couldn't bring a smile to her lips, when they'd brought her nothing but delight just a little over a week before. But smiling now, and the memory of Mama Joy and those cones, caused Kerry's heart to ache way too much.

When she and Mama Joy had put the display together, it was with much happiness and no idea of the sorrow to come. No, all they could think of then was the smiles of the passersby when they saw the new yarns displayed in the whimsical not quite ice-cream cones. Mama Joy knew the children in the neighborhood would love it. And she was right. They did. Folks came in and immediately asked for those yarns. Little faces glowed when they saw the display and brown eyes lit with delight upon seeing the colorful cones.

But like the dynamo she was, Mama Joy had already been anticipating the next display, looking forward to what they would be doing for the fall. She had been excited about showcasing something even better for the neighborhood kids come the end of August with the new shipments on the way.

Kerry felt a weight suddenly lay heavy on her chest. What would happen to those yarns now? What would they do now that Mama Joy was no longer here to help navigate the changes that the new season would bring? Kerry peered through the glass of the door once more, noticing the darkness in the shop, uncharacteristic for the hour of the day. If this had been a normal day, the lights would already be on in the back of the shop and right around this time

Mama Joy would be stepping forward to unlock the door and wave her in. Kerry let out a sigh as the fact that she'd never be greeted by that wave, or Mama Joy's easy smile, ever again took the air clear out of her lungs.

Oh well, she couldn't just stand here wallowing in her feelings. Instead, Kerry swallowed and physically forced them down as she reached out and gave the buzzer on the side of the door three short rings. She waited. One breath and then another. Two more rings. Longer and steadier this time. She moved to the side and rang the bell to chime up at the residence upstairs. *Come on, Jesse, where are you? Noah? Lucas?* She knew Damian would probably not be there, but she thought that maybe Noah and Lucas would have stayed over since they were all supposed to meet up here later anyway.

Disappointment blanketed her shoulders for a moment at the silent response to her ring. Why weren't the brothers together? Especially at a time like this? Sure, Lucas could have stayed over at the firehouse where he was stationed and lived most of the time, and maybe Noah went back to the place he was subletting with the other tour dancers, and knowing Damian, he didn't want anything to mess up his usual well-ordered routine so he'd probably gone back to his own apartment. But still, she expected Jesse to be there. Kerry felt her brows draw together. Who was she fooling? When it came to Jesse Strong, who knew what rock he was burrowed under this morning? The thought brought with it a sizzle of anger that shot quickly through Kerry's spine, followed immediately by an intense feeling of guilt.

She could at least cut Jesse some slack, today of all days. Yes, her thinking was perfectly logical, but it was uncharitable and uncalled for, nonetheless. Especially since Jesse was hurting just as much as she was—hell, probably even more so—with it being the day after Mama Joy's funeral. She may call Ms. Joy "Mama Joy," like most of the young people in the neighborhood, but to Jesse, Lucas, Noah and Damian, she was *their* mother. The only one that mattered. The only one in this world who stuck around and took the time to truly make them a part of her family. Kerry knew if she was feeling this level of grief and uncertainty, then what must Jesse and his brothers be going through having just lost the only mother they'd ever been able to call their own?

She pressed the shop's buzzer again, then hit the side buzzer one more time. Still no answer. Oh well, she guessed Jesse wasn't there. He probably hadn't wanted to spend last night home above the shop alone. And who knows, maybe he ended up staying over at Damian's. Kerry felt her lips tighten, knowing how unlikely that was, given how well the two of them got along. Nope, more likely than not, Jesse was crashed underneath whatever woman he was currently seeing or hooking up with. She sighed. There she was being petty once again. How was it that thoughts of Jesse brought out the "Call me Petty Patty" side in her so easily?

Reaching into her tote bag to pull out her spare set of keys to let herself into the shop, Kerry hesitated. *It shouldn't be too much of a problem just letting myself in. Right?* Mama Joy had given her the keys ages ago as a backup and Kerry had promised the brothers she'd meet them this morning to help with sorting things out while they discussed the future of . . . well, everything.

Kerry feared that after today the Strong brothers would officially state out loud what she'd assumed after hearing that Mama Joy had suddenly died. That Strong Knits and all that went with it would be no more. A Harlem institution here and gone in what felt like too short a breath, just like the amazing woman who had made it great.

With a last sigh Kerry finally let herself into the shop. The weight of the old wooden door seemed heavier than ever before. It couldn't be an easy decision for any of the brothers to make. The least she could do was have coffee on for them when they arrived.

As she stepped inside the shop, the light tinkle of the overhead bell made her half smile while bringing a tear to her eye and a painful tug to the center of her chest. She knew it was just her imagination, but it was as if she could still smell the scent of Mama Joy's cinnamon biscuits. The ones she'd make special on Wednesdays for her senior knitting circle, self-dubbed the OKG—Old Knitting Gang. Kerry was their honorary little sister and, in a way, their mascot from early on. She guessed now maybe Ms. Cherry and the rest of the crew would meet at the senior center or one of the women's houses. She made a mental note to get all their contact info so she could still help them with getting yarns online. Not that they'd let her get too far out of reach, mind you. They were just not that type of crew. The OKG felt more *Godfather* than Junior League, meaning that once you were in the family there really was no way out except one, and sadly, Mama Joy had made her way out.

Still, Kerry knew she owed much to both Mama Joy and her friends in the OKG. No, there wasn't much you could get past them, but she and many on the block were grateful for it. Around here, it wasn't always cool to go the "if you see something, say something" route. Not that there was anything wrong with that, but facts were facts, and there definitely hadn't always been the most amiable relationship between residents and the NYPD. Folks had to learn a different way to help each other out with neighborhood watches and small groups of friends who became family when 911 didn't always show up like the cavalry, and at times you didn't know who was the protector and who was the predator. So yeah, Kerry owed them and Mama Joy a lot, and it went further than yarn and double stitches.

At first they taught her to crochet, going from chain stitches to granny squares, then, as she grew in age and skill, moving on to knitting scarves and hats, then from there on to anything she could imagine. But more than the projects, it was the comfort she got just being welcomed into their group when she'd stop by early before school and then after school instead of sitting at home alone for hours on end, listening to the constant fighting between her upstairs neighbor and her horrible husband as Kerry waited for her own ma to get off work. Or more importantly, during those times when her ma had her own problematic love she'd dragged into their lives and Kerry just wanted an escape.

Either way, Mama Joy had long given up on believing or listening to Kerry's excuses for stopping in and just started setting a biscuit and yarn aside for her, having it all ready, the biscuit wrapped in a paper towel alongside a cup of sweet hot chocolate when she was little, and later coffee when her beverage habits changed in high school.

Kerry closed her eyes a moment. Would she really never hear Mama Joy's voice again? "Come on in, child, and get you some nourishment before you pass out. You need this strength with the way things are out there. A woman's got to have all her wits about her."

"Damn straight," Ms. June would chime in while not breaking stride in her stitchwork.

"Amen to that," Sister Purnell would say, topping off yet another hat or scarf for her church homeless drive or Ms. Cherry's Angel Tree kids.

Kerry smiled, the pain now excruciating. Little did Mama Joy know that just being in those women's presence was all the nourishment that she'd needed. Probably it was all anyone really needed when they took refuge in her little shop. Sure, people may have initially come for the yarns or the knitting or crochet needles or patterns, but it was Mama Joy's seemingly never-ending wellspring of love and sacrifice, which somehow didn't come off as a sacrifice, that kept her and everyone else in the neighborhood coming back.

A small smile or a hug from Mama Joy and, well, you felt like you'd just had the best meal of your life. Cinnamon biscuit or not.

Kerry felt lucky to have been on the receiving end of that hug or whatever Mama Joy was giving out. A fact that in the beginning was both a blessing and a sore spot for her mother. She was a single parent who worked two jobs that barely added up to one. And a young mother on top of it—who, yes, Kerry was sure, she guessed, tried her best to be mature. But at times the dip-and-do bug grabbed her and she didn't really want the responsibility that came with the constant mothering of an introverted kid.

Though Kerry's mother had her reservations about Kerry spending so much time in the shop, when her mother wanted time to herself or the apartment got a little tight for more than two, well then, Mama Joy and Strong Knits became just that much more of a tolerable solution.

Still, the sticking point that brought up problems between Kerry, her mother and any other neighborhood person with a curious mind and flapping gums was the other elephant in the shop, or four elephants, as it were. Specifically, Mama Joy's four adopted sons—Damian, Lucas, Noah and Jesse—and the fact that they were in and out of the shop while Kerry was spending so much time there.

Kerry thought of her mother, the neighborhood gossips and talk of her and the guys, and snorted to herself. As if her being around ever mattered to the Strong brothers.

Brought in from the foster system to live with Mama Joy when they were all in grade school, the boys ended up being adopted by Mama Joy and taking on her last name of Strong when they were in high school—and by then each was in some way ironically living up to the Strong surname. Kerry was constantly, even still to this day, questioned by her mother and anyone else with half a curious mind about her relationship with the guys and which one of them she was dating. As if any of them thought of her as little more than "Kerry Girl," the shop fixture and a general nuisance to be tolerated.

Though Kerry's mother was fine with her spending time in the shop and learning about knitting and business from Mama Joy, she could never quite get behind her daughter being in constant close proximity to the Strong brothers. Who knew—maybe her mother was right. With her track record for sniffing out heartbreakers and, let's face it, general assholes, she was a bit of an expert in the field. Not that her mother had learned anything, being currently lost in love on yet another potential would-be asshole binge. Kerry prayed that this one would be the last. She'd had it with her mother's disasters and, afterward, having to pick up the pieces. Besides, this last one had taken her ma clear out of state and given Kerry their apartment to herself. She loved her mom, but she loved having her own place almost as much.

It was then that a distinct beeping took Kerry out of her musings. *Beep . . . beep . . . beep, beep, beep.* Speeding up. Oh crap, the alarm!

Kerry ran behind the door to punch in the code. That would be everything she didn't need. She was not in the mood to deal with explaining to the NYPD why she was in a shop that she may or may not still be employed at while the owner was not only not present but recently deceased. Making sure the alarm was disarmed, she let out a breath, then looked around at the uncommon emptiness. The silence shrouded her as she walked forward and once again locked the front door, her eyes skimming across the flipped-over closed sign that had been in that position for the past week and a half, its possible permanence weighing heavy on her heart.

She shrugged. Nothing she could do about it. Whether the sign eventually flipped back or not was up to Jesse and his brothers. Well, mostly his brothers, really. What would Mr. Party All The Time seriously have to say about opening or closing the shop? What would he care beyond the fact that he'd have to find another place to park it when he was between women? As of late, when Kerry took notice, she couldn't help but observe that he'd been more out of the house than home anyway. Taking longer and longer stints staying with whomever he was seeing at the time.

Still, she thought, it wasn't as if Jesse didn't care. He wasn't that callous. He loved Mama Joy, loved her fiercely, in fact. All four of them did. But she knew they all had separate lives to live, and, thinking clearly, Kerry could not imagine those lives including keeping Strong Knits open. That hard truth said, she had to face the fact that it was time for her to move on and, once and for all, grow up and see her life clearly without the sanctuary of Strong Knits to fall back on.

Kerry headed back toward the small kitchen area, on the way passing some of the plants sent over to the funeral home as tribute. They were shoved over in the corner, as if they were purposely put down somewhere out of the way. Out of sight, out of mind. She could understand that. She caught sight of the peace lily sent from her own mother, who hadn't made it up from Virginia but had sent her regrets, and shook her head. Maybe she'd take that one home and at least get one off the brothers' hands. Or maybe she'd take it to the center when she went there to work later.

Kerry shrugged and turned, finally entering the kitchen and flipping on the lights, going to put her tote down on the counter-top. She suddenly stopped short as her eyes widened. The counter was packed with covered dishes in every imaginable shape and color. Most likely leftovers from the repast after the funeral yesterday. Putting her tote on the counter was almost impossible unless she squeezed it between a mountain of cold chicken and what appeared to be a twenty-five-pound ham. *Great*. That was a ham, and no doubt it was honey glazed with pineapple, and it had been out on Mama Joy's counter all night. Why didn't the guys put anything away? Kerry shook her head as she opted for placing her bag on one of the old kitchen chairs. She let out a long breath and turned toward the coffee maker. Coffee was very necessary. Now. She'd deal with the ham and the rest of the dishes later.

Purposely without thought, which of course she knew implied thought, Kerry picked up the coffeepot and brought it over to the sink to rinse and refill it with fresh water. She wouldn't look too closely at Mama Joy's knitted dish towels or the multitude of photographs that hung haphazardly on the walls, some in nice frames and others clearly made out of Popsicle sticks and macaroni shells from kids she'd known over the years who'd come into the shop or were from the community center where Kerry now worked part-time. There was even a photo of Kerry from her high school graduation, now eight years past, in its cheap faux wood frame, but hung with loving care. Kerry blinked back tears at the photo of the young woman, her dark hair pressed within an inch of its life, glossy beyond belief and curled to perfection, with shining dark eyes, and full burgundy lips spread wide in a warm, welcoming smile that seemed to say the world was open and full of possibilities for her.

Dammit! She shouldn't have looked. Looking led to feeling, and that was the exact wrong thing to be doing today. But how could she not? There was nothing but feelings all around this old shop, in every seemingly not-well-thought-out nook. And here it was, Mama Joy had gone and hung Kerry's photo right along with her own boys' graduation photos, just as if she were a part of their family too. She and Jesse graduating the same year, Noah the year before, Lucas and Damian just a couple of years before that. Kerry laughed to herself, a wry laugh that grated the back of her throat as she took in the kitchen wall. This whole gallery was so Mama Joy. She was the type of woman who never met a stranger. But that family was no more. Who knew, maybe they never really were in the first place—just something that only existed as long as Mama Joy did. Now would be the true test of that.

Kerry shook her head as a lump gathered in her throat, threatening to be followed by a sob. Nope, not this morning. Not today.

She turned back to the coffeepot, her eye catching on one photo on the way: Mama Joy sitting in her usual spot on the tall stool just off to the side of the front counter with all the boys around her. They must have been late elementary to middle school age. She guessed it was around when they had first been placed with Mama Joy by the people at Faith Hope group home, if she remembered the stories correctly. Though it was an old still photo, Kerry could clearly make out the boys all in motion around Mama Joy while she was intently trying to show them something with her knitting to little avail.

A much younger Damian stood taller than his younger brothers but, as usual, looked bored and slightly exasperated, his dark eyes showing little patience. Lucas, the next oldest, seemed to have gotten his yarn completely tangled, and Noah had put his knitting aside and was instead hopping on one foot, captured mid-spin in the photo. The only one paying any sort of attention, surprisingly, was the youngest, Jesse. He was mimicking Mama Joy's motions and to Kerry's astonishment had a pretty good-looking scarf started and a look of pure wonder in his soft green eyes.

What happened to that little boy? Kerry wondered, then snorted as the answer came almost as quickly as the question. She knew exactly what happened. *Boobs*. Sure, she shouldn't say "boobs," but that was what he and his brothers were calling breasts back then, and she could just about pinpoint the time that Jesse turned. It was when he put down the knitting needles and instead wrapped his hands around his first pair of boobs that it all changed.

Kerry stilled and found herself inadvertently looking down at her own perfectly adequate pair. She shrugged, then rolled her eyes before looking for the coffee filters in the mess of covered dishes. Who could blame Jesse? It wasn't as if he had to fight for the boobs to come his way. Hell, it wasn't as if any of the Strong brothers had to fight in that department. Since each of them had hit puberty and shot past six feet, they were like four boob magnets with eight good hands between them. As if all it took for the girls to come flocking was height, muscles, sexy eyes . . . oh hell. Who was she fooling? It honestly didn't take too much more than that. Not once a person got a look at them. Not that she was magnetized or anything. It's just that some girls were metallic in that way.

Photo by Katana Photography

USA Today bestselling author and native New Yorker **KWANA JACKSON**, who also writes as K.M. Jackson, spent her formative years on the A train, where she had two dreams: (1) to be a fashion designer and (2) to be a writer. After spending more than ten years designing women's sportswear for various fashion houses, Kwana took a leap of faith and decided to pursue her other dream of being a writer. A longtime advocate of equality and diversity in romance (#WeNeedDiverseRomance), Kwana is the mother of twins and currently lives in a suburb of New York with her husband.

CONNECT ONLINE

KMJackson.com

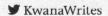 KMJacksonAuthor

🐦 KwanaWrites